Mina couldn't hear over the beating of her heart and the rush of blood in her ears.

"Are you okay?" Levi said, his forehead creased in confusion over her sudden change of behavior.

"I'm fine." Her voice sounded breathy and disjointed to her ears, but he only nodded.

Levi's gaze had become intense with emotion during the time they'd been sitting on the couch. Intent had softened his jaw and, she saw as he set both their bowls on the ice cream table, his shoulders. As he sat back up, the coming kiss dulled the world around them.

He leaned in to her, tucking a lock of hair behind her ear. "Are you sure you're feeling okay?"

"I'm sure," she reassured him, her lie failing miserably.

But Levi didn't seem to notice her failure. Or, if he did, he didn't care. Every skin cell burned as he trailed his finger along her jawline. The panic beating inside her couldn't hide the intensity with which she wanted his lips pressed against hers. The fear didn't stop her from leaning in to him, from meeting him halfway.

Dear Reader,

Love on Her Terms is one of those books that was born from many places yet somehow came together perfectly. There's no question this book is influenced by the many times I've watched the 1966 movie *A Man and a Woman* (my mom's favorite). And for years I'd wanted to write about a young woman who moves in next door to a cranky widower. She brings new sparkle to his life, but she has a chronic illness, and my hero's not sure he can handle it. Of course, the heroine's illness kept eluding me. Then while ruminating on a different novel where the heroine has HIV, a friend asked on Twitter if there were any heterosexual romances where one character has HIV. I knew then that I had to put the two ideas together! Sometimes—*okay, often*—authors need a friendly push.

My heroine, Mina, is also a graphic novelist so I can't resist recommending Scott McCloud's *Understanding Comics: The Invisible Art*. It's a wonderful exploration of the art form whether you've read comics and graphic novels or are new to the format entirely. Some of his theories made my jaw drop in awe. And seriously, if you do pick up the book and want to talk about it—shoot me an email! And for a real-life love story similar to *Love on Her Terms*, read *Blue Pills: A Positive Love Story* by Frederik Peeters. It's Peeters's graphic novel memoir about falling in love with an HIV-positive woman, who also has an HIV-positive son. As a librarian and book lover, suggesting books is one of my favorite pastimes, and these are two good ones!

Love on Her Terms was a powerful book for me to write and I hope it's just as powerful for you to read.

Enjoy,

Jennifer

JENNIFER LOHMANN

Love on Her Terms

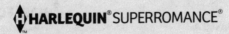

Recycling programs
for this product may
not exist in your area.

ISBN-13: 978-0-373-60999-4

Love on Her Terms

Copyright © 2016 by Jennifer Lohmann

All rights reserved. Except for use in any review, the reproduction or
utilization of this work in whole or in part in any form by any electronic,
mechanical or other means, now known or hereinafter invented, including
xerography, photocopying and recording, or in any information storage
or retrieval system, is forbidden without the written permission of the
publisher, Harlequin Enterprises Limited, 225 Duncan Mill Road,
Don Mills, Ontario M3B 3K9, Canada.

This is a work of fiction. Names, characters, places and incidents are
either the product of the author's imagination or are used fictitiously,
and any resemblance to actual persons, living or dead, business
establishments, events or locales is entirely coincidental.

This edition published by arrangement with Harlequin Books S.A.

For questions and comments about the quality of this book,
please contact us at CustomerService@Harlequin.com.

® and TM are trademarks of Harlequin Enterprises Limited or its
corporate affiliates. Trademarks indicated with ® are registered in the
United States Patent and Trademark Office, the Canadian Intellectual
Property Office and in other countries.

Printed in U.S.A.

www.Harlequin.com

Jennifer Lohmann is a Rocky Mountain girl at heart, having grown up in southern Idaho and Salt Lake City. When she's not writing or working as a public librarian, she wrangles two cats and a flock of backyard chickens (the dog is better behaved). She currently lives in Durham, North Carolina. She has one published comic strip, which you can find in a collection called *The Durham Comics Project*.

Books by Jennifer Lohmann

HARLEQUIN SUPERROMANCE

A Southern Promise
Winning Ruby Heart
Weekends in Carolina
A Promise for the Baby
The First Move
Reservations for Two

Visit the Author Profile page at Harlequin.com for more titles.

To Amy, Kirill and Yuri.
Thanks for all your support over the
past couple years and for bringing comics
and drawing into my life.

CHAPTER ONE

THE SOUND OF a heavy vehicle pulling into the driveway next door broke Levi Pardo's concentration, forcing him to look up from the newspaper spread out on the kitchen table. A small, ridiculously young-looking woman was hopping out of the driver's seat of a truck onto the narrow strip of grass between her driveway and his property. She'd parked too close to the lawn, which didn't surprise him. He was amazed she could see over the dash and touch the pedals at the same time.

He looked back down at the horoscope he'd been reading, some bullshit about expressing what you're feeling or else suffer the consequences. He didn't believe in astrology and found the *Missoulian*'s particularly annoying, but he still read two signs, Taurus and Cancer, every day. Habit, after years of marriage. Even if Kimmie wasn't around to care.

The woman moving in next door sure had a lot of energy, he thought, taking a sip of luke-warm, slightly oily coffee. He preferred to drink his coffee with flavored creamer, but he'd run out two days ago and hadn't yet made it to the store. Through his kitchen windows he saw the woman bound to the back of the truck and, with more power than he expected from someone so small, throw the door up and open. When a car drove up and parked along the curb, the woman leaped across the lawn like a pronghorn to greet her new arrivals.

Levi needed another sip of caffeine just to keep up with her. Maybe the process of unloading everything from the back of the truck would slow her down.

He shifted his chair over a couple of inches for a better angle. The house next door had been empty for almost two years and, as far as he knew, was as run-down on the inside as it was on the outside. It had good bones, though.

So did she, he thought, as the woman turned her head and faced his window. Long, dark bangs and a fringe of hair around her chin framed high cheekbones, a sharply pointed chin and a nose that looked like something out of a marble statue in those travel books about Greece that Kimmie used to bring home, back when she was feeling good and planning their adventures. Before he'd seen his neighbor's face full-on, he would have described her as cute. Short women were cute. Now *beautiful* was the only appropriate adjective.

Levi shook that thought out of his mind and turned back to his morning paper. He was about as interested in short women as he was in astrology.

TWO HOURS LATER Levi wiped down the kitchen counter, and, with the drape of a washcloth over the faucet, the second part of his Sunday ritual was done. Paper, first. Clean the house, second. It was midsummer, so he still had outdoor chores to do. He put sunscreen on his face and neck, covered his hair with a ratty Broncos cap, shoved his sunglasses on and went out to his garage for the lawn mower.

His ancient lawn mower, more Frankenstein's monster than anything resembling the machines currently lining the entrances of home-improvement stores, clanged as he pushed it down the driveway.

Even with his sunglasses and ball cap, he had to squint against the harsh sun.

He was leaning over to start the mower when voices caught his attention.

"I just don't get why you had to move *here*, of all places," an older woman's voice said, loudly enough that Levi could hear her, even though he couldn't see anyone when he looked around. He could picture the woman inspecting the neighborhood of old bungalows in varying states of repair with her hands on her hips and a slight sneer on her lips.

Though Levi couldn't understand what there was in this neighborhood to sneer at.

"Because the University of Montana offered me a job." A younger woman's voice this time, probably the bubbling one he'd seen driving the moving truck.

"So did the University of Richmond. If you had accepted their offer, you'd be near home." The older woman's voice again. Maybe the woman's mother. They must have been standing just on the other side of the moving truck.

Levi let go of the lawn mower's pull cord and folded his arms, giving in to the eavesdropping. He wasn't going to pass up the opportunity to get to know his neighbor, without the burden of going over and introducing himself.

"Which is exactly why I accepted the Montana job," the woman said, too bright and cheery for someone who was arguing with her mother. "Montana. Just the word conjures up adventure. Moose. Grizzly bears. Cowboys."

"Referring to grizzly bears as an adventure doesn't make me feel any more confident about your decision. Grizzly bears kill people," the older woman said.

"So does sitting, but you didn't offer to drive the U-Haul while I rode a bicycle alongside," the younger woman said smartly, while Levi bit back a smile.

"Don't talk back to your mother," a man said, a snap to his voice, which softened when he spoke again. "She's worried about you is all. We both are. If something were to happen, you'll be so far from home."

"Franklin married the most organized and efficient woman on earth. If something happens to either of you, she'll have flowers delivered to your room before you even get to the hospital." A laugh underpinned the woman's voice, though her humor had a sharp edge. Hidden, like the lid on a can of chili opened with a rusty can opener—familiar and domestic and safe, until you sliced a finger because you weren't paying attention.

"You know it's not *us* your mother is worried about," the man said, the sharpness of his voice less concealed than his daughter's. He sounded as if he'd cut himself on that can of humor before. "If something were to happen to you…"

"This is Montana, Mom, not the jungles of the Amazon. I'll be fine. Promise. There are good hospitals here. And my health has been good for years."

Levi shook his head. He shouldn't be eavesdropping, especially not on conversations involving hospitals. Resolving to return to his decision that he wasn't interested in short women, he gripped the pull cord and yanked until the ancient motor turned over, drowning out the conversation next door.

THE PROBLEM, LEVI THOUGHT, as he slipped a Pardo and Saupp Construction T-shirt over his head while looking out the window at the house next door, was that his new neighbor was always outside. It was hard to ignore a woman who seemed to think every beverage should be drunk on her front porch.

This evening, as she had for the past two weeks, she sat in the rocking chair with her feet up on the railing and a coffee cup in hand. The hems of her loose cotton shorts gapped. If he were at a different angle, he could follow the line of her skin down to her panties. She had nice legs. Not overly long, but shapely. He had no interest in women with thin legs.

She set her cup down and stretched her hands over her head. Her shirt lifted, and a little line of skin appeared between the elastic waistband of her plaid shorts and the bottom of her T-shirt. It was the type of movement he imagined her doing first thing in the morning, as she swung her legs over the side of the bed and welcomed the day. Intimate. Personal.

And he was staring out his window at her like a creep.

Levi jerked at the hem of his shirt, as if the movement could do anything to erase the image of his young neighbor with hair mussed by a long day. Not that that particular mental image was so bad, but he also imagined his hand slipping under the back of her shirt, her skin warm and soft on his cool palm and a glimpse of her face as she looked over her shoulder and smiled at him.

He reached up and closed the blinds.

He had to pick up his niece for soccer practice. Since he'd taken over coaching her youth soccer team two years ago, watching those girls tear up the field, fight, celebrate, fail and succeed had become the highlight of his fall. Solstice, his niece, seemed to have grown another three inches over the summer and would be all limbs. Helping her figure out how to manage all the new length in her arms and legs was a challenge he looked forward to.

THE NEXT FRIDAY, Levi climbed into his truck and looked next door with resignation. If he didn't want to watch his neighbor move about his life, he had to learn to ignore her better.

That and keep his kitchen blinds closed. Actually, all the blinds on this side of the house. Today she had come home from work, disappeared only long enough to change into shorts and grab a glass of what looked like iced tea. Now the ice in her tea was melting as it sat in the sun on her front porch while she was elbow deep in soil, shoving mums into the dirt. When she leaned forward, she stretched like a cat, her back long and her ass high in the air.

God, he definitely had to learn how *not* to watch her, because he didn't want to shutter his entire house. He *liked* the sunlight coming in through the windows, especially the afternoon summer sun. The big, south-facing windows were one of the reasons he'd bought this house.

He shoved the gearshift into Reverse, looked over his shoulder with barely a glance at his neighbor's ass, backed out of the driveway and sped down the street.

"YOU'RE LATE," DENNIS SAID, lifting up his eyebrow and his phone at the same time. Both pointed comments on the time.

"Barely." Levi slid into the booth and motioned to Mary for a beer. The two of them had been coming to O'Reilly's and sitting in this booth every Friday night for three years. The first six months, she'd come over to ask what beer he wanted. He'd said "whatever" enough times that she brought over whatever she or Brian, the bar's owner, felt like bringing to him. Sometimes he drank the entire beer and sometimes only a sip or two.

A little adventure, in his otherwise boring life.

A safer adventure than watching his neighbor.

Dennis coughed, a bad one that collapsed his shoulders in on his ears and shook the table. The kind of cough that would have his sister rushing to her husband to see what was wrong and Dennis struggling to both catch his breath and shake off Brook.

If he and Dennis were being honest with themselves, a surprise beer was probably the only adventure either of them needed, since the mine accident. And Dennis didn't even seem to need that. He always got the same bottle of Bud Light with a Jameson chaser. Had for years. Since before Missoula. Since before everything.

"You ain't been late since the day you were born," Dennis said, his bottle resting against his bottom lip. "And this ain't a big city, so you can't blame traffic."

"I've got a new neighbor."

Levi hadn't meant the comment by way of explanation, but he could tell by how Dennis lifted his eyebrows that it was the way his brother-in-law took the information. "He park in your driveway?"

"No. My neighbor's not why I'm late," he said, though he didn't have a better explanation for his tardiness, because "No matter how close I am to my new neighbor, I want to take at least one step closer, so it took me a while to drive away" would sound pretty stupid.

"Why'd you mention it, then?"

She was on his mind. "I'm not used to having a neighbor. It's distracting."

"So, not a sixty-year-old with a gut. You wouldn't be distracted by that."

"Ha!" Levi rubbed his own stomach. It was still flat but, at the age of thirty-seven, he was starting to think more about carrots and less about French fries and beer. "We'll both be lucky not to be that in twenty years."

"*I'll* be lucky to be that in twenty years." Dennis took a long pull on his beer, draining the bottle and signaling for another one. It was going to be one of those nights. Levi and the dishwasher would be hefting Dennis into the passenger seat of Levi's truck, and sometime around noon tomorrow, Dennis would text him for a ride back to get his car because Brook refused. And Brook would be texting him about letting Dennis get that drunk, because not only did she still think it was her job to monitor Levi's behavior, but she considered it Levi's job to monitor Dennis's behavior.

His sister had gotten taller over the years, but inside she was still a bossy twelve-year-old playing Mom while their dad worked in the mines.

But neither Levi nor Dennis would drive home drunk, so that was progress since their reckless younger years. At least they'd learned *something*.

Proof that stupidity wasn't guaranteed to kill you young.

"So, you gonna introduce yourself to this *distracting* neighbor?" Dennis asked, his second bottle of beer already half-gone. At least the whiskey was untouched.

"What for? To get roped into helping her with home renovations?" Levi shrugged. "That house needs a lot of work, and I'm already too busy as it is."

"So, she's cute."

"She's a child," he said, yanking his mind away from her legs and her nose and her ass and everything else about her he'd tried not to admire over the past couple of weeks.

"She bought a house, so I'm guessing she's at least twenty-five. Hmm. Might be more than cute—hot, even."

Levi shook his head. "It doesn't matter. I don't have time. Or interest. I've been married already. You should know. You were my best man."

Dennis shrugged. "Only 'cause no one else would do it."

A couple of beers between them helped them both laugh at the joke. At the time of Levi's actual wedding, Dennis—and everyone else—had been dead set against it. Kimmie had been too young, the chorus of noes said. And Dennis had only served as best man because Kimmie had cried when he'd refused. And then everyone had been mad at Levi for making her cry. No one had noticed at that time that his entire goal in his marriage had been to keep Kimmie happy.

All history.

"You gonna ask your neighbor out?" Dennis asked with disarming openness. Both he and Brook regularly pushed Levi to date women. Dennis suggested women like the girls who worked the registers at the hardware store or the ski shop. While Brook had a never-ending supply of friends who would be perfect for him.

Sometimes he said yes to Brook's friends, and he'd even gone on more than one date with a couple; but there had never been any spark that compared to what he'd felt for Kimmie.

Anything less would be doing both of them a disservice.

"I don't know her name." The least of the things he didn't know about her, though he was very familiar with the shape of her calves.

He had to figure out how to stop looking at her without closing his damn blinds.

"Don't see why that should stop you."

"I'm not interested in being married again." One time had been hard enough, even without the spectacularly tragic ending.

Dennis signaled for his third beer. Levi was still on his first. A part of him wished his friend would finish the shot sitting on the table so he would fall over, and they could both go home already, but his friend seemed determined to get drunk nice and slow. Which usually meant mean. He'd have to warn Brook.

"Hey, man, I'm not suggesting marriage," he said, draining the last of the bottle while Mary brought a new one.

No, Dennis never suggested marriage. But that was always Levi's first thought after seeing a woman who attracted him.

Or second, after the *she's got nice legs* thought.

He just wasn't interested in a stand, one-night or otherwise. Once attached, he stuck.

"Maybe *you* should ask her," he suggested to his brother-in-law, as useless a suggestion to

Dennis as Dennis's had been to him. "Brook wouldn't be at all mad."

Dennis's shoulders started to shake with a laugh, which turned into a hacking cough. It sounded worse tonight. They each waited until it passed, pretending it wasn't happening. The one time Levi had offered Dennis sympathy and a pat on the shoulder, he'd been angrily shrugged off, which only exacerbated the hacking fit. The next time they'd gone out for beers, both had been short and angry with each other.

Levi hadn't offered anything resembling sympathy for Dennis's coughing since.

Like Kimmie's suicide, they both found it easier not to acknowledge its existence. Kimmie died and Dennis had a chronic cough. Every Friday night, Dennis came out to the bar to drink and forget, climbing out of bed every Saturday afternoon back in the guise of a devoted husband and father. Levi had learned long ago how to hold on to your drink despite shit things happening in the world around you, rather than letting your drink hold on to you.

He tipped his bottle, watching the liquid slosh around while Dennis recovered himself. Levi was half-done with his beer. It would be his one and only tonight. His heavy drinking days were over, and the days he was willing to watch

Dennis pickle himself were numbered. Time to go home.

"Brook doesn't want to be with me when I'm coughing like this. And you think another woman would?" Dennis asked after he'd recovered from coughing and had been able to take another drink of his beer. He shrugged, and his smile was bitter. "Maybe you're right—Brook might not mind after all."

Levi shouldn't have brought the subject up. Coal dust from the mine accident lingered in every decision they made, obscuring any view at happiness. That was what this conversation was really about. Between Levi's dead wife and Dennis's dead lungs, could either of them be happy again? As much as Brook and Dennis suggested Levi ask women out and encouraged him to go on dates, he wondered what they would do if he found himself happily settled.

And, hell, what would he do if he wasn't spending his Friday nights with Dennis? They were in this wreck together.

"I'm going home," Levi said. No reason to finish his beer. He wasn't enjoying it any more than he was enjoying the conversation. "Finish your drink and I'll give you a ride."

Dennis shook his head. "It's Friday. There's more drinking to be had."

"Not for me." Could his friend hear his weariness?

"Hot date with the neighbor?"

Levi ignored the slice of resentment cutting through Dennis's question. "Finish and let's get going."

Dennis's face hardened into belligerence. "I'm staying." The alcohol had started to hit, and his voice sounded like an angry three-year-old's.

Levi slid out of the booth. "Fine. If you need a ride back here in the morning to pick up your car, let me know."

"Maybe I'll get lucky and take a girl home. Test your theory about Brook minding." Bitterness leaked from Dennis's mouth, lingering even after he wiped his chin with the back of his hand.

"Great." Levi tossed enough cash on the table to cover his beer and at least one of Dennis's.

On his way out, he stopped by the bar and told Brian and Mary that Dennis was staying. He also told them that Dennis's car wouldn't be running, and they should be prepared to call a cab or find someone to give him a ride. Dennis would be pissed, but there was no way Levi was leaving him able to drive home in a drunken, angry fit.

Maybe his friend would get lucky, and Brook wouldn't be too angry that they had to get his car from the bar parking lot on Saturday. Maybe she would even remember that when he wasn't busy playing an angry drunk, Dennis was a good guy.

Maybe Levi would get lucky, and his neighbor would still be up and sitting on her porch, reading.

CHAPTER TWO

MINA HAD MET all of her neighbors except one. Given how rarely she saw him outside, it seemed like he was determined she not meet him or even lay eyes on him.

Still, she wasn't used to not knowing her neighbors. Even in graduate school she'd made a point to meet all the people in her apartment building at least once. That way, she figured, even if they avoided her for the rest of their shared time in Chicago, they would be able to tell the paramedics her name if she were found gravely injured on the sidewalk outside the building.

Though how she would have managed being gravely injured on the sidewalk outside her apartment *after* being hit by a train was still a mystery.

Mina smiled as she crossed the property boundary. A death worthy of *Anna Karenina* was ridiculous, which was part of the pleasure of thinking about it. She was going to die from something prosaic and boring. A cold that turned into pneumonia. An allergic reaction. Basically, her own body turning against her. Nothing as spectacular as throwing oneself in front of a train after the betrayal of a lover.

She knocked on the door and almost laughed when her neighbor opened it, a death glare on his face that he didn't even try to hide as he said, "Yes."

Fortunately, death held little fear for her. It never had. Not even when in the form of a man who stood a head, a neck and a chest taller than her. Every other time she'd seen her neighbor, his black hair had been slicked back against his head, but this morning it was loose about his face, with locks hanging over his eyes. He obviously hadn't shaved since yesterday at least, and maybe since the day before. One day, once her garden was put in and her bathroom redone, she'd make a study of his facial hair.

Today, she stuck her hand into the void between them, a desperate cover for wanting to push his hair out of his eyes. "I'm Mina. I moved in next door a couple weeks ago and wanted to introduce myself."

His eyes were a surprisingly light brown, given how dark his hair was. She noticed this as she realized her hand…still hung in the air. She had offered him a strong handshake, like her dad had taught her. No weak wrists. People judged you on your handshake.

Or most people did. Her neighbor might never

shake her hand, and he wouldn't know that she'd practiced her handshake with strangers since she was five.

She was about to give up when his calloused hand slid into hers and gripped tightly enough that her knees went weak in the best possible way.

"Levi," he said, his voice deep with sleep.

It seemed his dad had taught him to have a good handshake, too. His grip revealed shapely forearms with just a hint of vein under the skin. Enough that Mina wanted to see more. More forearms. More biceps.

More everything of her neighbor.

Though there was plenty to see—or, at least, to imagine. His white T-shirt had a couple of holes scattered about the cotton and worn hems. His cotton pajama pants weren't much better. She sneaked a long enough peek to notice that the tie at the waist had been washed into a tight knot and he had to keep them loose enough to pull over his hips and butt without undoing the knot. What she could see of the hem of his pants was as worn as the hems of his T-shirt, maybe more so.

Had she woken him up? It was ten in the morning on a Saturday, so it was possible. But she'd seen him up earlier on Saturdays. And Sundays. And, from what she could tell when she closed her blinds before going to bed, he was also early to bed.

Oh, well. Too late now. If she'd woken him, the damage was already done. Best just to go on. Deciding to meet her neighbor on Saturday morning was yet another decision she couldn't redo.

"Nice to meet you, Levi," she said, returning her hand to her hip and her gaze to the scruff on his face.

When he rested his hand on his door, the movement raised his shirt a little, revealing both a little skin and some of the elastic sticking out from his worn pajama pants. Her gaze snapped back to his face. One eyebrow was up and, from the way he looked down at her, she couldn't tell if he was amused, irritated or both.

She looked down at his bare toes before she could feel self-conscious about knocking on his door and waking him up. He had nice toes. Long, with a dusting of dark hair on each of his big toes. Not enough to veer into Hobbit-hood, but enough to make his feet interesting.

"I moved here from Chicago," she said. The silence between them was starting to get on her nerves. Someone had to lead the conversation, and he wasn't going to do it.

He nodded.

Mina waited for him to offer up his own end

of the conversation. Maybe where he'd moved to Missoula from. Maybe that he liked Chicago. Or that he'd never been there. Or that both Montana and Chicago had bad winters, but Montana's was probably worse.

But he seemed to be done nodding, and he hadn't opened his mouth again. Since she'd knocked on his door, he hadn't said anything other than "Levi."

She could have looked at his mail to learn that.

"I teach at the university, in the Modern and Classical Languages and Literatures Department. I teach Russian. And a course on graphic novels. It's the first one they've offered. My suggestion, really, and the class is full. There was a waiting list, even." God help her, she was babbling. She'd gone beyond polite conversation with a neighbor and had hit full-on ramble.

"Graphic novels are what I do. I mean, they're what I write. I've written three, all based off Russian novels and folktales." She was wandering through her life and her history in front of this man who *still* remained silent. Of course, awareness wasn't enough to encourage sense and good behavior. Or enough to get her to stop talking.

She took a step back, teetering a little when her heel hit the back of his front steps.

"You can look me up," she continued. Distance. She had to put distance between her need to fill quiet with words and his gaping silence. She gripped the handrail. "Anyway, it was nice to meet you."

She had turned to go when she heard him say, "I can't look you up if I don't know your last name."

"Oh!" She spun around to look at him again. "Mina Clements. One *M.* I've got samples of my work on my website."

She slammed her mouth shut before she was tempted to continue. With a wave and a cascade of embarrassment washing over her, feeling like a complete fool, she hopped down his front steps and scurried back to her house.

LEVI CLOSED THE door with a soft click as soon as his neighbor—Mina—turned off his property and onto her own. She was even shorter up close. And younger-looking. And she had hazel eyes that danced with life as she talked.

Hell, he wasn't even sure what all she'd said. He was pretty sure he remembered her saying that she taught at the university, but he couldn't imagine that she was old enough. Did she teach people her own age?

Or maybe she was older than he thought she

was. Which meant *he* was older than he thought he was.

He turned away from the door, back to his coffee and the paper spread out on the kitchen table.

That he was older made sense, actually. He'd started noticing that he couldn't have extra fries without adding extra weight a year ago. Last year he'd noticed a creak in his knees when he got out of bed. And one benefit of living alone was that there was no one to watch or poke fun when he plucked the couple of gray hairs from his head.

Kimmie absolutely would have made fun of those hairs.

"When she was well," he said, flipping the paper open to the horoscopes and pressing the newsprint flat. Thoughts of how Kimmie would or wouldn't act always included a footnote about her health. Levi had never successfully been able to only remember Kimmie when she was well. Her depressive episodes sneaked into his memories so much that he'd stopped trying to halt them. After all, the weeks she'd spent in bed had been just as much a part of his wife as her laughter and sly sense of humor. Seemed almost like a betrayal not to remember them both.

"Remember her as she'd have wanted you to remember," people had said to him after her funeral. Well-meaning but ultimately stupid advice. Kimmie hadn't expected him to even be alive to remember her. She'd thought he'd died first.

The coffee burned down his throat when he took another swig. No second cup. Another side effect of getting older.

Not that he should be surprised. He'd spent a lifetime working with his body, and all those years, especially the ones in mining, were bound to have taken their toll. Yet he still had all his fingers and toes. He was able to laugh without coughing. And the only burn marks on his body were the ones he'd gotten being stupid around the stove.

A car started in the driveway next to his kitchen. His neighbor. No, Mina. She'd gone through all the awkward trouble of coming next door and introducing herself to him. He could at least call her by her name in his head while resisting the temptation to turn around and watch her as she drove off.

Maybe she really was a university professor. Teaching... He strained his brain to remember what she'd said. Russian and graphic novels.

Unlike the physical toll that mining took on him, he supposed people didn't get old prematurely teaching Russian to college students, even in Montana. He didn't exactly know what a graphic novel was, but he was sure the same applied. Mina Clements would be fresh and young-looking until the day she fell asleep at the ripe old age of ninety-seven and didn't wake up. And up until that time, she'd be inviting people into her life, whether they wanted to be there or not.

He skimmed the two horoscopes, only barely paying attention to their meaning. Between learning that it was time for him to open himself up to new experiences and that Kimmie should, if she were alive, let go of the past, the question of what a graphic novel was lingered. His mind had seized on the term *graphic*, wrapping arms around it and forcing him to face all the *graphic* things he'd been avoiding contemplating with his pint-size neighbor.

But women, even women from big cities, didn't go around introducing themselves to their neighbor and immediately saying they wrote pornographic novels and to check out their website. Missoula might be a more liberal area of Montana, but this was still Montana, and people would be offended.

Though even the offended would probably do just what Levi was about to do. He folded up the paper and tossed it into the recycling. Then he grabbed his tablet and searched the internet for Mina Clements. One *M*.

"Huh," he said to himself as he scrolled down Mina's page of books. "She writes comic books." There didn't seem to be any capes or superpowers, but his friendly neighbor wrote comic books.

Levi sat back in his chair and crossed his arms, looking at the image of a nose dressed in clothing standing in front of a large, ornate building. The drawings were black-and-white, with thick lines and harsh angles. Not funny or light or chatty at all. In fact, there was a darkness to the illustrations that he wouldn't have believed existed in the friendly woman with a strong, firm handshake and unguarded, bright smile that had him wanting to walk outside and greet the day with open arms.

He could tell she'd felt a little foolish as she'd walked away, though that wasn't his problem. He hadn't had anything to say, and he didn't want to get to know her. He hadn't invited her over here, didn't want her young cheer invading the life he'd made for himself. And when he wanted to feel like the world was a brighter place, he'd pick Solstice and her brother, Skylar, up for some soccer drills.

And, honestly, he *had* thought Mina had been a little foolish for standing on his front stoop babbling a bit.

But the woman who drew these pictures wasn't

foolish. Or silly. The woman who drew these pictures understood black humor and pain and isolation. The woman who drew these pictures was the kind of person he wanted to get to know.

Despite her external chipperness.

And, if he were being completely honest with himself, because he wanted to know how the woman who drew these pictures was the same woman who'd bounced down his stairs.

His chair legs squeaked as he scooted back to look out the window next door. What had previously been a plain, slightly barren lawn with more weeds than grass had now been broken up into flower beds. Mums, mostly. There wasn't much else one could plant in the fall in Montana that would flower, but Mina had added life and interest to her house.

He looked until he remembered that he wasn't interested. Then he tipped back in his chair and closed the blinds, dimming the room.

CHAPTER THREE

MINA ONLY REALIZED that she had a doorbell when she heard it ring for the first time. She wasn't that surprised that she had been too distracted to notice a small white button in the white siding next to her door, but she was surprised to see the outline of her cranky neighbor through the frosted glass window.

"Hello, Levi," she said as she opened the door. "I didn't expect to see you standing on my doorstep."

Inwardly she flinched at the slight implied by her words, but her neighbor didn't seem to notice. Or, if he had any reaction, the permanent shadow on his face from his stubble hid all the visible signs.

"I got some of your mail." He handed over a stack of envelopes, most of which looked like they would be junk and she'd be throwing them out anyway. "I saw that you were home and thought I'd bring it over, rather than leave it in your mailbox."

"That's nice of you. Thank you."

They stood on her porch as she waited for him to say something. The change of venue from his front door to her front door didn't make him any more loquacious. But he was here, and he'd done a nice thing, so she gave him a smile and took the reins of the conversation. "Does the mailman often put mail in the wrong box?"

Inane chatter. She could do better, but his silent presence seemed to knock all cleverness out of her. Between this and her babbling on his porch, he was going to think she was an idiot.

Levi looked relieved rather than dismissive. "No. But this house was empty for two years. He's probably not used to delivering mail here."

"Lucky for him, I doubt I'll get much." She held up the roll of advertisements and credit-card solicitations. "This looks like a lot of junk."

"There was an ad for Palmer's Drug in mine. Best drugstore in town. I tossed everything else."

"Oh. That's good to know, actually." Local pharmacies were often also compounding pharmacies and sometimes she needed the specialized service. Levi's visit was proving to be more than just an opportunity to appreciate the rough angles of his face and feel like a babbling fool.

"Any other best-in-town places I should know about?"

He shrugged, then looked around, probably at the disrepair of her porch. "I always go to Ace Hardware. Good people over there."

She laughed. "Will they come over and fix things, too?"

"Nah, but they give good advice. And this house has good bones. You take care of it, and it will take care of you."

Before she could say anything else, Levi nodded once, then turned on his heel and walked off her porch.

Mina stood in her doorway, watching him until he'd crossed over her lawn and onto his own. His butt looked nice in his jeans, but that wasn't the only reason she couldn't take her eyes off him. She also watched him because he was a puzzle of a man. If asked, she would have sworn that he was not a man to take such an ordinary task as returning a neighbor's mail and make it a personal gesture complete with recommendations. Not when he could have silently stuck it in her mailbox.

A WEEK LATER, Mina stood on her front lawn cursing her lawn mower. It was new and fancy, and the man at the hardware store Levi recommended had sworn it was easy to use. When she'd gone to the store, she'd "just been looking" and hadn't yet done any research into brands or reliability. But the salesman had promised next-day delivery and a thirty-day guarantee. He had sounded so reasonable, and she really had needed to mow her lawn or hire someone, so she'd plunked down her credit card.

Now she was the proud owner of a machine that wouldn't start. Silence was probably not what the man had meant by "runs quiet."

The lawn mower was electric, so it didn't need gas, but no matter how many times she followed the directions and tried to start the damn thing, it wouldn't run.

"Al sell you that?"

Mina jumped at the gruff voice behind her, releasing her hold on the mower and nearly falling backward. She turned to find Levi standing behind her, his arms crossed over a heathered green T-shirt.

"He should know better," Levi continued, his pink lips barely moving as he spoke; but the disapproval in his voice was clear, despite his quiet tone. "That brand is notorious for having bad starters and needing repair straight out of the box."

She exhaled a long puff of frustration. "It was cheap."

He nodded. "They are cheap, and, when it runs, that machine will be as quiet as Al promised. But you can pay a little bit more and get a quiet mower that will run every time."

"What do you know of lawn mowers? I've only ever seen you use a mower that looks like you made it in shop class from spare parts."

His shoulders bounced as he chuckled. "That's not far off. But fixing that thing has taught me more about lawn mowers than I ever wanted to know."

"Why don't you buy a new one?"

"Because Al has been trying to get me to buy a new one for years," he said, his voice flat, like she was silly for asking that question, but his eyes had the barest gleam. Her neighbor might have a sly sense of humor hidden under his stony facade.

"You could go somewhere else." She'd gone to the hardware store he had recommended because she wanted to support a small business, a decision she was rethinking right now.

"I could. But Al knows more about what's in his store than all the clerks at the other stores combined."

"He sold me a bum machine."

Levi bent his head in acknowledgment. "He also sometimes wants a bad decision off his lot so quickly that he forgets he wants customers to return."

She crossed her arms in front of her chest

and looked up at her oddly unhelpful neighbor. "Well, you can call him and tell him to come pick up the lawn mower. I want a refund, and I'll buy my new machine somewhere else."

Levi's lips twitched, and Mina wondered if he was going to smile, and, if so, was he smiling at her or at Al? Imagining him smiling at her didn't make her feel any less angry, though it meant she wasn't only angry with Al.

"You can do that," he said slowly. "Or I can help you pack it up, and we can return it. And see what discounts Al will give you in an attempt to keep you as a customer."

Mina gave the man standing in front of her a long, slow once-over. She'd seen Levi tinker with his lawn mower and glimpsed the expansive set of tools in his shed. Either he knew what he was talking about when it came to lawn mowers—*and Al*—or he spent a lot of money to look like Mr. Fix-It. Given the grease stains on his jeans and the slight bit of dirt under his fingernails, she decided to trust that he knew his stuff.

"I need an edge trimmer, too."

A slow smile crossed his face. "Al has lots of nice trimmers, and I'm sure he'll give you a good deal."

"Okay. I'll give Al another shot."

Together they got her lawn mower into the

back of Levi's truck. Mina grabbed her purse from inside her house, then climbed into the passenger seat. As Levi shifted into Reverse, she asked, "Why are you doing this?"

"Doing what?" he said, looking over his shoulder at the road and not once looking at her.

"Being neighborly and helping me out. When I stood on your porch and introduced myself, I was pretty sure you'd rather I hadn't bothered."

"Maybe I'm not helping you out. Maybe I'm helping Al out."

That cryptic statement silenced Mina the entire drive to the store.

ON THE WAY home from the hardware store, new lawn mower in the bed of Levi's truck, Mina asked the question that had been plaguing her the entire time they'd been shopping and Al had suddenly become informative, not just helpful.

"Am I coming home with a better lawn mower because you helped me and Al knows you, or because you helped me and you're a man?"

Levi's lips twitched, but he didn't turn his head to look at her. An annoying habit of his, and one that added to her sense that she didn't have a good read on him. Grumpy loner? Stoic, independent-minded Westerner? Helpful neighbor? All of the above? *None of the above?*

"Probably both. Al's of the generation that

thinks you should be inside making pie while your husband is outside pushing the mower. And you're a city girl, so he's doubtful that you'll mow your lawn, so why sell you a nice product when you're only going to hire someone anyway. But had you come into the store with a different man, Al might have flat-out given you a lawn service recommendation."

She grunted. His response wasn't what she wanted to hear, but at least it was honest. And it was along the lines of what she'd expected. Al had looked like a modern mountain hermit, with a grizzled face and coarse white hairs that stuck out of his face and head like electrical wires. "What about you?"

Levi flipped on his blinker and turned down the street leading to their neighborhood. "What about me?"

"What generation are you of?"

"One older than you." He must have noticed her roll her eyes because his lips curled in what was clearly a hidden smile.

"Do you think I should be inside making a pie while my nonexistent husband is outside mowing the lawn?"

"Does my opinion matter?"

Did it? She hadn't started teaching yet and was slowly making friends with her colleagues. So right now, Levi was as close to a friend as anyone else in Montana. "I guess I still don't understand why you're helping me."

"Huh," he said, and Mina realized *he* didn't understand why he was helping her, either. He probably saw himself as the cranky loner she had understood him to be during their first meeting. "I guess you should make a pie if you want to make a pie and mow your lawn if you want to mow your lawn. I won't be surprised if you end up hiring someone, but that's because mowing your lawn is a pain in the ass, not because you're a woman."

She laughed. "Will you come with me next time I need to buy an expensive piece of home equipment from Al?"

"Nah. You won't need me. Al may be from an older generation than both of us, but he's not so stupid as to drive a customer to one of those giant home-improvement stores more than once."

AFTER THAT TRIP to the hardware store, where Levi had caught himself watching Mina's hand instead of the road while he was driving—hoping her palm would suddenly rest on his thigh—he shoved his curiosity about her art and her cheer out of his mind and renewed his plan to avoid all thoughts of her. But catching glimpses of her outside had him reconsidering his stance on avoiding relationships because he was too old to risk heartache again. If he wasn't careful, he'd be shaving every morning just in case she touched his cheek—and double-checking his throat for patches of missed stubble.

But his resolve must have worked, because he didn't run into her again until Thursday, at the hardware store. She was in earnest discussion with Al over a cordless drill, asking him questions, and—as far as Levi could tell—Al was giving her good advice, rather than simply trying to sell her something.

Mina gave him a wave, and Levi raised his brows in return. When Al noticed, he looked over his shoulder and nodded. Levi nodded back, then caught Mina's secret smile at their shared joke.

Once Levi got home, he made sure all the blinds were shut on Mina's side of the house. He'd played friendly neighbor long enough and would have no part of whatever she was planning with her new cordless drill.

CHAPTER FOUR

THE PROBLEM, LEVI realized Sunday morning when he woke up and automatically started opening his blinds, was dark rooms and closed blinds reminded him too much of when Kimmie was feeling at her worst. She would close out the world and couldn't bear even the little bit of it that Levi would bring home every day when he got back from work. For weeks after her funeral, he'd kept the curtains open 24/7—the neighbors be damned if they saw him drinking coffee naked in the kitchen.

He picked up his pajama bottoms from the floor and pulled them on before padding out to the front door to get his paper. He'd mellowed a bit since Kimmie's death.

Once back inside, he tossed the paper onto his kitchen table and made himself some coffee before sitting down to the horoscopes. Sometimes he read the rest of the paper, but he *always* read the horoscopes. Not that the horoscopes ever said anything useful. Once a week—and today was the day—his horoscope told him to embrace a new future. Sometimes he wondered if the astrologer who wrote these simply had a list of generic recommendations for each sign that he or she rotated through.

Kimmie's horoscope recommended that she go outside and work in the garden. "Start early preparing the beds for your life for the winter," it said. "The warmth of Mother Nature will provide reassurance in changing times."

Clearly the writer didn't know that Kimmie had had a black thumb.

Levi looked up from his paper to the window, noticing that he'd sat facing Mina's house this morning, not with his back to it like normal. With his blinds open he could see the burst of fall colors her mums provided. Mina, crouched in her front yard, a drill next to her in the grass, was also in full view. She was holding two boards together and screwing down a clamp. When she finished, she picked up a level, held it against the join and shook her head.

He took several sips of his coffee while he watched her undo the work she'd just done and try again. Unsurprisingly, given the uneven surface she was working on, she had to take it apart once more.

He guessed she was making a raised garden bed. The task would be a lot easier if she had some help.

He flipped through the rest of the paper, idly reading the comics—even the terrible soap opera–like ones he should have given up on years ago—and checking the ads. There was nothing worth reading in the rest of the paper, but he skimmed the headlines anyway. For completion's sake.

Only when he'd finished the paper and his last bit of now cold coffee did he look up again. Mina had apparently gotten the two boards clamped together like she wanted. Now she struggled with holding the boards and predrilling holes for her screws.

Levi sighed. He wasn't the type of neighbor who liked to do more than wave from his truck when he passed someone on the street. He didn't want someone interpreting a friendly smile as an invitation to drop by and say hi.

Of course, Mina had already dropped by to introduce herself and before he'd worked himself up to even waving at her from his truck. And, despite helping her with Al, she hadn't invited herself over for dinner. She'd been friendly but not *intrusive*.

He sighed again, then stood and put his coffee cup in the sink.

With one last look at his neighbor's battle against the raised bed, Levi ran his hand through his hair and went upstairs to change into jeans.

She was too young. His heart was still too

tender, his memories of Kimmie too fresh. But with no one there to help her, Mina would spend the entire day struggling to produce a garden bed with lopsided joins that would set his teeth on edge every time he stepped out of his front door.

After buttoning his jeans, he dug a work T-shirt out of his drawer. In the long run, going over to help her was a bigger benefit to him than it was to her. Not only did she need the assistance and he had the skills to provide it, but that house had been sitting empty for two years. Helping her fix it up would improve his own house's value, not to mention what he had to see every time he looked out his windows.

He caught a glimpse of a bullshitting liar in the mirror as his head popped through the neck of the shirt. God, who was he fooling?

In the short bit of time he'd spent with Mina, he had felt more like his old self. The person he'd been before Kimmie's death, who made plans and had dreams. If he spent more time with her, that man he'd once been would come back, and it was that allure that had him hurrying down the stairs and out the door.

Against his better judgment, he was sure.

A LARGE, MAN-SHAPED shadow blocked Mina's view of the marks she'd made in the wood. She sat back on her heels, both in frustration at how long it had taken her to get the stupid boards flush *and* at the person blocking her view of the part of this process she was really looking forward to—using her new drill.

The shadow didn't speak, nor did it move. Finally, she turned and looked up into the sun at the man towering over her.

Her sometimes friendly, usually unfriendly neighbor, Levi, had come to watch her be foolish. A better show in person than from the window, no doubt.

"Hey," she said, throwing a little extra chipper into her voice.

"That'd be easier if you did it on the driveway. Your driveway's pretty level." Not much as far as greetings went, but what she could see of his shadowed face was open and friendly. Or as friendly as he got. His now two-day beard and sleep-messed hair didn't add much *welcoming* or *pleasant* to his look, but she'd always preferred brooding to charming.

"I know it would be easier, but if I did this on my driveway, I'd need someone to help me move it once it's built. And," she said with a shrug, "I figured it would be easier to get it level on the grass than move it by myself."

Looking up at him was giving her a crick in her neck. She put her drill down. Much to her surprise, when she looked back up, preparing to stand, his hand was out. She stuck her hand in his, felt a reassuring squeeze and then a pull that was surprisingly gentle considering how quickly she came to her feet.

"Thank you." She wiped the dirt off her knees.

"Why don't you have a friend help you?" There was nearly a smile on his face.

A hand and *nearly* a smile. Even though he hadn't said a word to her since their trip to the hardware store, Levi wasn't the cranky neighbor he seemed to so desperately want to be. Under the hair that had fallen down the front of his face again, there might even be a flicker of humor in his eyes.

Spooking him seemed like a possibility, so she didn't smile back. Or even *nearly* smile back. "I've only lived here a month. No friends yet."

His brows raised in surprise. "Really? You seem like the kind of person who makes friends in a day. And you've been here a whole *month*." He said everything but the last word drily, and she wondered if he were making fun of her until she remembered the near twinkle in his eye and the twitch of a smile she might have seen on his face.

"Well," she corrected herself, "no friends who could help me today. Ivan, the guy I share an office with, is going out of town this weekend.

Perry and Susan are at church, and I guess there was a *thing* after church. And Caroline doesn't *do* power tools. When I said I'd use the drill and she only had to hold the boards, she counter-offered with alcohol when I was done."

She glanced at the boards that were not yet the rectangle she'd thought they would be by now and laughed. "I think I'm going to need at least a beer. Maybe three."

Levi looked longingly across the two driveways to his house. For a long moment she thought he was going to shrug and walk back into his home. But he blinked, shook his head against some invisible foe and turned back to her. "I'll help you."

She didn't have to wonder if he wanted to. There was no smile on his face and no light in his eyes.

"What makes you qualified?" she asked, more curious than suspicious.

He raised an eyebrow. "I'm a contractor. Normally people pay for my help."

"Well, I didn't ask and you don't have to help me." Help was help, but *begrudging* help was almost worse than no help at all. "If I don't get it done today, Ivan can help me next week. He's already offered."

"Yeah, but if I leave you here, I'm going to know you're struggling, and I'm going to think about it every time I look out a window. I'll get nothing done." From his deadpan delivery, she couldn't tell if he was joking.

"So, really, I'm doing *you* a favor." His backward logic brought a smile to her face. "After you help me with this, you'll owe *me* a beer."

Surprise opened his face for a brief second before he barked out a laugh. "Yeah, I guess you could say that."

"That's a fair deal." She stuck out her hand to shake on it. And so she could feel his hand in hers again. Touch him again. Rugged, handsome, *and* he laughed at her bargaining skills. Suddenly she wanted to start touching him and never stop.

His hand lingered in hers, and with it the possibility of more intimate touches. Though, if that happened, she'd have to tell him about her HIV. And even if he didn't back away in horror—and most people didn't—he'd still want her to stop touching him so he could think about what she'd said. *That* everyone did.

Not that she blamed anyone for needing time to think, but, well, it always ruined the mood.

But Levi was helping her with her raised bed, not slipping his hand around to cup her head and bring her in for a kiss. There was no mood to ruin, only this stupid raised bed that she'd half destroyed in the process of building it.

As they sank down to the grass together, Mina kept her rash decision to build the garden bed at the forefront of her mind. The fact that she'd looked helpless enough for Levi to offer to help was a clear sign that she'd not thought the project through. And she knew better than to rush into things, men included—especially rugged neighbors with an air of tragedy about them. Lack of thinking things through made for bad decisions, and bad decisions made her parents worry. They would suggest she get on the job market again. They would call more. They would question every decision they knew about.

She'd moved to Montana for some independence, not to develop an unsubstantiated crush on a neighbor.

CHAPTER FIVE

LEVI GATHERED THE materials while Mina moved her car out of her driveway. Together they moved everything to the flat surface.

"You're right," she said as he tightened the clamps on the boards. "This does make everything easier."

"The driveway or another person to help?" Levi held his hand out for the drill.

"Both," she said, though she was shaking her head. "But you've only promised to stick around to build the thing. I neglected to ask you to help me move it in place."

"That'll cost you a beer." He gestured for the drill and grunted when she shook her head again. "What, I don't get beer for my labors?"

She laughed. "I'm not shaking my head at the beer. I'm shaking my head at giving you the drill." She crab-walked around the driveway, the weight of the drill obviously pulling down at her hand, until she was next to him. Then she bumped him with her shoulder. "Move over.

This is my raised bed and my drill. I get to use the power tools."

"I'll give up my beer in exchange for power-tool responsibility."

The way her nose wrinkled as she pretended to consider his request made him want to laugh. "No dice," she said, with another nudge. "I'll pay you two beers for a lesson in power tools."

He gave up with a bark that didn't quite cover up his laugh and scooted to where he could hold the wood steady while she drilled.

It took Mina a few times with the drill to figure out how to control the power. Levi was pretty sure she was muttering and swearing under her breath each time the drill slipped and she had to release her fingers, but she managed to control any cursing by the time the whirl of the tool stopped. And each time she wrinkled her nose in frustration, took a deep breath and leaned forward with renewed concentration. When she had finally gotten all the holes pre-drilled and the screws in to attach the first short side of the bed to the post, she looked up at him in triumph.

"You didn't give me any instruction, so I'm not sure I owe you the beers. But I got it done anyway, and I'm feeling generous. One beer, not two."

He smiled at her continued reevaluation of

their bargain. If he didn't pay attention, he'd end the day having built a raised bed and offering to make dinner, too. "Your first lesson in power tools is that it would have been faster if you'd let me do it."

"Does that mean you'd rather not have any beers?" She took the clamps off the board, then slid down and started clamping that end to the post.

"No," he said, slipping into his role as assistant. To his surprise, he was having fun. "Just being honest. I have experience with this. You don't."

"But I'll never get experience if I don't do it. And if I mess it up, the store has more boards I can buy."

"But you can't pick up another helper."

"Like I said, Ivan can help me next weekend." She said the man's name again, as if he should know who Ivan was. Her boyfriend? He hadn't seen anyone regularly coming to the house— or noticed her spending nights away. Not that it mattered to him if his cute neighbor had a boyfriend. He was over here to be *neighborly*—trying something new like the horoscopes always suggested—not because he was interested in anything else.

Liar, liar, pants on fire, as his nephew Skylar would say.

"Besides, I don't see you leaving in a huff because I won't let you hold the power tools." Her smile had turned into an impish smirk, and Levi knew he was staying, beer or no beer, power tools or no power tools.

"I said I'd help you build this bed, and I will," he said with conviction that surprised even himself. "I'm a man of my word." He paused. "Around household projects, at least."

"A caveat of household projects? Is that a promise or a warning?" Figuring out how to put her whole body into the push of the drill didn't seem to change her ability to keep that playful smile on her face.

Levi hadn't enjoyed watching a woman's face move so much since...well, since he'd first met Kimmie all those years ago. That realization hit at the same time Mina finished drilling and released the body-weight pressure she was putting into the wood. The sudden change knocked him off balance and on his ass, his hand flying out behind him for an equilibrium he couldn't seem to find.

When he looked up, Mina was staring at him, her mouth and eyes wide in surprise. Amusement shone in her eyes. She recovered well enough to close her lips, but one corner of her mouth stayed lifted in surprise. Levi pushed himself back upright, chuckling at his clumsiness, and it seemed to be all the break Mina needed to laugh herself.

"Are you all right?" she asked.

"Yes. I didn't expect..." He'd expected to spend the afternoon thinking about his house and his chores and being anywhere other than here. He *hadn't* expected to have an offer to get more wood so they could build another raised bed lingering on the tip of his tongue. "You moved sooner than I expected."

"Well, Levi of no last name and worn hems, you're less grumpy than *I* expected."

Levi laughed, not a bark, not a chuckle or an acknowledging grunt. The laugh escaping his mouth was a full belly laugh that made his stomach muscles hurt but lightened the weight of his head on his shoulders. "Worn hems, huh? I guess my pajama pants are a bit old."

"So is the T-shirt you were wearing."

"You don't let up, do you?"

"Not when I'm winning," she said, her face bright with both the sunlight shining down on her and the pleasure radiating from within her.

"Let's get this bed finished so I can have the beers that you owe me," he said, emphasizing the *s* on the end of *beers*.

As they built the rest of the raised bed and dug holes for the posts, Mina chattered along, much like she had when standing on his front porch. Chatter was her default setting, he realized, and it had only been mindless and haphazard on his porch because he'd been silent, and she'd been nervous. Now, as he occasionally asked questions and bantered back, her conversation was still light, but it was also interesting. Levi had never expected to care about the glories of Russian curses, but so long as Mina was the one talking about them, he was eager to become an expert.

THE LEGS OF the wheelbarrow sank into the grass when Mina let go of the handles. The bed was done. It was even full of dirt. Levi had called someone he knew who ran a rock and soil yard, and they'd gone in his truck to pick up a load of topsoil and compost mix. She might, *might*, be able to squeeze in a few fast-growing greens and harvest something before the bitter cold weather set in.

But that was a task for another day. Despite the cool air hinting at fall, all the work they'd put in meant dirt stuck to the sheen of sweat on her skin like those minuscule brambles that stick to your socks after a hike. Her hair had fallen out of the bobby pins and was adhering to her face in clumps. And sniffing herself wasn't required; she knew she stank.

Levi grimaced as he ran his hand along the

back of his neck and gave his shoulder a few hard rubs. The world could be deeply unfair. Mina was pretty sure she looked like something the cat dragged in. Levi, who had to be just as dirty and probably also stank, looked rugged and capable. The streak of dirt across his cheek made the light brown of his eyes stand out, and his teeth looked whiter when he smiled at her.

"I'm going to be sore tomorrow," he said with another rub at his neck.

"Since you weren't happy giving over responsibility for the drill, I assume you do this sort of thing on a regular basis." Maybe she just liked to imagine what he would look like chopping wood. "Or was that just because you're a man and like to be in the driver's seat?"

He let out a low sound, somewhere between a snort and a chuckle. The outright laughter that had caught her by surprise earlier was gone but not forgotten. She didn't need it to know he was having a good time. "I supervise more than I hammer, so if you want to drive, I'm man enough to be a passenger and enjoy the scenery."

"How long have you lived in Missoula?"

"Three years."

"Is that long enough for you to be able to show me some cool places? Places I wouldn't discover unless I had also lived here for three years?"

She had tried to make her question airy—and tried for a light smile to match—but she could see in the cock of his head that he was trying to understand if she was truly asking or being flirty. Hell, *she* didn't know if she was looking for suggestions from someone who'd lived in the city longer than she had or if she was hunting around for the likelihood of a date. She'd promised herself that from now on she'd get to know someone casually before getting serious. No more rushing into relationships or hopes or dreams. Rushing led to hurts, and she was trying to cut down on hurts.

But emotional caution just wasn't and never had been a strength of hers.

"I know some places," he said finally, each word carefully measured out as if he was also trying to figure out what she was asking *and* what he was offering. "And I know locals who know more places."

"I've not met many locals. The university seems to be full of transplants like me, at least among the professors." Different universities had different cultures and different feels, but the hodgepodge of people from around the globe remained the same. The academic job market was tough, especially for someone who studied a language, and everyone took what they could get.

"But before I ask you for more favors," she said, giving them both an out, "I should probably get you that beer I promised. I'll make you dinner, too, if you're interested. You helped me out a lot today, and feeding you is the least I can do."

Again he looked at her, obviously evaluating her words with a slow blink.

"It's just dinner, I promise," she said with a low laugh to cover the awkwardness. "I'm not trying to put a down payment on future yard work."

He snorted. "I don't believe that, but I also don't care. Give me a chance to shower first, and then dinner sounds great."

"A shower is a good idea." Maybe cleaning the dirt off her body would clear the confused dust out of her mind. And, if she decided she really was trying to explore the potential for a date, at least she wouldn't be worried about armpit smell.

"Give me at least a half an hour to get myself cleaned up, and you can come over any-time after that. I'll leave the door unlocked, but give a knock so I don't jump when you walk in the door."

"Deal," he said. Then he smiled, and his face and shoulders relaxed. Hers did, too.

FRESHLY SHOWERED AND in clean clothes, Levi stood in his kitchen watching the clock. It had been twenty minutes since he'd left Mina's front yard, and he figured he had ten minutes to kill before he could walk through her front door without risking her still being in the shower. He emptied his dishwasher, then turned his attention to the paper still lying open to the astrology section.

He was supposed to try to embrace a new future today. If Kimmie were alive, she was supposed to go outside and garden. Not that he believed in the nonsense of the stars covering his fate, but today's horoscope seemed uncomfortably close to the truth. Kimmie couldn't go outside and garden, but Levi was alive, and getting outside seemed good advice for all the living.

And then there was that new future...

Levi glanced up at the window to where Mina was out of the shower and closing her curtains. She didn't look embarrassed at all as she caught him looking while she was wearing only her towel. Instead, she smiled and waved. He waved back, then reached up and closed his own blinds.

Dennis was right that maybe he should get out and explore the world of women. Brook was right that he should do so with more seriousness. He'd never imagined that he'd be in his midthirties and single. He'd been excited to marry Kimmie and talk about having kids. He'd *wanted* to settle down. He still wanted to. But it wouldn't happen if he avoided women who seemed more interested in relationships than in just sex.

Mina didn't have to be *the one* or even *the maybe*, and dinner tonight didn't have to lead to anything more than friendly greetings between neighbors, but he'd never know unless he tried. Mina was the first woman he'd felt more than a sexual interest in since Kimmie, and she was at least a good place to start, even if she seemed impossibly young.

He sniffed at his shoulder, which smelled like dryer sheets and deodorant. He reached up and unbuttoned his shirt, draping it across the chair as he headed to the bathroom to shave. Cologne would be overkill—besides which, he didn't own any—but shaving for a woman was a nice gesture, even if dinner was just dinner.

After his shave and before heading out the door, Levi stopped by the kitchen, folded up the paper and tossed it in the recycling bin before the stars carried him away from reality.

CHAPTER SIX

MINA WAS PUTTING the butternut squash and leeks into the oven to roast when she heard a knock at the front door, followed by a squeak of the hinges.

"Hello?" Levi called, his footsteps quiet and uncertain on her wood floors.

"I'm in the kitchen," she called. "Head to the back. It's a small house—you can't miss me," she said, shutting the oven door and grabbing a towel for her hands. Levi's head stuck around the corner just as she was tucking the towel back on the oven handle.

He'd shaved. She was, momentarily, speechless. The sharp contours of his face and squareness of his chin were worth a moment of silence, but that wasn't what stopped her tongue. Not only had he taken the time and effort to shave, but he was wearing nice jeans and a neat dark blue button-down that showed off a trim, muscular figure, especially with the sleeves rolled up and his forearms on display.

Levi had gone to some effort. Like this was a date.

"I feel underdressed," she said, recovering her speech and looking down at her worn gray yoga pants and white tank top. Since she wanted to get the vegetables in to roast as quickly as possible, she'd just rinsed the sweat off her body. Barrettes and sweat were keeping her hair off her face, and shaving... Well, the state of her leg hair was better not considered. Probably for the best. Looking at him now, she needed to put brakes on her libido.

He shrugged. "You look fine to me" was all he said, but there was warmth in his eyes, so she brushed away her feelings about looking sloppy. "What's for dinner?"

"Butternut-squash lasagna and a salad. It's not a quick meal, but it's one of my favorites, and I had all the stuff on hand. Plus, it's filling after a long day of working outside."

"No meat?" he asked with the disappointed face of a child who's been denied candy.

"No." She shook her head with a laugh. "I have sausages in the freezer, but they would have taken too long to defrost. The lasagna will be good, I promise, and if you miss the meat, I'll make sure the sausages come out for the next time I cook you dinner."

"Next time," he said, his voice caressed with

approval. "I like that idea. Where did you learn to cook?"

With that simple question, Mina eased into conversation, talking about cooking with her mom when she was a kid and some of the terrible food experiments and impossible diets she'd tried in both college and graduate school. "I don't know how I found the time or energy to eat a raw food diet, but I managed it for six months."

She didn't mention that she'd tried many of these diets in an attempt to keep her flagging energy or stave off upset stomachs or to control all the other side effects of either HIV or the meds that kept her virus count low. Desperation over a chronic illness had been her motivation to prepare raw carrot crackers every week. Then there had been the macrobiotic diet. And the gluten-free one. And hopping back and forth between several other less popular options before she'd settled back into moderation and mostly vegetables.

"I don't like the sound of a raw food diet. There's no way that could include enough meat for someone born and raised in Montana," he said, one side of his mouth kicked up in a half smile.

Good—she wasn't boring him. Mina was a talker. She talked when she was nervous; she talked when she was relaxed; she talked when she was tired… She just talked. She even talked to herself as she wandered her house. The near never-ending stream of chatter had driven more than one boyfriend crazy—at least that was what they said. But there had been a few that had been amused. She could hope Levi was the latter.

She sneaked a peek over her shoulder at him as she stirred the béchamel sauce. If she was reading his shave and nice shirt correctly, well…the more she talked, the more his eyes seemed to shine and his lips stayed in the *amused* position.

This could lead somewhere. If she was thoughtful and deliberate and purposeful, she could turn one dinner into two.

Mina, if you're thinking about anything past dinner, then you're already rushing into something. Get through dinner first, then worry about what comes next. Good advice, but not nearly so much fun.

"The lack of meat wasn't the problem I had with eating raw foods," she said, steering her mind back to the conversation.

"Not born and raised in Montana."

"No. And far too interested in trying new fads to stick with the tried-and-true method of eating meat and three square meals. Though that's how I grew up." She turned her attention away from the handsome man standing in her kitchen and back to the food. The béchamel had thickened, and it was time to layer the lasagna and get it in the oven.

"Do you need help?"

"No. Grab another beer and we'll go sit in the living room while this bakes. It's more comfortable in there."

Mina joined Levi in the living room as soon as the lasagna was in the oven. He was on the couch, not in one of the two armchairs, and he'd sat near the middle of it. Unless she chose one of the armchairs, she'd have to sit near him.

She joined him on the couch and put her beer on the coffee table in front of them, turning her body toward him. He'd turned toward her, too. They weren't touching, but she was close enough to smell the brisk notes of his aftershave and to see some stubble along his jawline that he'd missed. His intense gaze sent good shivers down her spine, shivers that reinforced that she hadn't been wrong about his more intimate intentions.

After her diagnosis, Mina had become more thoughtful about her interactions with men. She hadn't yet managed to make accurate predictions about their intentions from her careful study of their movements, but she kept trying.

Trial and error would surely pay off eventually, and she'd be right about a man one day.

If nothing else, the careful study of men slowed her down a little.

"I'm glad you came over and introduced yourself," he said, his rich voice coating her skin in warmth.

She smiled. "Me, too."

"I checked out your website. That was the first time I'd heard about graphic novels. The drawings were neat and, uh, darker than I would have guessed."

"Yeah." She laughed. "I'm so bubbly and short that everyone expects me to have light, fluffy drawings. Something cute, with bunnies. When I do talks and festivals, the most common comment I get after 'I love your work' is 'I thought you'd be taller.' It used to bother me, but I've stopped worrying about it. Honestly, my art used to be lighter."

Levi took a drink from his beer bottle, and his Adam's apple moved as he swallowed. How had she not noticed what a sexy part of the male anatomy the neck was until now? "What changed?"

She shrugged. "My drawings were always macabre and obsessed with the strange, but in college my lines got darker and thicker and I started having fewer curves in my art and more sharp corners. It's better, actually. One of the things I tell my students is that they don't have to be an amazing artist to write comics or graphic novels, but their art has to match their subjects. Like Kate Beaton, who draws these hilarious comics with random historical and pop-culture references. Her drawings appear to be rough sketches and, if you ignore the adult content, almost something a kid would draw. But it makes the punch of her jokes that much stronger. Or Tom Gauld, who wrote this beautiful book on Goliath, where Goliath was an innocent victim. The bare landscapes mean the reader focuses on Goliath's simplicity and how he is used by both his friends and his enemies. Scott McCloud has this great book where he talks about comics with a focus on form versus comics with a focus on idea or purpose, and I was really so focused on form that I forgot my ideas."

When she took a deep breath, all the words she had to say about comics clouded up her lungs, and she had to exhale slowly before she could say another word. Just to be safe, she waved all the excess words out from between them. "Anyway. Before, well, before my art and my subject matter were a mismatch. Not completely wrong for each other, but wrong enough that the stories lost their power."

"Do you have more of your books?" he asked, his brows raised in genuine curiosity.

"Sure," she said, pleased. "You want to see?"

"Of course. I've never known anyone who made money drawing pictures."

"Oh, I don't make much money. It's certainly not a living." She doubted that she'd ever make a living doing it. Russian stories were interesting to people, and people liked her art, but it wasn't commercial, really.

She pushed herself off the couch and headed over to her bookshelf, feeling his gaze on her the entire way. When she got back, he set his beer on the table and accepted the two volumes from her.

While he examined her books, she examined him. The ridges of his spine starting at his hairline and disappearing into the neckline of his shirt. The curves of his ear and softness of his earlobe. A faint scar across his cheek that she hadn't noticed under his previous scruff.

Her scrutiny didn't seem to make him uneasy. He didn't seem to notice it at all. He was a steady man, she realized, and someone could easily mistake his composure for shallowness, but his stillness suggested the lastingness of a mountain lake, not the transience of a rain puddle.

Better, he was taking the time to really study her art and the words, not just flip through and look at the pictures.

The timer beeped. Mina got up and went to the kitchen to take the lasagna out of the oven. While it rested, she set the table as Levi continued to study her books. When she called him over for dinner, he asked a few questions about her art, then sat back and let her talk. Still flattered by his interest, Mina monopolized the entire dinner talking about herself, her theories about comics and all the plans she had for books to come. And it felt right, because when she stopped chattering to take a breath, Levi asked her a question and then looked interested when she jumped back in.

She felt, well, she felt comfortable being herself with him, which was the best thing you could want in a man.

After they finished eating, Mina directed Levi around the kitchen as she washed dishes, and he dried and put them away. Then she offered him the choice of five different kinds of Sweet Peaks Ice Cream from her freezer. As he looked at the row of cartons on the countertop, he had the faintest possible smile, and she felt silly in the best, warmest possible way.

This casual, no-expectations dinner was quickly turning into something else. At least for her, and she was pretty sure she wasn't misreading him.

Which meant it was time to relax. Be funny. Friendly. Open. Charming.

With their bowls of ice cream in hand, they returned to the living room couch, almost in the same spots that they had been sitting before. *Almost*, because now they sat closer to one another, their knees not quite touching as they faced each other.

There on the couch, their knees a hope and a prayer from being intertwined, Mina couldn't hear the question Levi asked her over the beating of her heart and the rush of blood in her ears. She asked him to repeat himself. She tried to smile and tried to make it look natural. The world must be smiling down on her, because suddenly she thought of a question to ask him, something to take the pressure off her and give her time to take a deep breath.

Time to stop the panic welling up inside her.

More important, time to stop herself from acting on the panic.

"Are you okay?" Levi asked, his brows crossed in confusion over her sudden change of behavior.

"I'm fine." Her voice sounded breathy and dismantled to her ears, but he only nodded.

"Let me take your bowl," he said, and she released her grip on her ice cream. She wasn't finished with it, but she had stopped tasting it several minutes ago.

Levi's eyes had grown hot during the time they'd been sitting on the couch. Intent had softened his jaw and, she saw as he set both their bowls on the coffee table, his shoulders. As he sat back up, the coming kiss dulled the world around them. Mina stopped being able to hear the tick of the clock on her wall, and the outlines of the furniture got fuzzy.

He leaned into her, tucking a lock of hair behind her ear. "Are you sure you're okay?"

"I'm sure," she reassured him, trying to lie to them both and failing miserably.

But Levi didn't seem to notice her failure. Or, if he did, he didn't care. Every skin cell burned as he trailed his finger along her jawline. The panic beating inside her couldn't hide the intensity with which she wanted his lips pressed against hers. The fear didn't stop her from leaning into him, from meeting him halfway.

Just as his lips were a whisper away from hers, the panic that had risen inside her surged out, shoving charming and flirty and casual out of the way. "I have HIV," she said, then sat back against the cushions before he could reject the kiss. Reject her.

"What?" he asked. His entire face had folded in on itself in confusion.

"I'm HIV positive. I thought you should know, before we, well…" That last part was a lie. She didn't think he should know before they kissed. He didn't *need* to know before they kissed. HIV wasn't spread through saliva. They could make out all night, and he wouldn't be any more at risk than if he'd sat in a church praying.

But Mina had never mastered the timing of *the tell*, if there was a way to master it. She'd read books and articles on living and dating with HIV. She'd read everything she could find in an attempt to find the balance between telling someone about the skeletons in your closet early enough in the relationship, so you could judge if they were a person who could handle your particular set of baggage, and not telling them so soon that you were pushing them away.

She *always* told too soon. Or too casually. Or didn't prepare them for *big news coming*. Like everything else, she rushed into it.

"Okay. Um, thanks for telling me, I guess." Levi leaned away from her, looking her over for a long minute. Then he nodded once with a finality that might as well have been a slap across the face and stood. Mina watched as he gathered the ice-cream bowls and walked into the kitchen. When he returned, she hadn't moved an inch.

"I'm going to head home. If you need help building another raised bed—"

She braced herself for the final rejection.

"—give me a call."

"Okay." Her voice was barely audible to her

own ears, even though she had no heartbeat to drown it out.

He nodded again. He shut the front door behind him, and the possibility of their relationship clicked closed, too.

CHAPTER SEVEN

LEVI'S BLINDS WERE still open when he got home. The lights were on in Mina's house, and he could see right through from his kitchen into hers. The ice-cream bowls were on the counter where he'd put them.

Mina only had good ice cream in her freezer. Dinner had been delicious, even if there hadn't been any meat. Levi pulled everything out of his pockets and plopped his keys and his phone on the table, before dropping into a chair facing her house. He'd *enjoyed* himself at Mina's. She'd been funny and interesting, and her face moved when she talked, and he hadn't wanted her to stop talking, because he hadn't wanted to stop watching her face move.

But then he'd been leaning in to kiss her, and she'd told him about her HIV, and the animation in her face had turned into pill bottles on the bathroom counter and blinds that were always closed and doctor's visits and the heavy weight of watching someone slowly withdraw until the day you came home, and they weren't there at all.

Levi rested his forehead in his hand, feeling the weight of his head and the way it pressed his elbow into the table. He'd caught his skin on the table in a weird way and he should move his elbow, but the pinching kept him from disappearing into the past. Into what he should have done better, the times he should have reminded Kimmie to take her pills and the times he'd reminded her too much. Into the last day when she'd said, "Don't go to work today. I feel like something bad is going to happen," and he'd been frustrated because he couldn't find his keys, and he'd said, "You always feel like something bad is going to happen."

Only this time, Kimmie had been right.

He dropped his palm to the wood with a slap, his head bouncing once before he righted it and stared again at Mina's house.

Knowing what he knew now, knowing how everything ended, he still wouldn't go back and change anything about the day he'd walked up to Kimmie and asked for her phone number. He'd loved her more than he thought was possible—still did. Every minute they'd been together had been the best minute of his life.

A love like that was possible, and he believed lightning could strike twice.

But he didn't know if he could go through the pain of loving someone who was slowly dying again. He had doubted he was strong enough for more heartbreak. Was he strong enough for worse?

The screen on his phone flashed on with his sister's face, then vibrated on the table.

"Hey, sis," he said.

"I've been trying to call you all day. Where have you been?"

"Yeah, sorry." He'd felt the phone vibrate in his pocket but hadn't wanted to interrupt Mina to even check who it was. "I was over at my neighbor's, helping her build a raised garden bed. She made me dinner."

"Oh? The neighbor Dennis mentioned?"

"Don't go getting any ideas," he warned, hearing *ideas* she already had in the *oh*. If she got ideas, she'd call and text him nonstop to ask how the relationship was going. Eventually he'd turn off his phone just to get a break.

At some point when they were kids and she'd been stuck being Mom, she'd apparently gotten the idea that Moms smothered, and she hadn't let go.

"Nothing is going to happen," he said, before she could start planning his future wedding. "Mina is HIV positive."

"Oh." This *oh* was flat, not yet judgmental but

edging that way. Brook was no longer getting any ideas. "I guess it's best, then, that you're not yet over Kimmie's death."

"What?" He regretted answering the phone, regretted saying anything. He *especially* regretted saying anything about Mina. Her disease was not his sister's business, and it had not been his information to share, even if he'd thought Brook would understand his hesitation.

Which she clearly didn't. "Maybe it's not so bad if she's one of those poor souls who's had it since birth or got it from a blood transfusion or something. But what do you know about your neighbor? Maybe she got it from sharing a needle or she slept around in college or... I don't know. How else do people get AIDS?"

"I think there's a difference between HIV and AIDS," he said slowly, realizing he didn't know for sure. He didn't know the answer to any of his sister's questions. And the question of how Mina got HIV didn't matter.

Did it?

"Well, you're not going to be seeing her again to find out, are you?"

"Brook, less than a minute ago you were hopeful I was over Kimmie, would fall in love with Mina, get married and produce nieces and nephews for you to spoil."

"All I said was 'Oh.'"

"Yeah, but we both know where that *oh* was going."

"Well," she huffed, "you had always wanted to get married and have kids. Maybe you could marry someone with HIV, but you couldn't have kids with them. It would be wrong to knowingly bring kids with AIDS into the world."

I think HIV and AIDS are different. He didn't bother repeating himself. She hadn't listened the first time, and she wouldn't listen a second. "I think someone with HIV can have children who don't have the disease. Isn't that part of what they talk about on the news when they talk about AIDS in Africa?"

"Honestly, Levi, you think a lot of things, but what do you know? About the disease or your neighbor?"

He bristled at her tone. She was his older sister, and her tone had likely been condescending since the day he was born.

At least, that was how he remembered it.

Most of the time he was able to remind himself that she was his sister, and she cared about him, and she fussed and bossed over everyone she cared about, from Dennis to her children to their aging father.

But tonight, he wasn't in the mood. "Look,

Brook, I get that you want me to get married again—"

"You *liked* being married," she interrupted. "Even if…"

"Yes. Even if Kimmie had entire weeks where she didn't leave the house, I did like being married. But I'm thirty-seven years old, and I get to pick the women I date." Even as the words came out of his mouth, he felt like her baby brother.

"And if you want to hear about any of them, you have to reserve judgment. At least until you meet them. And you have to *pretend* that I'm an adult and might pick out someone good. After all, I picked Kimmie."

Silence reigned through the phone as Levi waited for Brook to point out that Kimmie's clinical depression had eventually killed her. He could *feel* his phone shudder at the effort his sister was putting forth to keeping her mouth shut.

"Kimmie was great," she said finally, her voice soft with affection. Because Kimmie had been great. She had been unable to be a light in her own life, but she'd been the sun, moon and stars for many others.

"Good night, Brook. Go remind Dennis to take his high blood pressure medicine or something."

"I worry."

Whether it was about him, or Dennis's health,

or any number of things, Brook didn't say, and it didn't matter. "I know."

"Someone has to."

"But it doesn't always have to be you."

On that note they finished their goodbyes, and Levi ended the call. Then he slouched in his chair to catch his breath. Talking to his sister for ten minutes was more exhausting than an entire day spent building a raised bed with Mina. For all Mina's chatter and energy, Levi had felt better *after* building the raised bed than he had before.

This was why he didn't call his family and only occasionally answered the phone when they called him.

His breathing back to normal, Levi glanced up at his windows. Mina's blinds had all been closed, and her house was dark.

It was too late to go over and apologize, but he could at least prove his sister wrong about the baby thing. He sighed. He knew the growing list of items he needed to apologize to Mina for, though he didn't know what he wanted out of it. To be back on her couch kissing? To be friends and neighbors? To make the barest effort at not being a total ass?

Or did he need to apologize simply because he was wrong and sorry about it?

Levi rolled his eyes at himself. No matter

what he was sorry for and why, he could at least be less ignorant when he apologized. Gathering his phone, he went in search of his laptop.

IT WASN'T UNTIL Friday that Mina was finally able to be outside after work, hands shoved in the new dirt in her new raised garden bed. Even though the nights were getting cooler, the sun had shone on the dark dirt all day, and it pressed warmth and possibility against her skin. She didn't even care if the greens she was planting grew into anything edible, so long as she had the excuse to be out here, away from her thoughts and her work and her problems.

The past week had been rough. Classes were starting, increasing the amount of work she needed to do and the amount of time she had to spend on campus. Departmental meetings, syllabi, double-checking on the assigned readings and that the bookstore and library both carried what the students would need, etc. The meetings were the worst. She could work on the syllabi from home, but the department wasn't yet willing to hold meetings through Skype. She'd always suspected that her emotions played a big role in the side effects of all her meds, and this week had done nothing to disprove her theory.

She'd spent more time on the toilet than she cared to admit to herself. Today wasn't just the first day she'd been able to be outside in the sun, it was the first day her stomach had felt like it belonged to a normal human being. Or mostly normal. She'd gotten accustomed to the base level of nausea her meds caused.

She patted the soil down over the seeds, trying not to let her feelings press down too hard.

Her emotions and her side effects fed off each other, making everything worse. She felt self-conscious about the time spent in the bathroom, which brought her thoughts back to Levi walking out on her, almost without a word. She'd stay later in her office, hunched over her desk, hand cramped from her tight control on her drawing—which meant her drawings were shit. And she'd both wish she were home where she would be more comfortable and be glad that she couldn't see if Levi's truck was pulling into his driveway and wondering if she'd catch a glimpse of him.

It had taken her three days of concentrated effort on what her therapist had said about thoughts just being thoughts before she had been able to say, "I'm better off knowing his true stripes now," and mean it. Only then had she been okay with leaving her office and spending time at home, in her garden and near her own bathroom.

Of course, when her emotions had settled down, so had her nausea.

"Hey, Mina," a woman's voice called from behind her. Mina stood and turned around to see her neighbor Echo standing on the sidewalk with her fluffy little dog on the other end of the leash, the dog's tongue flipping in and out of its mouth in exaggerated, adorable pants. "Nice garden bed."

"Thank you." Mina took advantage of the opportunity for a break. She and Echo had spoken a couple of times when her neighbor walked past with her dog. The woman seemed friendly and interesting and worth getting to know a little better.

"Was that Levi I saw helping you build it?"

"Yeah…" Mina replied, not sure where this was going.

Echo looked right and left, as if checking for spies in the bushes. "I've barely gotten Levi to say hi to me when Noodle and I walk by."

Noodle? The dog with the papillon ears and dachshund body and Pomeranian coat was named Noodle? Echo might be even more interesting than Mina had thought.

"I'm not sure he wanted to help," Mina said, feeling the lie stick on her tongue as she tried to make Sunday sound like *no big deal*. Echo caught the lie, too, because her eyebrows lifted up to her hairline.

"Okay, so he wanted to. And he's brought over my mail and helped me buy a lawn mower, but there's nothing more."

Given the continued elevation of her eyebrows, Echo understood the subtext of *there might have been something more* as easily as she'd recognized the lie. "I want to hear about this. You have dinner plans?"

Other than pasta with butter and Parmesan cheese? "No."

"The store had some nice-looking salmon. I bought myself a piece for tonight and a piece for tomorrow, but one indulgent dinner with a friend is better than two indulgent nights in by myself. Come over for dinner and a glass of wine, and you can tell me all about how Silent-Neighbor Levi ended up building you a garden bed."

"Honestly, Echo, there's not much to tell." And Mina wasn't certain she was comfortable sharing what information there was. After all, blurting out "I'm HIV positive" rarely went as well as she hoped with possible friends, too. And she still hadn't figured out how not to overshare.

"Do you not like salmon? Or wine?" A teenager rode by on a bicycle, and Echo's little dog barked and jumped about like the devil himself had been on those two wheels. "Or little barky dogs?"

"I like salmon. And I like wine. I'm okay with little barky dogs that aren't coming home with me." And she needed to make friends. So she needed to trust a little. Dinner and boy talk wasn't a bad place to start. "Is there anything I can bring?"

"Bring dessert. Come over in about an hour."

"Okay. Thanks."

"Gossip in the neighborhood." Echo tapped the tips of her fingers against one another. "This is doubly exciting because no one ever tells me anything." The movement of her fingers stopped, and she looked down at her dog, who looked up expectantly. "Probably because gossip is always a trade, and I only like to take. Greedy, my ex-husband always said."

Mina laughed at the blatant attempt to reassure her. "I'll be over in an hour, with ice cream." She was less sure about bringing gossip.

CHAPTER EIGHT

MINA STOOD ON Echo's front stoop, ice cream in a plastic bag in one hand while attempting not to clench her nerves too tightly in the other. Once, in another lifetime, she would have been bouncing with excitement at a new friend. Her body still remembered those times, and wanting them back was the reason she'd made a point to introduce herself to as many people as she could in her new town, including her cranky, handy-with-a-drill-and-friends-with-the-hardware-store-guy neighbor.

But that Mina had a different, naive understanding of the world. She'd grown up in a happy household, with parents who loved each other and their children. Maybe they were too intrusive in their kids' lives, maybe they just cared a lot; it didn't matter. All Mina had known about the world was that it was a place full of nice people you could trust.

The world had acquired shadows since her diagnosis. She didn't want to go back, really, because shadows added depth and interest, but she occasionally wished she could sink into her old happy-go-lucky self, the one who found the world to be full of friends rather than potential hurts. The one fascinated by the macabre but who didn't understand it.

She took a deep breath and knocked. Noodle started yapping from deep inside the recesses of the house, a sound which got louder and louder until the front door opened, and the dog spun and leaped at Echo's feet.

"Welcome," Echo said with an expansive wave of her hand and a surreptitious sweep of her foot to push the dog out of the way. "Let me take the bag from you and get the ice cream in the freezer. Come in."

"It smells delicious," Mina said as she stepped through the doorway and waited to be sniffed and approved by the dog. "What is it?"

"Salmon in a cilantro sauce. Given how much cream is in the dish, it *should* be delicious. There's rice and sautéed squash, too."

Mina followed Echo and the aroma to the kitchen, waiting off to the side while her neighbor put the ice cream in the freezer.

"Dinner's pretty much ready," Echo said, balling up the plastic bag and tossing it to the back of the counter. "The table's even set. And there's a bottle of wine out there, if you want to pour us some. I'll feed the beast, so she doesn't try to get in your lap, then bring the food out, and we can serve ourselves."

The table was set with matching floral china, silverware and what Mina assumed to be crystal. Despite the casualness of the invitation and Echo's manner, she felt underdressed in her jeans and cream tank top with a big black bow. It was the flats. A girls' night in with crystal deserved heels.

"Like my china?" Echo asked as she came from the kitchen into the living room. Noodle was chomping happily on kibble in the background. "When my ex left me, I got to keep all the trappings of having once been married. The china, the crystal, the silverware. For a long time after I moved, it stayed in the cupboards, and I ate off regular plates and drank out of cheap glasses. Then I decided I was worth fancy, and I haven't looked back."

With a closer look, Mina realized Echo was not only older, but older than Mina had thought. "It's nice. I won't feel underdressed, then."

"Feel like you deserve better. And sit, sit. Let's eat."

Maybe it was the wine, maybe it was the good food, and maybe it was that Mina felt like herself for the first time in a week, but she relaxed into dinner and conversation with Echo like they were old friends. Well, not quite like old friends, because they were sharing basic bits of information with each other such as where they were from and what brought them to Missoula. But, much like she had felt with Levi on Sunday, Mina was immediately comfortable with Echo.

They laughed and joked as they cleaned up the kitchen together and scooped ice cream into bowls. Mina had purposely brought over different kinds of ice cream than she'd had last week, not wanting to make dinner at Echo's feel too much like dinner with Levi. Not that she would confuse the neighbors, but one of those dinners hadn't turned out as she'd planned.

They ate their ice cream at the dining room table, and this time Noodle got to help with the cleanup. When those bowls were put in the dishwasher, Echo poured them each a full glass of wine, and they moved to her living room for a chat.

"So," Echo said as she curled her legs around her on the couch, and her dog settled into her lap. "Tell me how Levi came to be at your house swinging a mighty hammer."

Mina sank into a deep armchair with plush cushions and a high back and sides. She'd probably had a little too much to drink, because the armchair felt like the closest thing she'd had to a hug in ages. "I don't know. I introduced myself to him shortly after I moved in and was trying to meet my neighbors. He helped me get a good deal on a new lawn mower, and I was outside struggling with the raised bed when he came over to help. He said he couldn't concentrate if he knew I was outside struggling so much. He seemed gruff and standoffish when I first met him, but after that he just seemed gruff."

"I've lived here for two years, and he's still standoffish to me." Echo's lips were pursed in disappointment, and Noodle looked up at her with disgust at the heavy pat on the head she got.

"Did you want something more?"

Echo shrugged and went back to petting Noodle in a way that made the dog relax in her lap again. "In reality, probably not. In my fantasy world, yes. I was newly divorced and thought the solution to my problems was someone who would stick around. Levi always struck me as the kind of guy who sticks."

"Yeah. He does seem that way, doesn't he?" It was the jawline, Mina decided. And the broad shoulders. The handiness with tools and that stupid hodgepodge lawn mower of his. A man who would stick with that lawn mower had to be a man who would stick in a relationship.

That was the same kind of reasoning that

made a known jerk seem like a nicer person because he got a chocolate Lab puppy. That kind of reasoning got women into relationships that went nowhere but in downward spirals.

Or out the front door.

"Do you know something about him that I don't, Mina?" Echo was looking intently at her glass of wine, as if the light bouncing off the crystal held the secrets to the universe.

Mina wasn't the only one who'd had too much to drink tonight. She was grateful that tomorrow was Saturday, and she could sleep off whatever headache she was sure to get.

Which didn't stop her from reaching forward and pouring more wine in her glass. At Echo's gesture, Mina topped off her glass, as well. She drank deeply out of the garnet courage, giving the buzz time to reach her brain and cloud her thinking. She *wanted* the edges of her mind to go fuzzy, to stop thinking, *can I trust this person?*

If she didn't say anything to Echo, then she continued to be just-Mina. The friendship would develop as if Mina were another neighbor, and, depending on how close their friendship got, eventually Mina might tell her. Maybe Echo would be upset that she hadn't been told until then, and maybe she wouldn't be. The problem was *you never knew.* Rarely did the opportunity come up naturally for Mina to hear someone's ignorance or otherwise on HIV, and, as she'd learned the hard way, people's words and their actions could be diametrically opposed.

Mina took another sip. But alcohol never could dull her mind. All it ever did was make her riskier.

A lesson she'd also learned the hard way.

Or not learned, she reconsidered with another sip of her wine. She hadn't become a teetotaler.

"He came over for dinner after we finished the garden," Mina said. "And I thought something was between us." She shook her head. "No," the word slurred out. "There was definitely something between us. But I have a health problem, and I thought he should know before, well, before anything."

She shrugged her heavy shoulders. "He thanked me for telling him and walked out. Though he put his dishes back in the sink. So that was nice."

"That rat," Echo said, plopping a heavy hand on her dog, who barked, either in sympathy or irritation, Mina couldn't tell. "I didn't think he was that kind of guy."

"Better to know now." Mina robotically repeated the words she'd been reassuring herself with for an entire week. They didn't help any more now than they had on Monday morning.

Any dulled pain was more likely to do with the second bottle of wine they were on.

"Did I tell you why my husband left me?"

Mina's mind skipped over their conversation for the night. Though she was pretty sure she wasn't remembering everything they'd talked about, she didn't think she'd have forgotten hearing that. "No."

"I had breast cancer. Young. We caught it early, and I was about as lucky as I could be for treatment." Echo looked down at Noodle and scratched behind the dog's ears. Noodle turned her black eyes up at her owner with more love and affection than Mina thought she had ever seen in another living animal.

"Jackson stayed with me through the treatment. After I got the all clear, things just didn't seem to be right between us. He was distant and afraid to touch me. He'd never been afraid to touch me, even when I was sick and physically fragile." Her petting on the dog sped up in tune with her emotion and the anger Mina could hear building in her voice. The dog grunted, then rearranged her head on Echo's lap and settled in, like they'd done this before.

"When I asked him about it, he said he couldn't look at me without thinking I was going to die. And it scared him. He didn't think he could go through that again. We argued a lot. I even insisted that we go to counseling, though I knew he was a stubborn fool once he made up his mind.

"I asked him how long he'd been thinking of leaving me, and he said since I came home and told him my diagnosis. He knew then, that if I survived, he'd never be able to look at me the same way again."

"That's real sick," Mina said.

Echo's hand stopped its motion on Noodle, and her head jerked up. "It is, isn't it? I moved to Missoula for a new start, and he's still living in Billings, and I hear he's dating someone. I don't know how he thinks he'll be able to guarantee that she'll outlive him."

"Maybe he snuck some blood from her and has sent it in to be scanned for cancer risk."

Echo snorted. "He'll be surprised and disappointed when she's one of those people who get cancer, even though they don't have a genetic history of it."

"Or has a random, deadly accident," Mina said, her dark humor helped by all the wine she'd had.

Echo giggled, then slapped her hand over her mouth. "Oh, dear. It was really terrible of me to laugh at that."

"I won't tell. And you can always blame the wine," Mina said, reaching forward and topping off their glasses. They were both in for a bad morning anyway, might as well finish off the second bottle.

"Do you wish he'd told you earlier, when you were diagnosed?"

"No." Echo shook her head. "Maybe it would have been more honest, but it was easier to go through the cancer with his support."

"I have HIV," Mina said, the wine and the ease of the conversation loosening her tongue.

"Oh."

"I'm not... You can't catch it from me having dinner over here."

"I know that much, at least." Echo waved her off. "And that's why you felt you had to tell Levi before you even..."

"Before we kissed. Even if you can't catch it from kissing."

"I understand better why he ran off."

Mina was stunned into absolute stillness. Given the conversation they'd had so far, she expected some sympathy from Echo.

"Oh, don't look at me like that," Echo said, waving wildly in the air. "Leaving without giving you a chance to talk was a rat thing to do, and you don't want to date a rat. Maybe he really can't handle dating someone with a chronic disease, but he should have at least been up-front before not letting the door hit him on the way out."

Mina settled back into her chair. This was more what she'd expected from her new friend.

"Dating is a series of gambles where each person slowly lays their hidden, scared cards on the table, until one of you calls or you both go all in." Echo had started to really get into her speech. Even through her drunken haze, Mina could see that her neighbor's arm waving had become exaggerated. Probably because of *Echo's* drunken haze. Noodle looked up suspiciously at her owner but didn't get off Echo's lap.

"You're at a disadvantage because you have to show your cards first thing, before a guy's even gotten a chance to know if the benefits of going all in are worth it. Post-kiss, Levi might have decided you were the best thing that had ever happened to him. Pre-kiss, well…"

Indeed. "So far I've not found a guy who thought the benefits were worth it."

"No boyfriend since… Uh, were you born with HIV?"

"No." Mina didn't elaborate, and Echo was either too drunk or too kind to press on. "I've had boyfriends, but they weren't all in."

"All in" seemed to imply someone who did more than pat themselves on the back for slipping on a condom and having sex. Someone who was willing to listen when Mina was having bad med days—or weeks—or be understanding about her yeast infections. The men she'd dated had wanted a medal.

She'd been lucky, though. While she'd endured private snubs and comments, no one had yet exposed her private life and her virus online. She hadn't yet been subject to internet bullying, death threats and the many other scary things strangers threw at another stranger for no reason other than they could, and it gave them a power trip.

I've not been bullied online. Thank God for small blessings.

"You know," Echo said, looking sad for the first time tonight, "even someone who says they're all in doesn't stay that way. 'In sickness and in health,' the vows said. Jackson stuck with me 'in sickness' once, but he'd never agree to do it again."

"That's rat behavior, too." Mina knew her relationship problems were unique—or as unique as could be when 1.2 million people in the United States shared the same disease—but facing relationship problems wasn't unique at all. Everyone had them.

"How come you're not bothered by my disease?" Mina asked. Over the years she'd told many people for various reasons about her status and gotten responses from shrugs to pity to judgment to fear. Echo's response was as cool as the best health-care practitioner's and much warmer.

Echo shrugged. "Maybe the alcohol? Maybe I need a friend and you seem like someone worth getting to know. Freaking out would probably cost me a friendship."

"Well, I appreciate it." Mina had known that moving to a new town would eventually mean more *tells*. She hadn't expected to tell two people in such rapid succession, and she hadn't expected the polar opposite of responses. She certainly hadn't expected the equanimity Echo displayed, not ever.

"There any wine left in that bottle?" Echo asked.

"No." Mina picked it up and shook it. "We drank it all."

"Can you get home okay?" Echo shoved at Noodle, who resisted long enough to make her displeasure clear, then hopped off.

Home was across the street and four houses down. Mina could make it that far. "I think so."

"Wanna stay the night? I have a guest bedroom. The sheets are clean."

"I'll be okay," she said, standing and wobbling a bit. "I'm sober enough to remember to take my meds and, well, forgetting to take my meds is bad."

The last time she'd gotten this drunk had been years ago, when the guy who'd given her HIV had shown up at a bar and was making the rounds, hitting on women. When she'd confronted him on the way to the bathroom, his only response had been "Are you going to tell them?"

No had been the cowardly truth that she'd tried to drown in shots of Buttery Nipple and Rattlesnake. She didn't remember how she'd gotten home, and she certainly hadn't taken her meds. Her morning had been spent hugging the toilet and listening to her roommate yell at her.

"I'm not gonna stumble past you sprawled out in my driveway in the morning when Noodle needs to go out to pee, am I?"

"If that happens, let me continue to sleep. I'll need it."

Echo shook her head, then looked sick. "Depending on my morning, I might let Noodle crap on the floor."

"Hey," Dennis called from across their usual Friday night booth. Judging by the irritated curl of his friend's eyebrows, Levi was pretty sure he'd been trying to get his attention for a while. "Did you hear my story?"

"Yeah, I can't believe it, either."

"You know, you're a shitty friend."

"Tell a different kind of story, and maybe I'll pay attention," Levi said defensively, even though Dennis was right.

He sighed. "Or tell it again and I'll pay attention this time. My mind is wandering."

That was also a lie. Levi's mind wasn't wandering. It was camped out in front of his neighbor's house, waiting for a sign that she was home, something he'd not seen once this week. It was like she was avoiding him. Which, if she was, he understood. While waiting for her, he'd been trying to avoid himself all week and hadn't succeeded. No matter how hard he worked or how many weights he shoved on the bar at the gym, he and the cruel way he'd reacted on Sunday night were there.

"I think it's your new neighbor." Dennis took a swig of his beer. It was a good night. He was only on his second bottle of beer. The shot of whiskey remained untouched. "I saw her walking across the campus once. She's cute. Too young for us."

God, he'd forgotten his first impression of Mina—that she was cute but too young for him. Somehow, in looking at her artwork online and thinking of the chronic illness she lived with, youth didn't matter any longer. Had she been born with HIV? And, if she had, had she ever been able to be *young*? Did he care?

"I should have stayed around to talk with her," Levi muttered. He should have done everything about that night differently. Or everything after Mina had told him.

"Like, you were standing on her front lawn and she said, 'Hey, let's talk' and you said no?" Dennis lowered his beer to the table, his mouth open in disbelief. That he didn't say anything else was proof Brook hadn't shared Mina's secret. Not that he'd expected his sister to do something so terrible, but he'd done it, and he wouldn't have expected it of himself, either.

"You just told me she was too young for me." Levi waved away another beer. Maybe Mina was too young for him, but he was too old to keep drinking until the world blurred. And these days the world blurred at fewer and fewer drinks.

His oldest friend shrugged. "She looks too young for you. But age would be the least of my concerns if she were inviting me into her house."

"Yeah?" Levi asked, knowing he'd regret this. "What would top that list?"

"The plumbing just don't work like you think it should."

Levi raised his eyebrows at his friend, who looked all-knowing.

"She's young and maybe has expectations. Remember when you were young and…"

Levi interrupted with the only thing he could

think of to stop this conversation dead. "Don't forget that you've been married to my sister for twenty years, and I don't want to hear about it."

Dennis took a swig from his beer. "Stuff changes. That's all."

"I don't want to talk about my neighbor or my dick with you. Separately or together."

"Fine." Dennis called for another beer. Levi asked for a glass of water. He didn't need to drink more, but he also didn't want to leave his friend stranded. Especially not when Dennis was in a good mood.

"When ya' gonna pay up on the fantasy league?" Levi asked. If Dennis was going to make him uncomfortable with questions about Mina, Levi would return the favor and bug him for money.

CHAPTER NINE

MINA HAD MADE it out of bed enough to get down to the kitchen and take her morning meds before collapsing on the couch in a sprawl. She'd hoped to stay that way, eyes closed and clinging to the cushions all morning, but her head was knocking too much to embrace her hangover and all the pain that went with it. When the knocking was followed by the doorbell, she realized it wasn't her head.

It was her front door.

She rolled off the couch into a heap, then dragged herself up and opened the door. The bright morning sun had her blinking back a reinvigorated headache and swallowing her nausea. Stupid, she now realized, to have spent all week with an upset stomach and then to have drunk enough wine to invite vomiting just as the side effects of her meds seemed to have settled.

But the damage of both the drinking and *the tell* was done; there was no escaping the consequences. Mina raised her hands to her brow to block some of the light and stared uncomfortably at Levi, who was standing on her front porch. She swallowed and searched his face for judgment, but all she found was concern.

"Are you—" he hesitated and sniffed "—okay?"

"Yes. I would just really like to be back on my couch right now." If she were lucky, a big hole would open up under her couch and suck her down to a place where no one was playing drums in her head, and Levi wasn't standing on her porch while she looked and smelled like something the cat dragged in last week, then buried under the trash can for the dog to dig up.

"Can I come in?"

If she were still drunk, this would be easier. "Why are you here?"

"I wanted to apologize and talk to you."

"Can you come back?" After she'd showered... and brushed her teeth for a half an hour.

"Are you sure you're okay?"

"I'm hungover, Levi." God, he had to be able to smell the stale alcohol on her. She hadn't brushed her teeth in twenty-four hours. But at least she hadn't barfed on herself. Small mercies and all that. "I had dinner with Echo. We drank too much. I need a minute before I hear any apology."

"Oh." Levi's face was still stoic and cranky, but the relief that poured off him softened his hard edges like a waterfall softens a cliff. Despite her headache and nausea, she wanted to dive right into him and swim around for a while.

Even though he'd left her.

"I was worried."

"Oh," Mina said, the word exiting her mouth on a soft puff of air. It had been a long time since someone had worried about her.

No, that wasn't true. Her parents and her brother and her doctors and the nurses and everyone else she interacted with because she was HIV positive worried about her. They worried about her T-cell count and her virus count and the side effects of her meds and her mental health and if she got her flu shot. The men she'd dated had worried, too—about the condom breaking and what their friends would think. Everyone's worries revolved around her HIV, like there was nothing else Mina could possibly be into that might be cause for concern.

HIV or nothin'.

Levi, though, was worried about her hangover.

"Wait. What did you think happened to me?"

"Honestly, I don't know. Maybe you couldn't answer my knock because you fell in the shower. Then you opened the door and, well, you look like shit."

"Come in. If you want to talk, we can talk, but first I need to shower and brush my teeth."

MINA STEPPED INTO her dining room to the smell of coffee. Levi was examining one of the favorite drawings she had on her wall, the one with a cockroach playing a French horn, the bug's body parts labeled in Russian. She'd picked it up at the Small Press Expo, and the whimsy in its clean lines never failed to make her smile. He looked from it to a comic of two tongues experiencing their first French kiss and shook his head before turning around.

She still felt like her face was green around the edges, even if her eyes were less bloodshot and she definitely smelled better; but with the look of appreciation in his eyes, she didn't think he noticed. Either that or he had some strange fetish for women in gym shorts and *Brothers Karamazov* T-shirts.

"Is that coffee I smell?" she asked, pleased to hear that the shower had also rescued the post-drunk quiver from her voice.

"I thought you'd probably want some. And a glass of water. I don't know if you have tomato juice." He walked into the kitchen and went right for the cabinet with her mugs. He must have either snooped or paid careful attention when he was over the other night. Given the large cup of coffee he poured her, she'd forgive him the snooping. "Do you take anything in it?"

"Usually some sugar, but not this morning. Or not yet."

The crockery was hot against her skin as she wrapped her fingers around the mug and bent her face to the restorative steam, sighing. "Thank you." However, the first sip didn't feel as good in her stomach as she'd hoped, either because of her queasy digestion or her dancing nerves. Maybe both. Still, she took another tentative sip.

Levi poured himself a cup. "Do you have stuff to make pancakes? Or an omelet? Your stomach would probably feel better with some food in it."

"An omelet, no." She shuddered. "I don't think I could handle it. Pancakes, maybe. But you wanted to talk. So let's talk."

"I'll make pancakes while we talk," he said, his body quivering with pent-up energy. She realized that with the exception of the night he'd been over for dinner, she'd always seen him working on something. Mowing his lawn or helping her with her garden bed. Levi was a tinkerer. A doer. Something she liked in a man.

She gave a wry chuckle, stopping when her

stomach rebelled. "Well, don't be insulted if I don't eat any."

Levi pulled the canister marked Flour close to him. She directed him to the drawer with the measuring cups and the mixing bowls. Once he'd gotten everything out for breakfast, he said, "I'm sorry," still staring down at the pre-pancake operation.

He must have realized he wasn't looking at her, because his head flipped up with a start, and he turned to face her, waiting until their gazes caught before speaking again. "I'm sorry for running out last Sunday, without even a word."

"Is that something you do often? Run out on people?" She clutched the mug between her hands, letting its warmth comfort her.

He shook his head as he turned back to his breakfast-making. "No. The opposite, really. You have no reason to believe me, but I'm generally known as the kind of guy who sticks, long past when he should."

"You're right. I don't believe you. But you're here apologizing, and that's a step in the right direction." Wanting desperately to believe, she stepped farther into the kitchen, leaning against one of her countertops, the mug of coffee still clutched in her hands.

The deliberate way he put butter in the microwave seemed as much about procrastination as making pancakes, but if it was, he didn't allow himself to wallow in it. With the microwave buzzing in the background, he faced Mina, again waiting until she met his gaze. "My wife committed suicide. She was clinically depressed. She had been fighting her illness for as long as I knew her, and then one day, she lost the battle."

The microwave dinged. Coffee and the glimmer of an understanding had settled her stomach enough that she could help make breakfast, even if she wasn't yet sure she wanted to eat it. She stood on her toes and looked in at the half-melted butter. Then she set the timer and sank back down against the counter, her nearly empty cup in hand.

Levi took a deep breath, and she realized that probably wasn't the worst he had to say. "And I'm ashamed to admit that when you said you are HIV positive, my first thought was 'Fuck. Am I only attracted to women who are going to die?' And I didn't want to face that battle again."

Mina reached behind her for the glass of water Levi had poured for her and took a long drink while various reactions raced through her head. Finally she settled on the one response among many that she knew was true. "I'm sorry about your wife."

She could sort through all her other feelings later.

"Thank you." His shoulders dropped immediately. When he dumped the flour into the bowl and it puffed in his face, he seemed to relax. The microwave beeped again, and, as if they had been making pancakes together for years, Mina got the butter out, setting it on the counter next to him.

"You didn't think I was dirty or diseased or…" She let the *or* speak for the nasty words that she didn't want to repeat.

"No. When I left your house, I was only thinking of me. You, and what the disease meant for you, never crossed my mind." Regret, and maybe embarrassment, colored the tone of his voice, but his face remained unreadable. "I reduced both you and Kimmie to your illnesses, and I'm sorry about that."

The sincerity in his voice had her wanting to reach out for him, so she gripped her cup tighter. "Who are you thinking of now?"

"I need a griddle," he said, then opened the cabinet Mina pointed at and got out the pan. The clang it made on the stove when he set it down made her wince and reach for another drink of water.

"Me," he continued. "I'm still thinking of me, and I'm thinking that I've never met anyone like you. I'm thinking that I want to get to know you better."

Mina wrestled with pleasure and disappointment while he cracked two eggs into milk he'd measured out, and she continued her silence while he poured in the cooled butter. She liked him. She wanted to like him more. But she also wanted him to be thinking of her.

Eventually she wrestled honesty to the ground and held on to it. "Okay."

She wasn't the only one struggling with her emotions. No matter that his face didn't reveal anything, the methodical way Levi sprayed the griddle with oil and carefully plopped two scoops of batter on the hot surface had more to do with an internal struggle than pancake-making. He seemed too practiced at the pancakes to need to think so hard about the griddle. So she wasn't surprised when he said, "That's not the only thing I have to apologize for."

"Oh?" Tension pressed the air from the room against her skin.

"I told my sister about your HIV."

"It was not your secret to tell," she said, her words brittle, breaking on the tile as they fell out of her mouth.

"I know. She called me right when I got home from your house on Sunday. I was still shaken. Which doesn't excuse what I did." The tops of the pancakes started to bubble. Levi pulled a spatula out of the crock by the stove and flipped them.

"You were only thinking of yourself," she said.

"I wasn't even thinking, which is worse. I'm sorry."

Disbelief stopped her from being able to say anything, so she stared at him in silence as the pancakes he was making sizzled on her stove until he stacked them onto a plate and slid them into the warm oven. In the little bit of time she'd known him, he'd walked out on her once and told her biggest secret to his sister.

And he was standing in her kitchen making her pancakes, and she hadn't thrown any at him.

She didn't know which surprised her more.

"Did you just come over here to make me pancakes and apologize?"

"I didn't expect to make pancakes," he said, nudging the new batter he'd plopped into the pan into nice circles. "I came over here to apologize."

"And?" she asked, her fingers tapping on the cabinets at her side.

"And to ask you about your illness. Maybe to ask for a date."

"Only maybe?"

One of the pancakes hit the side of the griddle as he flipped it. "I don't know. It was hard to lose Kimmie." He paused, and she could see him fighting to slip his reserve back on, like it was a sweater that didn't fit anymore. "I hadn't believed it could happen. No matter how bad her depressive episodes got, suicide seemed like something that happened to other people. So facing a relationship—even a date with a pretty girl—where premature death is in the cards, I just don't know. It's cowardly, and I'm sure it's foolish, but if I'm not honest now, how will you trust me?"

His back straightened, and despite little movement in his face, she could tell he'd recovered himself. "I'd like to hear about the disease from you, not the internet."

"This is still all about you. What about me?" Honesty was nice, but it wasn't enough. People could be real mean in the name of *I'm being honest*.

"You?" He looked up from his pancake-making in surprise. "Even if I had all your creativity and imagination, I don't think I could have ever imagined someone as intriguing as you moving in next door."

The warm air that slid out of the oven door when he opened it to add pancakes to the stack melted some of her irritation, but not all of it. "And you didn't leave on Sunday because you're afraid of catching the bug?"

He shook his head. "No. I don't know much about HIV, but I know the condom part. You tell me what else I need to know."

"I don't need to *convince* someone to be in a relationship with me just because I have HIV." She'd fallen for the trap of settling for less before.

"I didn't ask you to. I just want you to educate me about HIV."

There was still a small, hurt part of her that wanted him to define the difference between convince and educate, that wanted him to *beg* her for the information. But most of her wanted to get back to where they were on Sunday night, with his face a breath away from hers and her body tingling with anticipation. Being suspicious of how much she wanted it didn't mean she was willing to argue semantics.

"I wasn't born with HIV, if that's part of what you're asking," she said, getting the most damning portion of her story out before he could imagine her as some innocent lamb done wrong by a blood transfusion. Not that she deserved to be HIV positive—or that anyone deserved to get this disease—but people had funny notions about sex and cosmic punishment, and if Levi was one of those, she wanted to know that as soon as possible. "I got it because I had unprotected sex with a man I trusted. I was a little drunk, and in the back of my mind I knew better, but that doesn't change what I did."

She gave a hollow laugh at her past self. "I remember being so glad I wasn't pregnant, because besides not using a condom, I wasn't on the pill, either. The guy ended it pretty much immediately after, so it took my roommate three months to convince me to go to Planned Parenthood and get on the pill, which meant STD tests." She looked up from her hands to catch his eyes and dare him to judge her. "It's a good thing I wasn't pregnant."

Instead of recoiling in disgust or raising his eyebrows in disapproval, Levi just nodded and flipped the pancakes. "When my wife and I were first dating, and young and stupid and hotter for each other than we should have been, we had unprotected sex. I remember being relieved that she wasn't pregnant, too."

"Thank you."

"For the pancakes?"

"For not telling me how stupid I was at nineteen to be having unprotected sex." She'd been moralized against by those who thought she was justly punished for having sex before marriage and moralized against by those who had forgotten all the stupid things they'd done when they were nineteen—because the effects of their stupidity hadn't lingered.

"Oh, I figure you know it was stupid. Just like I know it was stupid to water-ski drunk. Doesn't mean I didn't do it when I was nineteen."

She laughed, something she hadn't thought she'd do during one of these conversations. "You could have drowned!"

"Yeah." Levi pulled the oven door open and set two more pancakes on the plate. "That only occurred to me later, after my sister yelled at me. I had only been worried about impressing the girl I was with."

Mina looked at her cup and rolled it nervously between her palms. "I had wanted to impress the guy, too. Be all cool and casual, like I wasn't worried about things. Easy. Not easy to have sex with, but easy to be around. Not one of those demanding chicks." She paused as something clicked in her mind. "Of course, at the time, I confused the two."

"Okay. So you did something stupid when you were young." He scraped the last bits of batter into the pan. After watching him make batches and batches of perfectly round pancakes, she was charmed to see two blobs spread out on the griddle. The imperfection made him seem more human. "What else do I need to know?"

"Um—" she shrugged "—if we get to that

point, sex will be low risk, but never *no* risk. My virus count is very low, and I haven't missed a dose in, God, years, but even with condoms, there's always a chance."

"Okay," he said, nodding and flipping the two imperfect pancakes. "Where do we go from here?"

"Well, I've told you all of this, but I still don't trust you. You both walked out on me and shared my health information. The latter is a very big deal. There aren't enough pancakes in the world to make it a minor mistake."

"How about a date?"

"Did you hear what I said? I don't trust you."

"You have good reason not to trust me. You don't know me. If you go on a date with me, then you can get to know me."

"You make that sound easy."

He shrugged, then leaned down and pulled out the pile of pancakes from the oven. Perfect, round, delicious-looking pancakes. She wanted the two funny-looking ones he'd just made.

"It's not easy. But I want to get to know you better, and the only way to do that is to ask. So go out to dinner with me."

"Okay," she agreed, the pull of the couch from last Sunday more than she could resist.

"Great." He looked up from the pancakes he was placing on a plate, a satisfied expression on his face that burrowed deeper in her soul than any smile. "Now, which one do you want?" he asked, holding out both plates.

"That one," she said, and he offered her the plate with the imperfect pancakes on it.

CHAPTER TEN

MINA HAD NEVER planned a first date and then sat down with that person and shared breakfast. Having had roommates, she'd shared kitchens with men pre–first date before, but those had been men who had slept with her roommates, and those were often one-night stands. This breakfast was much nicer. They'd returned to their previous status of Levi asking questions and Mina doing all the talking.

The singularity of it all had Mina skipping the farmers' market later that day in favor of sitting at her desk and sketching. As was her habit, she read over the last sketches she'd done. Her sketchbook wasn't a journal, per se, but a running story told in comics of a woman just like herself going through the things Mina was going through. She'd started it soon after her diagnosis. The counselor whom her college had found for her had recommended it as a way to understand what was happening to her, and she'd kept it up. *The Adventures of Mina +* continued, and probably would until, well, until one of the complications of the disease caught up with her and she died.

Or she was hit by a bus.

She smoothed the pages of the sketchbook, knowing where the lines for the panels would go and letting the feel of the paper against the palm of her hand tell her where the drawings would go. Then she got out her pencil and drew the squares. She wrote "The Tell, Third Time Is Not the Charm" in the first panel and then prepared to draw the humiliation of sharing her disease and watching a man walk out on her.

She hadn't yet figured out how to draw any conversation where she let that man take her to dinner, at least not one that anyone would believe.

A WEEK LATER, Levi sat in O'Reilly's and looked at the text message he'd gotten from Dennis.

In Bozeman for a job interview. Staying the night. Forgot to let you know.

Mary brought him his beer, and Levi drank it in one long gulp, like he used to do when he and Dennis were young and stupid, and too much beer didn't give him heartburn. Dennis never forgot about their Friday night at the bar. Never.

Not once since they'd moved to Missoula, since Kimmie's death—since everything.

And the couple of times Levi hadn't been able to make it, Dennis had given him hell. Bad friend, everything they'd been through, and all that. The mine accident, Kimmie's death and Dennis's cough wove between their feet, binding them to each other and preventing either of them from stumbling too far from one another.

But Bozeman? For a job interview?

Levi hadn't even known that Dennis had been looking for a new job, and especially not one in Bozeman, of all places. Taking Brook and the kids and moving three hours away. No more coaching soccer practice. No more Fridays at the bar. No more running into his sister at the grocery store and getting a cup of coffee with her on the spur of the moment, so he could hear all the news about the kids and Dad.

He and Brook had always lived in the same town. Always. After the accident, when both he and Dennis had been looking for something else to do, they'd come to Missoula together. They hadn't even talked about it. Dennis had said he had friends in town who could help them find jobs, and that had been that.

Mary brought another beer. Levi had drunk half of it before realizing that if he didn't stop, he'd be the pathetic one trying to figure out how to get home. He pushed the beer to the other side of the table and signaled for the waitress. He needed a glass of water and a burger.

Was Dennis giving up? After everything they'd been through together, now he was picking up and leaving?

WTF. I postponed a date with my neighbor for tonight.

Mina. She was hanging out at the edge of his mind. Another go at the life he'd wanted, with all of his family together. A wife, his sister, maybe kids. Hell, maybe their dad would even visit. They could make that happen. It could be possible. Recently he'd been spending more time with Solstice, his niece, really getting to know her as a person, not just as his sister's kid. He looked forward to getting that time with Skylar, too. Taking him for hikes and maybe out hunting or fishing.

Or whatever that kid wanted to do. Levi wanted to be with him as he grew up. The *how* didn't matter.

Dennis moving ruined all of that.

Levi tapped his fingers on the cracked wood while waiting for Dennis's response. The burger came before the text did.

We all got problems, man.

He turned his phone facedown and shoved it next to his beer. Apparently he was the only one who thought they had some responsibility to each other, especially after all they'd been through.

The burger might as well have been softened cardboard for as much as he tasted it as he wolfed it down. And he only noticed that the fries made his hands greasy; not if they were hot or not. Then he guzzled the glass of water and the rest of the beer and headed home.

ON SATURDAY NIGHT, Levi stood on Mina's front porch, a bouquet of flowers in one hand while the other knocked on her door. It had been a while since he'd been on a date—a real date—but he remembered that Kimmie had liked getting flowers. Until he learned what Mina liked, flowers couldn't hurt.

Though, if tonight went well, the fact that he'd shaved right before coming over had been just as smart.

Mina opened the door, wearing a flowy, floor-length cotton dress in a dark blue with earrings that dangled past the cut of her hair, though they didn't quite reach her shoulders. Between that and her sandals, she looked ready for the beach.

"Aren't you going to get cold?" he said, before leaning over to drop a kiss on her cheek.

"Levi, it's nice to see you," she responded, stepping away with amusement on her face. "Thank you for the flowers. Let me get a vase for them."

When she turned, his jaw dropped. The straps at the back of her dress came together along her spine. The dress wasn't incredibly revealing, but he'd never considered how sexy shoulder blades could look on a woman before.

Especially one walking away from him.

He started after her, catching up with her in her kitchen, where she had set a vase filled with water on the counter and was cutting the bottoms off the flowers' stems.

"Sorry. I meant to say, you look great."

Her eyes sparkled with what seemed like amusement, and the red of her apple cheeks deepened. "I know. I can tell by the look on your face that you like my dress."

"I do." He stopped himself before asking again if she was going to get cold. He had a spare flannel shirt in his truck if she did.

She must have read the question on his face, because she laughed. "I'm bringing a cardigan. Don't worry. But it's sweet that you're trying to take care of me."

The night air had to have been chilly on her

shoulders as they walked out Mina's front door, but after she locked up, she straightened her shoulders, settled her head on the top of her neck and walked on in front of him to his truck. He would have to figure out how to sit at dinner so he could see the slope of her shoulders from the back. And how her face moved in tune with her emotions.

"You drove to my house?"

"Well, there wasn't much driving. Mostly I just parked in front of your house." He had figured the gesture would delight her, probably more than the flowers. Her chin ticked up, and she made a pleased noise at the back of her throat when he opened the passenger door for her.

It was a short drive to the restaurant he had picked out, so there wasn't much time for Mina to talk about the many activities happening in her busy schedule, which had caused their date to be postponed an entire week. Levi was pulling into the parking lot of the restaurant when she mentioned something called a "drink and draw."

She should drive next time, so he could watch her face as she talked.

"Hold that thought," he said. "I want to know what that is, but let's get our table first."

While Mina walked toward the restaurant,

Levi rested his hand on the small of her back, keeping just behind her. The temptation for more, for walking his fingers around to hold the curve of her hips or reach and grasp her hand in his, was strong, but he resisted. The parking lot on the way into the restaurant on their first real date wasn't the place. Especially since he had broken her trust and needed to earn it back. A hand resting on her spine, feeling the heat of her body from under her dress, was a nice middle ground.

After they entered, he kept a little closer to her as they wove their way through the tables behind the hostess. The space was small, and all the tables were full. Which was fine by him. Mina, with her curves and her smile and that intoxicating view of her back, was the kind of woman he wanted everyone in town to see him with.

"So, drink and draw," he said as they sat down. "What's that?"

She glowed from within as excitement lit her eyes. "It's collaborative, group comic drawing. Everyone meets at a coffee shop or a bar and sits around drawing, only there are exercises like panel passes, where one person draws a panel of a comic, then passes it to the next person, who draws and passes it to the next, and so on until the comic is finished. They're a good chance to practice story and explore new styles."

She smiled at the waiter who poured water in

their glasses and told them the specials. Mina ordered a glass of wine, and he ordered a beer.

"What's good?" she asked.

"Everything. This is the best pizza you will get, not just in Missoula, but the *best*."

"You know I went to graduate school in Chicago," she said, looking up at him from her menu, the amused twinkle of her eyes visible through her long bangs. Everything about her was animated and alive. As far as he was concerned, she could talk about anything, so long as she kept talking and her face kept moving.

"It's a different kind of pizza than that, but good. You won't feel like you're missing out."

"Well, everything does look good."

"You teach a graphic novel course at the university, so why also the drink and draw?" he asked.

"Levi!" said a surprised and pleased voice walking past their table. His neck tensed in apprehension as his sister turned to face them.

"Brook, hi." He tried to sound excited to see her, but her reaction to Mina was unlikely to be pleasant. They'd texted a couple of times since their phone conversation but never actually addressed his neighbor and her HIV. Or Brook's judgmental reaction.

The only way out was through. "Brook, this

is my neighbor and my date, Mina," he said, putting an emphasis on the word *date*.

"Mina, this is my sister, Brook."

"Nice to meet you," Mina said, her hand out in greeting. She was a handshaker; it was one of the things he liked about her. Had liked about her since she stood on his porch babbling about being new in town and he felt both irritated that she'd interrupted his morning and that he didn't want her to go away.

Brook was pulling her hand out from her side and the introductions seemed like they would go smoothly when his sister's palm stopped at her hip. Seconds seemed to pass, even if it was only the blink of an eye, before his sister stuck out her hand for Mina to shake. Mina's smile froze on her face, a chill rising to her eyes and extinguishing the life in them.

His sister did shake Mina's hand. Eventually. But no one watching the interaction could have any doubt that there had been a moment when Brook had thought about putting her hand back down, leaving Mina's hand unshaken. And an insincere "Nice to meet you, too," hadn't helped.

"Did I overhear that you work at the university?" Brook asked, her voice tinny.

"I'm a professor of Russian language and literature. I also teach a course on graphic novels." Mina's entire body turned from the warm, lithe thing it had been before into peach-colored and thin, brittle glass. Like if he tapped her, she'd shatter into a million little pieces.

"Do their parents know?"

"Brook. I'm on a date. You shouldn't be doing this." The fake innocence in her voice made his skin crawl, and he wanted her gone. "I'll call you tomorrow."

"I assume their parents know that their kids are taking a graphic novel course," Mina said, staring intently at his sister, her tone leaving no doubt that she knew exactly what Brook had asked about and didn't think it worth her time to acknowledge. "But with college kids, you never know. Was taking a frivolous class the worst thing *you* did in college?"

"Brook," Levi said again, his voice low with warning. "We'll talk tomorrow."

"Fine. Call me tonight, if you get a chance," his sister said. She lifted her chin, and a hard smile spread over her face. "I'll be home early."

"I won't be."

At that goodbye, Brook pursed her lips, straightened her shoulders and walked off to meet her friends for dinner.

"I'm sorry about my sister," Levi said, as soon as Brook was out of earshot. "She…" An excuse for the way his sister had behaved hung on the edge of his lips, but he swallowed before he could rationalize away how mean Brook had been.

Mina shrugged, her attempted indifference barely able to make her shoulders rise a fraction of an inch. "It's okay." The bright tone in her voice was just as fake as his sister's had been and more heartbreaking.

"It's not. If I hadn't told her, she would have been so excited I was on a date that she would have greeted you with a hug."

Mina shrugged again. He wished she would stop, because she wasn't able to cover up her hurt with the movement, and he would feel more comfortable if she would just stop trying. He didn't say anything about it, though. His comfort was not Mina's problem right now.

"I've gotten worse," she said, her tone throwing away her pain before he could catch it.

"That doesn't make me less sorry."

"Well," she said, "this is a first date. It might not matter."

Levi wished she'd stop shrugging. He wanted to reach across the table and smooth the worries away from her brow, rub her shoulders until the muscles of her back relaxed and hold her in his arms so that she couldn't hear the cruel words people say—words that put such a stony look on her face. And so she wouldn't see people hesitate before shaking her hand.

But she was right. They were at a restaurant, on a first date, and he could tell by the wary way Mina kept one eye on where his sister sat and one eye on him that she didn't trust either of them.

If he wanted his *sorry* to matter, if he wanted anything to matter, he had to make it past this first date, to date number two and three, to hanging out at her house and binge-watching Netflix, to... He didn't let his mind go further. That future was unknowable, even to the people who wrote Kimmie's favorite horoscope websites.

"Well, I'd like to make it to a second date," he said, his words bringing a little life back into her smile. "And a third. Tell me more about teaching." Then he reached his hand across the table, palm up in invitation. When she placed her hand in his, he folded his fingers around the warmth and softness, never wanting to let go.

CHAPTER ELEVEN

"YOU SHOULD PARK in your own driveway," Mina said, though she couldn't deny the fluttering of pleasure in her chest that he was pulling up to the curb in front of her house. That small, silly gesture had meant more to her than the beautiful flowers.

"Nah. This is a date, and a date gets brought home, not brought next door to her home."

She could see the muscles of his face twitch in the light of the streetlamps. Levi wasn't the grouch she'd first thought him to be, but his emotions were subtle, and she'd have to work for them. Which was fine—he would have to work for her, too. Meeting his sister in the restaurant had been painful.

"Stay here," he said, his large, strong hand giving her knee a quick pat. The pleasure in her chest expanded as her date walked around the front of his truck and opened the door so she could step out.

"I like this old-fashioned courting." Feeling cared for rather than coddled, she slipped her hand into his and accepted help out of his truck. Then she tucked herself against the warmth of his body as they walked up to her front door. The dry night air was chilly on her bare shoulders, but she'd rather be slightly cold and lean against the man next to her than get her cardigan out of her purse.

They stayed touching, even as she fumbled at the door with her keys. Levi pulled away for only a moment, as the lock clicked and the door opened, and Mina flipped on the light.

The moment felt more real with the light on. In the restaurant, she'd been debating how insulted to be by his sister and how much she was going to blame Levi for it. In the car, with the chill of the fall air sneaking in through the cracked windows and the sharp scent of wildfires off in the distance—their smoke obscuring any hope of stars—everything had taken on a surreal feeling, as if some other Mina had been in that truck.

But now she turned to face him, his eyes locked on her as he closed the door behind him. The intensity of his interest tingled her skin. Tightness in her belly traveled down her thighs to her feet before boomeranging back to the more sensitive skin between her legs and around her nipples. Levi must have felt it, too, because they seemed to step into each other's arms in one choreographed movement. Before she could

think, or even breathe, she was wrapped in his
arms. Her head tilted up, and his lips pressed
against hers.

She tensed.

Levi didn't lift his head from hers, but a question lingered between them. *May I?* his hesitation seemed to say. A far cry from *Should
I?* Mina walked her fingers up his neck until
they were in his hair. The movement grounded
her, reminded her who she was here with and
why. Fear of being hurt or hurting had halted
her movement forward, but this was a man she
wanted to put her trust in.

She wanted to believe.

She grasped his hair and pressed her breasts
up against him. His fingers on her waist tightened once, before his palms flattened out.

Mina understood the desperation in his hands
as he held her to him. She felt that desperation, too. The need and the wanting. In the back
of her mind was a tiny reminder to wait, that
rushing into sex got her into trouble. But those
worries were swept aside when she opened her
mouth, and his tongue tickled the top of her
bottom lip.

She sighed and opened herself up to him. They
stayed locked, leaning against her front door, all
tongues, and lips, and hands, savoring the kiss.

The smell of him changed up close and with

the combined heat of their bodies. He smelled spicier and richer, almost like expensive dark chocolate. A taste to relish, rather than to rush through.

There is time. The thought struck Mina as his hands moved down to grasp her butt, and he pulled her closer. She lifted up on her toes and relaxed into his hands, letting him bear most of her weight. If they did this right, there could be time for everything, no need to hurry to get to it all.

Like that's not rushing wedding bells, she reprimanded herself.

Levi was the one who broke the kiss. In the dim light of her entryway, his eyes were dark and heavy with desire. The anticipation that had been building inside her pulsed.

"Hi," she said, though whether it was to Levi or desire, she didn't know.

"Hi." His answering smile started slow, then widened to lighten up his entire face. It took her breath away.

"Hi," he said again, smoothing her hair away from her face. Their previous kiss had been passionate, new and exciting, but his hand on her face had the exquisite tenderness of a long-time relationship. Passion, sure, but love was there, too.

Again you're rushing into this. It was too early

for love to have anything to do with her feelings for Levi. All the bubbly warmth spreading through her body and tingling between her legs was lust. She hadn't had sex in a long time, and the orgasms she gave herself didn't have the same depth. But if she didn't pull back, she'd end up hurt and confused. And, unlike the night she'd told him about her HIV, any recovery would be slow in coming. She knew this, because she still latched on to every hope like a drowning sailor to a lifeboat.

Or, more accurately, a moth to a flame.

Sex and orgasms she could want. That was real and that was now.

"Do you want a drink?" The words felt clichéd, but in all her years of dating, she'd never figured out a better way to ask a man to stay.

"I don't want to leave." Desire had deepened his voice, and her toes curled in response. "But I don't want a drink."

"Um, I don't have condoms."

His lips twitched, but he didn't step away. "Stupid of me. I thought that if we got to this point, you would be prepared."

"Waiting until the third date, taking things slow, had seemed like a good idea, earlier today." She'd stood in the aisle of the grocery store, her hand on the blue pack of Trojans, wondering if she should. Eventually she'd decided that it would be prudent to wait a date or two for sex—to give both of them a chance to feel comfortable—and she'd left the box on the shelf. Insurance, she'd thought, like not shaving your legs or wearing holey underwear for a date. A reminder that this *should not happen*.

At least, not yet.

But now she was standing in her entryway, her arms wrapped around Levi, one of his hands on her butt, the other resting on her neck, his fingers caressing her jawline, and insurance seemed like it had been a terrible idea. Sex seemed like the much better one.

He barked a short laugh. "That's one way to plan."

"I'm regretting it now."

"It was probably a smart decision," he said, bending down to drop a kiss on the top of her jaw. "I want...well, I want us to trust each other. We might both need to take this slower than we would like."

"You're not... This isn't..." She didn't want to ask the question. She didn't want to feel like she should ask the question, but it lingered in the back of her mind and would fester and rot if she ignored it. She'd learned that the hard way. It seemed like she had to learn everything the hard way.

"About your HIV? No." The very fact that he

addressed the question so directly told her that he was being honest. "You're the first woman I've been really interested in since Kimmie died. You're right about us taking our time. I want to enjoy every moment."

His voice caught, and the hand now resting on her shoulder felt gentler than it had before. Like he had found something fragile in her bones that he hadn't known was there. She would wonder again if his hesitation was about her disease, but his gaze was somewhere off in the distance.

Or maybe in the past.

He loved his wife. The realization gave Mina comfort. When she rubbed her hand against his biceps, he shook his head, smiled and looked down at her. And the night was going to be okay. She could hope for the best in this relationship.

"Go home, then," she said with a pat on his shoulder, "before we both think a trip to the drugstore is needed."

She loved to watch him smile. For the first couple of weeks of their acquaintance, his face had been neutral at best, and now she was standing close enough to notice how his smile lifted the corners of his eyes as well as his mouth. With his easy smile, any worry left in her heart. Mina stepped back into his arms for a hug. He kissed the top of her head. She pressed a kiss against the base of his neck.

"Slowly, then," she said into the fabric of his shirt.

"But if we see each other often, then it will seem fast."

"Go home."

He smiled again, dropped a kiss on her mouth, then left. She watched him walk across her lawn to his house, seeming to forget that his truck was parked on the street in front of hers.

CHAPTER TWELVE

MINA HAD A sleepless night. Once the glow of the date had worn off, she had succumbed to the temptation to think about all the things that could go wrong. The only benefit of her restlessness had been that she'd gotten up and drawn. Anxious feelings of love and rejection were perfectly suited to her newest book project, an illustrated collection of poems by Lermontov and Esenin. The pictures were avant-garde and risky and not really a comic at all, but she'd seen the characters as she'd read the poems, and she was self-publishing this one.

Even now, washing her coffeepot and mug, she was tempted to look out the window. To see Levi sitting in his house, maybe his phone at his ear. To check that his sister wasn't scaring him out of a relationship. To reassure herself that he was *there*, and the possibility that he'd be a fixture in her life remained a possibility.

Hope was painful. It had a way of clenching your heart and holding it hostage. Hope pulled Mina in multiple directions. It made her want to wrap her arms around her body, using the pressure to withstand the tightening of her ribs. But that was a protective response, and it wouldn't get her anything other than sore elbows and shoulders.

Instead, she rinsed soap off her mug and placed it in the dish drainer. She found it harder to follow the other path hope illuminated, even though she knew it was the smarter one. She had to keep her arms by her sides and her eyes on a positive future. She had to breathe through the rigidity until she could relax, waiting out the moment when hope broke through the surface and flowered into faith and trust. She knew from experience—not all of it good—that a relationship only blossomed if she believed.

So Mina concentrated on the hot water coming out of the faucet as it sluiced over her hand. She reminded herself again that anyone who could be easily talked out of a relationship with her by his sister wasn't worth her time, no matter how good a kisser he was and how soothing his smile.

As she pulled the stopper out of the sink, she let her worries drain away with the dirty water. They were still gurgling together when her phone rang.

"Hi, Mom," Mina said, after only a split-second debate over whether to answer the phone or not.

"Hi, honey. How's Montana?" Her mom's voice was fast and high-pitched, a dead give-away that she was worried.

"Good. Why do you ask?"

"You've not posted to Facebook recently, and so I don't know what's going on in your life."

"Mom, Facebook is hardly a good way to know what's going on in my life. Besides, I've been busy with work and making new friends and the house and everything."

"New friends?" The same hope Mina had just been battling cracked through her mother's voice.

"Yeah. And I went on a date last night."

Mina heard her mom's breath catch and thought she could hear her mom's mouth open and shut. She imagined her mother waving her hand at her husband, trying to catch his attention and give away that their daughter had *big news* without saying anything Mina could overhear.

"And he knows about my HIV." Better to get all the news out to her mom at once. Her mom wouldn't get up the courage to ask the question for another couple of weeks. Until then all their conversations would revolve around how to share the news, when to say it, the last time Mina had had a boyfriend and how he had taken the news, as well as how he'd treated her afterward.

Mina would rather talk about her drink and

draws than the complications something as microscopic as a virus lent to her love life.

She pictured her parents in the seemingly never-ending moment of silence. Her mom continuing to gesture toward her father, the confusion on his face as he mouthed that he didn't understand what she was trying to tell him and her hand movements getting more and more erratic until finally she whispered in frustration, "Mina's got a boyfriend."

"Not a boyfriend, Mom. We had one date." And only one kiss, but a thousand tender gestures over the course of the evening.

"But he knows," her mom said, confused.

"I told him before our date." She left out the details of the tell; her mother would only sigh and remind her to think before she spoke.

"You know I think it's important you tell someone before...well, before you're intimate." Mina's mother had never been comfortable talking to her children about sex. HIV had changed the type of advice her mom felt she should give and brought "the talk" that should have happened over a decade ago into the forefront of their relationship. Not that her mother was any more comfortable with the conversation, just that she didn't think she could avoid having it any longer. *Intimate* was the compromise. The soft look in Levi's eyes as he'd looked at her last night had been more in-

timate than the last time Mina had had sex—
not something she was going to share with her
mother, though.

"But I think you need to get to know a person a little better before disclosing your status."

"You don't know how well I know Levi,"
Mina pointed out.

"No, I don't. But you've not been in Montana
long enough to know someone very well. Not
well enough to know..."

Her mother couldn't bring herself to finish
that sentence, so Mina finished it for her in her
head. *Not well enough to know if they will confuse a disease with a character flaw.* Not that
it was possible to ever know anyone that well.
Of the two cousins Mina had been close to her
entire life, one had reacted to her positive test
result with a hug while the other had remained
a Facebook friend where a "like" on a post was
as much interaction Mina could hope for.

"It was only a date, right? You weren't intimate with him already?"

The heart of the misunderstanding between
them was when they each thought the tell should
happen. Mina and her mother agreed that the
tell should happen before sex. Some people argued that, if you practiced safe sex, disclosure
until a more serious relationship had developed
wasn't necessary. But Mina fell into the camp

that believed it might not be medically *neces-sary*—especially with a low virus count like she had—but disclosure after the fact was a sure way to end the relationship in tears and distrust.

Where Mina and her mom disagreed was how well you had to know someone before sex. Mina fell into what she thought of as the modernist camp, where sex and a relationship were not synonymous. The pre-modernist camp, represented by her mother, seemed *okay* with premarital sex—or had given up the fight long ago—but believed anyone you were sleeping with was by definition your boyfriend.

It was a generational difference, one that Mina probably wouldn't have noticed if sex hadn't suddenly become something her mother felt she had to talk about with her. Still, this was where Mina's life was.

"We didn't have sex, if that's what you're asking."

Her mother sighed. "Your father and I worry about you is all."

Woven through her mom's simple statement were all the past relationships Mina had had, post-positive. The men she'd been mad for, who had freaked when she'd disclosed her status, ending all possibilities of anything more by claiming they'd just wanted to be friends, and she'd misunderstood. Or worse, discovering they suddenly had a girlfriend back in Iowa.

Still, those weren't as bad as some of the men who'd nonchalantly said, "No problem," then pretended like her virus didn't exist. They wouldn't talk about it. They didn't want to see her take her meds. They pretended her nausea was bad chicken. At least she'd known where she'd stood with the men who bolted. With the men who'd stuck around but were never fully present in her life, she'd felt like she was constantly pretending to be someone else. Someone *healthy*, whatever that meant. She felt as healthy as anyone else. Sort of.

Mina had never been able to fall asleep in the arms of those men, something she should have understood as a sign of trouble.

"I know. And I appreciate it. I won't tell you not to worry, but I think this is one of the good ones."

Unreliable men straining for degrees of distance weren't the only men in her past. There had been two, both while she was in grad school, who had been supportive and open and loving. But neither of those two men had ended up being *the one*, and she hadn't been *the one* for them, either. Still, memories of those men and those relationships had been what kept her willing to keep trying.

"Whatever happens, just know that we love you."

"I do. I love you, too, Mom. And make sure to tell Dad."

Mina and her mom finished their goodbyes, and she hung up, ready for a day of errands, grading and trying to keep the complexities of life from intruding on living.

"Levi, I called you several times last night," Brook said as she answered the phone.

"I told you that I would be out late and that I'd call you today." His sister had left two messages on his voice mail and texted him five times. He'd ignored them all, but he couldn't ignore her forever. Especially when the only way to deal with his sister when she was being passive-aggressive was to cut right to the chase. "How you treated Mina last night was unacceptable."

"I thought you'd decided not to go on a date with her. Because, well, you know."

"Because she's HIV positive. If you're going to be afraid of touching her hand, you should at least be honest about why." Anger clamped down on his ribs. "Be. Able. To. Say. The Words."

If Brook noticed the irritation in his voice, she ignored it. "She drank out of your beer glass. And you shared a pizza."

"We shared more than a pizza." He regretted the way he took her bait and demeaned the kiss he'd shared with Mina as soon as the combative words were out of his mouth.

"Did you have sex with her?"

"Brook, that is absolutely none of your business. In fact, my entire relationship with Mina is none of your business."

"You're my brother, and I care about you. I've cared for you since Mom left. I saw you after Kimmie died."

"Is that what this is about?" he asked, the hope in his voice clear, even to himself. Mina was, well, Mina was amazing. He could sit on her couch with her head in his lap and listen to her talk for hours. She was warm, loving, creative, funny and hot. Not only would he want to sit and listen to her for hours, but he would want to sit and look at her for hours.

Brook was his big sister. As kids, they'd parked themselves on the front steps of their house and cried together the first time they'd come home to an empty house. She'd taught him what it meant to care about someone, and when Kimmie had been suffering through her worst depressive episodes, Brook had been there for him. His sister's support had enabled him to be there for Kimmie.

"Of course. What else would this be about?"

Brook sounded so reasonable that Levi was immediately suspicious again.

"You didn't want to shake her hand, Brook. You can't get HIV from shaking her hand."

His sister was silent for several seconds before she responded. "I'm not worried about *me* getting HIV."

"Well, I'm not worried about *me* getting it, either. Go online."

"I did," Brook interrupted. "Right after we talked on the phone."

Levi rolled his eyes. "Don't read scaremongering websites. Read… Never mind. I'll send you links to read."

"How do you know the websites you read are the ones telling the truth and the ones I read are lying?"

"Don't be this person, sis. I don't know what your problem is, but call me back when you get over it." His piece said, Levi swiped the phone off, missing his landline, which was much more satisfying to slam.

CHAPTER THIRTEEN

ON THURSDAY WHEN he saw Mina's kitchen light come on, Levi texted, Hey. Good day?

Two classes today. Russian lit and my graphic novel class. The gn course turned in their first assignment.

Working tonight? Texting wasn't new to Levi, but texting while dating was. If someone had asked him a few weeks ago what he thought of texting the woman he was seeing, he'd probably have sounded like a grumpy old man complaining about kids these days.

Instead, he loved it.

Yes. :-(Need to return the pieces Tuesday so students have time to read comments before next assignment is due.

Want company? I'll make you dinner. Since she left for work before he did, he came out and wished her a good day each morning. He had

gone over to her house on Monday night, and
they'd shared dinner, a drink and some kisses.
And texting made all of this incredibly easy
to arrange.

If his dad said to him that a man didn't woo
a woman this way, well, he'd just tell him that
Mina had started it. He was just enjoying it.

Hmmm... I do need dinner.

That was all the encouragement Levi needed.
Hded to the store for supplies. Be there in thirty.

THE PLASTIC BAGS in his hands crinkled as he
lifted his fist up to knock. He stopped noticing
the way the handles cut into his skin the moment the door opened, and Mina stood there in
a smile and her T-shirt, but no bra.

"Come in," she said, opening the door and
stepping back. "What's for dinner?"

"Spaghetti and a green salad okay?"

"Of course it's okay! You're bringing dinner
to my door and cooking it for me." She closed
the door behind him, and then he followed her
to the kitchen. Her dining room table was covered in papers, a laptop open in the middle of
them all.

"Sorry about the mess," she said, catching

where his attention had gone. "I also have quizzes to grade for my Russian language course."

"With all that grading, three classes sounds like a lot to teach." He put the bags on the counter and looked over at her.

"It is." She wrinkled her nose, and her head waved from side to side. "But we're a small department, and I'm the low woman on the totem pole. Plus, I really wanted to teach a graphic novel course, so that got added on."

"How much work do you have to do tonight?"

She shrugged. "A lot. But the only thing I need to get done are the quizzes. And I was hoping to work while you cooked. I don't have many left."

"All right. Get to work, then."

When she lifted up on her toes and pecked his cheek, satisfaction spread throughout his body, warming him from his toes to the tips of his ears. And then he got to work, too.

Every time Levi found a break in dinner prep, he'd glance over to where Mina sat at the table. Her head was bent over her papers, her hair obscuring her face. He smiled at her concentration.

This was nice, he thought, as the water came to a boil. Comfortable. He reached for the box of noodles and dumped the whole pound in. Dinner would be more than enough for the two of them, and they would have leftovers, which he always needed. Making dinner while Mina worked was something he could imagine doing regularly.

Like he had with Kimmie.

Giving the pasta a quick stir, he shied away from that thought. He didn't want what he'd had with Kimmie with another woman. He wanted something new and different. Worse, comparing Mina to Kimmie would cause nothing but problems. He'd gotten himself into trouble by thinking about their two illnesses the same, and this thought was better, but not great. No matter the details, comparing the two women sold them both short.

Cooking dinner for Mina might be similar to what he'd had with Kimmie, but the feeling of contentment swelling in his chest every time he looked over and saw her head bent over her work was very different. Not better, different. More solid and suited for the man he was now, rather than the man he had been four years ago.

While the pasta cooked, Levi cut up vegetables for the salad. He was so immersed in getting all the carrot cubes close to the same size that he didn't notice that Mina was finished with her work until she came up behind him and rested her hand on his back.

He jumped. And the pressure of her finger pads against his skin was enough for a tingle of arousal to race through his nerves.

Kissing her wasn't enough. Or it was good enough for now, while he was giving her time to trust him. But he thought about her every night, usually with his hand under the covers, giving the barest hint of realism to his fantasies.

"Done with work?" he asked, putting down his knife and bending over to give her a kiss.

"Yes. I even cleaned up the table."

He was glancing over her head when the timer for his pasta dinged. "Just in time," he said with a smile. Cooking for Mina while she was working at her table was nice. Having her next to him was nicer.

Seated at her dining room table, it took only one question for Mina to launch into a story about her students and the homework she'd assigned in her graphic novel class. Spaghetti noodles bopped on the end of her fork as she talked and forgot to eat. Her eyebrows danced. Her cheeks rose and fell as hints of dimples that never fully appeared graced her face. She was completely animated and a sight to behold.

When he imagined them in bed—and on the couch and in the kitchen—he imagined her just as animated. Her hands everywhere on him at once. Her lips and cheeks and eyebrows springing about her face with pleasure before freezing when she came.

As their relationship moved forward—and he

hoped it would—he should go to the hardware store and tip Al for selling Mina a dud mower. If Levi hadn't come over to help her with that mower, he might still be sitting in his house, with his back to the kitchen window, being a dumbass about the neighbor he couldn't take his eyes off of.

"Oh," she said when she noticed that he was done with his dinner, and she had barely touched her own food. "I've been talking too much."

The change in the tone of her voice brought his mind out of his fantasies and back to reality. Fortunately, he hadn't gone too far afield. Mina was in both.

"I like listening to you."

She waved her left hand at him, her right still holding the same fork with all the noodles wrapped around it that had been hanging there—uneaten—for a couple of minutes. "You're being nice. I pour out words like faucets pour out water, only without a handle to turn me off."

He snorted. When she said things like that, how could she doubt that he wanted to listen to her? "You assume I want to turn you off."

"Well, sometimes I need a knob to turn myself down at least. My dinner has already gotten cold. And it was really good hot. If you find the lever, could you tell me?"

"Maybe. But maybe I'd want to turn you on instead." He couldn't help but smile. "Do you want your food reheated?"

"No. That's silly. You made it for me and I've been too busy talking to finish it. It's good cold, too. But I'm going to ask you a question and then stuff my mouth, and I'm not going to say another word until I finish eating. All the conversation responsibility will be yours," she said menacingly.

Pronouncement made, Mina added more spaghetti to her already full fork. "How was your day?" she asked, then shoved the too-large pile into her mouth, her brows raised in a challenge.

"Good" was all he said in reply. Then he waited.

Mina waited and chewed. Patiently at first. Then her chewing got more fearsome, and her eyes got bigger with the playful scold that was clearly coming. Still chewing the massive amount of food she'd pushed into her mouth to make a point, she motioned with her hands, as though encouraging him forward.

He still didn't say anything. His day had been good. That was all he had to say. Plus, he liked watching her squirm a little.

She must have realized his game, because

she lifted an eyebrow and slowed her chewing. He cocked his head, waiting to see how long she could manage. Very pointedly her chin rose and fell until she couldn't keep the food in her mouth any longer, and she had to swallow.

She let out a puff of exasperated air and said, "I wasn't going to win at that game, no matter how I played it, was I?"

"No," he said, chuckling. "That game was designed so that only I would win."

"Well, you have to say something. Otherwise I'm going to try and fill the silence, and then I won't eat."

"What do you do when no one is here?" He wasn't much of a talker, but he would for Mina, because she asked. Though he was genuinely curious.

She shrugged. "I turn on music. This is the first time I've lived by myself. I went from my parents to the dorm to graduate school and roommates, so there was pretty much always someone around. I like having my own space and getting to decide what to do with it, no roommate with the ugly couch they're attached to, but I miss the company sometimes. It's why I stay at work so late a lot of the time."

"I get that. I—" He paused, not sure how much he would be able to say, but he wanted to share pieces of himself with her. "I turned on music, too, after Kimmie died. Being alone was hard."

"Do you want to get married again?"

The bluntness of her question surprised him, as did the fact that she felt the need to ask it. "I do. I hadn't been looking. Maybe the right person hadn't come past me, or maybe I wasn't ready, and one passed me by. But, yes, I do."

The small satisfied smile on her face was a clue that he'd given the right answer. Which was good, because it was also the true answer. Then she put her fork down, leaned over the corner of her table and kissed him.

Her lips brushed against his, and maybe that was all she had meant it to be. A kiss. But the brief contact had him wanting more. His chair squealed against her wood floor as he maneuvered his body so he could put his hand on the back of her head and press her into him. She tasted like tomatoes and garlic, and there was the sharp tang of vinegar from the salad dressing on the edge of her lips. He leaned into all of it. Into her. Into the smell of her. Into the softness of her hair and the softness of her lips and the liveliness inside her that made her glow.

Another chair squeaked on the floor, and their knees were pressed up against each other. A muscle in his back started to throb from the torqued position he was in, but her hands on his shoulders holding on to him like he was her favorite drawing pencil in the room distracted him.

But he must not have been the only person contorted into a strange position, because she slipped away from him and said, "This isn't very comfortable," before climbing out of her seat and onto his lap.

She fit perfectly.

His cock pressed against the fly of his jeans and the crotch of her jeans, and the pressure of it all was almost enough to make him explode. The muscles of her thighs moved and gripped as she leaned into him, nibbling on his neck, her hands clutching the short hair at the nape of his neck. He leaned his cheek on the top of her hair, encouraging her to stay there. To stay here. To give him more of a chance to smell the flowers in her shampoo and to feel her teeth graze against his skin.

Sharp alternated with soft as teeth alternated with lips, and every time sensations changed he seemed to get harder.

As he kissed the top of her head and breathed in the sensation of her being here, of them being here, wisps of her hair got up his nose. And suddenly his shoulders relaxed, the tension that he hadn't realized was there gone.

Her fingers walked down his back and sides,

leaving small fires in their path. Returning the favor, he trailed his fingers down her back, pulling at her shirt until his palms were in contact with her skin. Soft, delicate skin, made more interesting by a constellation of small moles his fingers traced along her spine.

"Oh, Levi," she said, her breath in his ear sending shivers rocketing along his skin. Then she enhanced the feeling by shifting her hips and rubbing against his cock.

The sensations were almost too much to bear. He jerked his hands out from under her shirt and grabbed her face, kissing her with all the desire that had been building up in him for the past couple of weeks. Her mouth opened, yielding to the pressure and his tongue. They moaned together, hungry lips and tongues mingling. Their noses bumped. Their teeth bumped. The kiss was messy, tripping a fine line between affection and trying to touch and feel each other every place at once.

She yanked his shirt up, breaking their kiss long enough to scoot back on his lap. Her fingers fumbled with his fly. Then her hands were under the elastic of his briefs, and his cock was straining for her touch. Straining and desperate for her.

Their lips met again, filled with desperation and desire. He wanted her. He wanted all of her. Now. Immediately. As much as he could get of her.

Like a child, trying to eat all the candy without stopping to taste it.

There was almost an audible snap when he broke the kiss, leaving them both panting.

"Is everything okay?" Mina asked.

"I'm not…" He paused, unsure of how to say what he meant without sounding like a teenager in the back of a station wagon.

The hell with it. "I'm not ready," he said.

She cocked her head, her brows crossed in confusion and her eyes full of questions. "Not ready? What do you mean?"

He drew in a long breath. The pent-up desire between them heavy in the air. "Like I said before, you are the first woman I've wanted to sleep with—make love to—since Kimmie died. And I don't want to rush it."

Her mouth opened and shut a couple of times, his explanation clearly not helping her understand why he'd pulled back. "Is it the HIV?"

"No," he said flatly, tamping down any irritation that she would ask. Of course she would ask. She was probably used to that being a reason for a physical relationship to grind to a halt. "I want you so much that it's all I can think about at night."

Her hands popped out of his jeans like something in his pants had bitten them. "I still don't understand."

His erection poked out of the fly of his underwear and his pants like a comic joke. A hello without a reply. All his fault, of course. "I want to make love to you. Have sex. Sleep with. Fuck. All the variations. But I want to enjoy the buildup, too."

"We can go back to making out after we have sex. No one says we can't." Her face was screwed up, not just with confusion but with sexual frustration, as well.

He lifted an eyebrow.

"Okay. Some couples don't," she amended. "But..." Her top teeth grazed her bottom lip. Finally, she puffed out an unfulfilled sigh. "I wouldn't want to be pressured, and so I shouldn't pressure you."

The *but* was left unsaid, though Levi still heard it.

"It's nice to be wanted," he said, holding the words out as an offering, even though they both knew it was a poor one.

"I guess," she said. "No, that was rude. It is nice to be wanted. I'm frustrated and horny, and I feel a bit rejected, even though I don't think you mean to reject me. But you want me, and that's better than the alternative."

Not knowing what else to say, Levi kept his mouth shut.

"You're ready to move on after Kimmie's death, right? I don't want to get my hopes up, if you'll never be able to love again."

He flinched, but it was a fair question. Worry crept into Mina's eyes as he didn't answer right away, and the temptation to give her the answer she wanted pulled at his tongue, but he didn't give in. If this was going to be something special—and he hoped it would be—then he had to give her answers, and he had to give her true answers.

Finally, he opened his mouth, and her shoulders instantly relaxed, even though the concern didn't leave her eyes. Apparently any answer was better than the unknown.

"Yes. I can't pretend that I'm not scared. Like I said before, Kimmie's death was hard, and I'm scared to go through something like that again. But I would feel that way no matter who I was with." He sighed through the painful and wonderful memories flooding the space behind his eyes.

"But I loved my wife, and, even knowing how it ended, I wouldn't trade the years we had together for anything. If all I learned from that is not to get into another relationship, then I didn't learn anything. And I failed everything that Kimmie meant to me and that I meant to her."

"That answer was beautiful, but it didn't answer my question. You *want* to be ready for another relationship. But *are* you?"

"Yes," he said, leaning into the word so that the force of his body, mind and soul came out in the three letters. So that she would know and understand and believe. "I just need some more time. Especially before we have sex."

She nodded, slowly, though he wasn't sure she actually understood. He didn't understand, either. He just knew that he wanted to have sex with her now and forever. But not *now*, and the distinction made him crazy.

"Okay. I believe you, but I need to think about this a little. And I can't think about it with you here."

"I understand. Don't…" He paused, but the only way out of the discomfort he'd caused was to get through it. "Don't think too long, please."

"I won't. I'll text you in the morning."

It was his turn to relax from the stress of the situation he'd created. "And I'll come out to say good morning before you leave for work."

"You'd better," she said, before dropping a quick kiss on his lips and hopping off his lap.

He stood and tucked himself back into his pants. "Do you want me to help you clean up?"

"No. Washing dishes is a good thinking activity. Go. I'll be all right. We'll be all right. And we'll see each other in the morning."

He followed her to her front door. "Good night, Mina."

Before he stepped out the door, he grabbed her by the back of her head and pulled her toward him for a kiss, putting as much passion and desire into that kiss as he could. He must have succeeded, because she melted into his arms, and they sank against the doorjamb in a pile of arms, legs and lips.

"Tease," she said, as she finally broke away.

He smiled, nodded and closed the door softly behind him.

"Good shower?" Mina asked as Levi walked into his kitchen pulling a T-shirt over his head. She had texted him to say she was coming over with dinner. She'd brought the makings for stew, and she was browning beef in a big pot.

"I feel better," he said, dropping a kiss on her upturned cheek. He was so happy to see her, he wouldn't have cared if she'd brought over bags of fast food, so long as he got to spend the evening with her. Though there was something especially satisfying about seeing her in his kitchen, a wooden spoon in her hand, a smile on her face and the smell of meat wafting through the room. He could get used to sharing a home with Mina really quickly.

"You still look exhausted. What would you have done for dinner, if I wasn't coming over?"

"God, I don't know. Frozen pizza? Grilled cheese?"

"Good thing I'm here, then." Her cute grin was nearly a satisfied smirk. "What about work was so tiring?"

He shrugged. "Right now, everything. After years of no one spending money on their house, now everyone wants to renovate, and we took on one more project than we should have. I spent the day tiling a bathroom. I *hate* tiling, especially a mosaic pattern like the one I did today. All those tiny little pieces..." He trailed off as she hopped between the cutting board and the pot. "Can I help you?"

She set the knife down. "Oh, God, yes. Can you cut the onions, carrots and celery into precise quarter-inch pieces?"

His mouth fell open. He didn't realize she was teasing him until she laughed.

"Hand over the knife," he said, his hand out and a smile on his face. "What size do you want them cut?"

"Nice and chunky. And the potatoes, too. You can peel if you want, but I usually don't."

He looked over at the mound of red potatoes on the counter. "Peeling sounds too much like work."

"More tiling tomorrow?"

"Yeah. The guy who normally does our tiling should be done with his other project, but it's better if I finish the job I started. We'll put him to work on the tiled backsplash for the kitchen."

"How'd you get started in contracting anyway?"

The knife seemed to drop extra hard as his shoulder fell from a shrug. "When I was working in the mines, I did construction and other handyman projects on the side. For extra money."

He'd been saving for the trip of a lifetime for him and Kimmie. A trip where she'd need her passport and they'd both laugh as they struggled with a foreign language because neither of them had paid much attention to their language tapes.

"When I moved to Missoula," he continued, "I got in touch with a guy Dennis and I went to high school with. He gave me work, and I've been slowly buying into the business as he's been not-so-slowly turning into a ski bum. It's good work."

Sometimes he wondered what this brilliant woman with a PhD who could call herself Doctor and did get called Professor was doing with him, a man who had barely finished high school and had only had jobs that involved his hands and back.

But when she looked at him like that, with admiration in her eyes, he didn't wonder. Not that he understood *why*, but when she had that look in her eyes, he decided understanding was overrated, and appreciating her affection was the best route.

Especially when the twinkle in her eyes made his heart race.

"I've always admired hard work and a man with strong hands. Especially the strong hands. A girl can come to get attached to a good pair of hands and nimble fingers."

"I…" The doorbell stopped him from saying anything more, which was fine, because he was stumbling over what flirty thing he could offer in return. Flirty wasn't something he had much experience with.

"I'll see who's at the door."

"Don't forget that I need use of those hands when you get back," she said with a wink before turning back to the counter.

Levi had again been too busy trying to think of something flirty to respond with to wonder who would be on the other side of the door, but he hadn't expected to see Dennis.

"What's up, man?" he said as he stepped aside.

"I need a break from home," his friend answered. "What smells so good?"

"Mina's making stew. Do you want to stay for dinner?"

Dennis took off his jacket and hung it on one of the hooks by the door. "Brook's mad at me, so dinner's chicken nuggets. Which the kids are excited about."

"Whatcha do to my sister?" Brook was just as likely to be in the wrong as Dennis, but she was his sister, which trumped Dennis as best friend.

"Nothing."

Mina looked up as they got to the kitchen. "Hey, Dennis." They'd met each other at the grocery store last week. Dennis had been friendly. Brook had been herself.

"Hey. Stew smells good."

"You're welcome to stay for some, but it'll be a while." God, she looked cute standing next to the stove, poking around in the pot. Her cheeks were flushed from the heat of the stove, and a couple of strands of hair stuck to the side of her face.

He could come home every night to Mina standing in his kitchen and die a happy man. Nothing else required. She didn't even have to be cooking.

"Thanks," Dennis said, reaching into the fridge for a beer. "I'll do that."

Between the click of the bottle cap being removed and the way Dennis settled himself against the kitchen counter, he was going to be here a while—well past dinner.

"Brook's making chicken nuggets, huh. And you didn't do anything." Brook prided herself on making home-cooked meals for her kids, nightly proof that she wasn't going to up and leave them like her mother had done.

Dennis took a long swallow of his beer. "She's mad that I applied for the job in Bozeman. She's mad that I interviewed for the job in Bozeman. She's mad that I think the interview went well, and one of my references has been called."

Mina set the lid on the pot, then turned to look at Dennis. "Didn't you talk about moving before you applied?"

His friend shrugged, which was answer enough.

"Come on, man," Levi said, getting his own beer out of the fridge. He'd need it for this conversation. "That was dumb."

"Doesn't it ever bother you that the whole reason we're in Missoula is because of the mine accident?" Dennis's face was tight and hard. "Fuck. Everything I've done for the past three years has been because of that accident. *This* is for me."

"But you're married," Mina said, confusion crinkling her face. "And you have kids."

She didn't know—she couldn't know—what it had been like to be trapped in the mine, then to feel trapped in the town, where everyone knew and asked and commented and pitied. Pitied him for Kimmie's death and pitied Dennis because they knew about his lungs. They'd moved to Missoula to get away, but neither of them had really left the accident behind.

"I don't get why you didn't tell Brook, but I get why you want to leave," Levi said.

It was Dennis's second chance, one where he didn't sit across from the friend he'd been trapped with every Friday night, coughing and reliving the experience. Levi looked over at Mina still standing next to his stove, the way her head was cocked making her neck look long and kissable. She was his second chance, one he hadn't thought he was ready for until now.

THERE WERE MANY reasons why it was nice to have the guy she was interested in living next door, but its single biggest downside was that he never stayed the night. Not having far to go seemed to mean that walking home was easier than climbing under the covers. So, not only did none of the kissing lead to actual sex, but also none of the making out led to a moment when she could lie satiated, warm and naked in his arms.

Taking it slow meant a physical relationship like she'd had in high school. There were orgasms, and they were great, but the fact that their relationship remained unconsummated left her feeling frustrated. Levi hadn't exactly been what her mother would call "perfectly polite," but that didn't mean Mina wasn't frustrated as she lay in bed at night, her hands under the covers.

All of these things combined meant that when Mina spied Echo walking past the house with Noodle after work, she burst out of her house to join her neighbor for the walk.

"Oh, good," Echo said as soon as Mina joined her on the sidewalk. "You, lady, have a lot of explaining to do."

"Explaining?" Mina asked, falling into step next to her friend.

"Uh, the whole neighborhood noticed that Levi's car was in front of your house all night two weeks ago. *All night.*"

"Echo, he lives next door. Maybe he parked there because his garage was full of…equipment."

Echo laughed so hard that Noodle barked. "You couldn't even come up with something believable."

"He didn't stay the night," Mina said, not sure why she was being defensive. She was old enough that she didn't have to defend herself when a man spent the night, even to her mom.

"The sex was so good that he forgot he'd parked in front of your house?" Echo asked with delight in her voice. "Why'd he park in front of your house in the first place?"

"For our first date. It was sweet. He opened the car door for me and walked me to my door."

"I always thought Levi seemed like an old-fashioned guy. Those quiet and hot guys are the ones you want to catch. So attentive."

"Yeah," Mina replied, not really feeling it.

"What? He's not attentive? I've seen him cross that yard a couple times this week. And come out in the morning to say goodbye before you leave."

"What are you? James Bond?"

Echo shrugged. "I walk the dog and have eyes. Plus, the action happening at your house is way more interesting than the Campos. And you didn't answer my question."

They stopped so Noodle could inspect and pee on a mailbox.

"Levi wants to take things slow," Mina said under her breath, halfheartedly hoping Echo wouldn't hear her.

"'Slow' means…"

They started walking again. "'Slow' means no sex."

"Is it the HIV?"

"Thank you," Mina said, as sincerely as she could.

"For what?" Noodle's dart forward jerked to a stop as Echo halted and peered at Mina, honest questioning in her eyes.

"For not dancing around my illness. For not pretending it doesn't exist." Mina needed a support network in Missoula. While she thought her parents worried too much, she knew it had been a risk to move so far away from everyone she knew. And she hadn't wanted to find out that the friends she was making would prove ignorant if something went wrong, and she needed them most.

It was heartening to realize that she already had two people who knew and whom she believed she could rely on.

Levi's sister was a wild card that she didn't want to think about.

"Thank you for not reacting like I'm a leper."

"Oh, that." Echo shrugged. "Getting breast cancer so young taught me how people are often afraid to face your illness, because doing so means they have to face their own vulnerability. And it's not 'taking your mind off everything' if your friend sticks her fingers in her ears and says la-la-la every time the subject of chemo comes up. That's real lonely."

"It's still nice. I appreciate it." Mina's words felt hollow to her ears, but there weren't strong enough words in the English language to communicate her gratitude.

"Again, you didn't answer my question. Hey, Mrs. Jorgenson!" Echo yelled with a wave to an elderly woman digging in her front yard. "How are you feeling?"

The older woman waved back but didn't say anything.

"You can talk all you want about the no sex," Echo said matter-of-factly. "Mrs. Jorgenson never wears her hearing aid."

"There's nothing to tell. Levi says he wants to take it slow. That I'm the first woman he's been interested in since his wife died. That he wants to enjoy every step."

"Do you believe him?"

"Yeah."

"That was halfhearted."

"I'm frustrated is all." And, if she was being honest with herself, worried that there was something else going on. Not a fear of being infected, but his sister's influence. Or maybe he was worried what people would think if her disease got out and people knew about their relationship, or maybe the love that he felt over his late wife, the love she'd admired and respected so much after their first date, was getting in the way.

Mina Clements, if you really think any of those things, you need to ask him about it and break the relationship off if they're true.

But everything else is so good, she replied to her common sense.

"Sexually frustrated *with* a man in your life is very different from sexually frustrated without."

"Yeah. I'm learning that the hard way." Echo stopped and Mina was surprised to find they were in front of her house. "Thanks for listening to me."

"Are you kidding? I talk a big game, but I'm still terrified to try and date after my divorce and with the missing boob... I'm hoping your courage will rub off on me," her friend said as she rubbed her hand on Mina's shoulder like there was a genie hidden under there.

It was Mina's turn to shrug. "I believe all the trouble will be worth it. I still want something like what my parents have. Sure, they fight sometimes and both enjoy vacations away from the other, but they support each other, giggle and kiss when they think no one's looking and honestly love each other. It looks...nice," she finished lamely.

"It sounds nice." Echo sighed. "My parents are still married but not happily. Your way sounds better."

"Have a good night."

"You, too," Echo said with a smile. "Get inside, put on some sexy underwear and text Levi a description. See if that helps."

Mina laughed and called out a goodbye as she walked to her front porch.

CHAPTER FOURTEEN

ONCE IN HER BEDROOM, Mina sat on her bed and looked at her dresser drawer. She had sexy underwear in there, a couple of pairs of lacy, barely-there panties and matching bras that weren't particularly comfortable but perked her breasts nearly up to her eyeballs.

She scooted back on the comforter, resting her head against mounds of pillows. Then she reached to her nightstand for her phone.

I'm looking at my dresser, contemplating a pair of red lacy panties and a matching bra. Interested?

Levi's response took half a second.

Of course I'm interested. Tell me more.

There's not much to tell, because there's not much to them. But I think you need to see them for yourself to judge.

I've been working all day. Give me twenty minutes to shower and shave. Then I'll be over to help you enjoy them.

Her mouth twitched as she considered what to write next.

Leave the door unlocked. I'll come over there and meet you after your shower.

The single emoji smiley face that returned made her grin. Pleased, but understated. Which was one of the reasons she liked him so much.

I'm bringing condoms, she typed.

The notification light on her phone didn't blink for a full two minutes. Mina knew, because she was staring at the clock on her phone and watching the numbers change. As the minute changed from five to six, she wondered if she had overstepped. The minute changed from six to seven.

You're being dumb, Mina. The problem with texting, as opposed to talking on the phone or in person, was that you couldn't tell if the person on the other end had gotten up to use the bathroom or shut a window or look for their glasses.

Not that Levi wore glasses.

She was usually able to keep dating anxiety

under control, but the longer she sat looking at her phone, the dark wood of her dresser visible out of the corner of her eye, the more quietly her vulnerabilities whispered. And quiet meant they were more insidious.

Have a box. Keep that box at your house. We'll need them there. ;)

With that, Mina's entire body started to tingle. She hopped out of the bed, rushed over to her dresser and pulled out the underwear she'd promised.

THE TEXT "I'M bringing condoms" made him hard. And with it came the realization that he'd been acting stupid. He'd been putting off sex in search of the perfect moment. The right move. The time when they'd squeezed every last moment of pleasure out of the sexual tension between them.

Or maybe that was him being kind to himself. Maybe he was afraid that once she was under him and he slid into her, he'd never want to let her go. And he'd want nothing more than to make sure she was happy all the time. He'd be done. Finished. Wiped out.

That thinking clouded the fact that Mina made his life better. She made his life bigger. They were in Big Sky country, but with Mina by his side, the sky wasn't so much big as it was infinite.

It wasn't fear he was feeling, but awe and inspiration. And the gut-clenching hope that he was worthy of all she would bring him.

Plus, sex was awesome, and being so horny was distracting him at work. Sex with Mina and being able to relive it later would also be a distraction, but at least it would be a better one.

Have a box. Keep that box at your house. We'll need them there. That didn't look too inviting. He added ;) and hit Send. The hell with it. He was an old grouchy widower and cute texts weren't his style.

That Mina seemed to like him anyway made him the luckiest man in the world.

Levi tossed his phone on the unmade bed, stripped off his dirty clothes and headed for his shower.

HE HAD ONE towel wrapped around his waist and was drying his hair with another when he walked out of the bathroom and realized he wasn't alone in his bedroom. Damp and chill settled into his skin when he lowered the towel from his head to his shoulder. There, sitting on his bed like something out of a dream, was

Mina, in the red lace underwear she'd texted him about and nothing else.

"Damn," he said.

"Hello to you, too." A slow smile spread across her face. "I guess you like it."

"I do." The understatement of the year. The red made her skin look extra creamy and slightly pink, like she was the one who had just stepped out of the hot shower. He started at her toes and worked his way up her shapely legs and the thighs he'd been thinking about every night since he'd seen them clad in shorts that barely covered her ass.

Her breasts looked like little apples, and he took a deep breath to stop himself from rushing over to the side of his bed to lean in and give them a nibble right then. He'd start there and nibble his way down her body, spending time around her belly button and at the back of her knees so he could feel her legs wrapped around his head.

Suddenly aware of the tent in his towel, Levi dragged his gaze from Mina's luscious body to her face. Her smile had turned into a satisfied grin.

He didn't know how long he had been standing there staring at her. "I didn't think you were actually going to wear the underwear over here. Or lie on my bed waiting for me."

"Oh, I took pity on the neighbors and wore clothes. The underwear was underneath."

He laughed, delighted. Because that was what she did to him.

"I can put my clothes back on," she said, mischief and pleasure dancing together in her eyes. "Come back another time in different underwear."

He took one determined step toward the bed. Then another and another, until his knees hit the mattress and he could run his hand over the rise of her breasts and down her smooth skin to rest on the curve of her hip. "Oh, you should come back another time in different underwear, but putting your clothes on now would be a waste of effort."

"And you are against waste." She said the words easily, like the relaxed conversation that seemed to slide out of her in all situations. But as he glided his hand around her hip to the soft skin of her ass, her muscles tensed, and she sucked in a breath.

"Yes," he said, experimenting with the movements of his hands and the way her body responded. He had to stoop to reach the curve of her knee, and the trailing of his fingers there had her knees and back bending, along with her gasping.

He turned his attention back to her face, to

her closed eyes and the way her head was tilting back, revealing the vulnerable undersides of her neck. He'd nibble there, too.

"But I'm very much in favor of your red underwear. I'm in favor of all of your underwear, both on you and off you."

"Oh, are you?" Her voice was breathy and distracted.

"Yes." He leaned over and pressed one kiss to the crest of her right breast. Then to her left breast. His entire body was tense, and his dick was practically dancing with desire, but he was keeping this slow. Waiting for some perfect moment had been a stupid idea that had frustrated them both, but that didn't mean he couldn't concentrate on making this perfect for her.

His hands replaced his lips, and he started kissing his way up from her breasts to her mouth. When she started to wrap her arms around him, he slid his palms up, guiding her arms up over her head and grasping on to her hands, holding them there.

And smiled when he felt her leg snake out from its spot on the bed and lock in place around his knees.

"I would say I've got you," he said, his voice rough with desire, "but I think it's just as accurate to say you've got me."

The light in her eyes danced with pleasure. "It's one of the things I like about this relationship."

Levi lost his balance when he leaned forward to kiss Mina, tumbling on top of her. When he landed, he grunted, and Mina let out an "ooff."

"Sorry about that." He lifted up on his arms to roll off her, but she stopped him by wrapping both her legs and her arms around him, her skin cool against his shower-warmed body.

"Don't be," she said with a wiggle of her hips that settled his cock nicely in the V of her thighs. "If you hadn't fallen on top of me, I would've pulled you down soon."

His nose flattened against her cheek as he kissed the line of her jaw. So he kissed her nose; then he pushed against her arms with enough force to lift his head and catch her gaze. Her eyes were a bright hazel that sparkled in the light from his lamps. "Thanks for coming over tonight."

"I was sick of waiting."

"It seemed like a good idea at the time," he said, because it was true. "But it seems like a stupid idea now."

"Not stupid. I can feel how excited you are to have me here," she said with another well-placed wiggle. "You should kiss me some more, or I'm going to think this is all talk."

He raised a brow at her. "I'm never talk."

She giggled. "Okay. *Or* that I ended up in the bed of your doppelgänger."

She'd barely gotten the words out when he bent his elbows, lowering his face down to hers. "Not my doppelgänger," he said with his lips hovering bare millimeters above hers, her breath warm on his skin. "And I'm going to make sure you never want to find that man, if he exists."

Then he kissed her, and the world around him blurred into nothingness. Every sense that he had sharpened into focus around Mina. Around the smoothness of her legs against his. The smell of her shampoo and her soap and her lotion all mixed into something that was uniquely her. The quiet humming noise she made at the back of her throat when he ran his tongue along the edges of her lips. The pressure of her hands against his back.

His arms shook with the effort of keeping himself hovered over Mina, but he ignored it and deepened the kiss. When Mina's hips shimmied under him, his hard cock slipped through the gap of his towel. Touching the silky fabric of her panties was almost heaven.

He broke the kiss, lifting himself up a little higher so that he could look at her again. This close he could count the long lashes framing her dark eyes and see the barely-there dimple in her cheek when she smiled. Balancing himself on one arm, he ran the other hand up and down the side of her body as she lifted up to kiss his neck. Her lips were warm, her tongue was wet, and her breath on his skin raised goose bumps all down his body.

"I'm going to kiss every last inch of skin on your body," he said, shifting his weight back as he lowered himself down to where he could return the favor.

Her hips bucked against his. "I'm looking forward to that, but..."

Her breath caught when he ran his tongue between the lace of her bra and skin. There, between the rises of her breast, she smelled musky and sweet and salty. "But?" he asked, sitting back on his heels. He walked his fingers around to her back, enjoying the movement of her chest when she arched her back to give him access. The bounce of her breasts when he unhooked and pulled off her bra was even more satisfying.

"God, you're beautiful."

"I'm eager... Oh." She sighed when he caught one nipple between his lips and gave a gentle nibble.

"You keep starting sentences and not finishing them," he said, his lips now on the underside of her left breast, the weight of which pressed deliciously against his cheek. "Which is too bad, because I like listening to you talk." He followed his kisses with his tongue, and she gasped. "Maybe even as much as I like doing this."

Then he moved on to the next breast. "Maybe more."

He just caught Mina's face out of the corner of his eye as it scrunched in frustration. He was pretty sure it was the good kind of frustration. "I'm eager for you to be inside me," she said quickly, probably so that she could say what she wanted to say before he moved his fingers to the warmth between her legs. As soon as he slipped his fingers under the elastic of her panties she started to moan.

He was pretty sure all conversation was over at that point. He sure as hell wasn't able to say much more.

Mina was wet and warm, and he would be happy to spend the rest of his life with his fingers tangled up in her curly hair. Her moan changed to a low noise at the back of her throat when his two fingers dipped into her folds and explored. As his fingers found their rhythm, and he adjusted for pressure, he listened for changes in her breath and adjustments she made to the movement of her hips.

When he felt her thigh muscles tighten around

his wrist, he knew she was close. Hell, he was close, and the only stimulation his cock was getting was a damp bath towel. He didn't need more. The smell of Mina's arousal filling the room would have been enough to stoke his wet dreams for years, but he was also storing away the noises she made and the movements of her body for times when she wouldn't be around.

For a brief moment, Mina's body stilled, and she stopped making any noises at all. Then she cried out, her head rocking back and her neck exposed and long. The muscles of her pussy were tight against his fingers, a softer cousin to the hold her legs had on him.

A breath later, she relaxed with a sigh. "Oh, that was good." She sighed again. "Your turn. You get your condoms, and I'll help get everything off."

Levi leaned over to the nightstand and opened the drawer as Mina wiggled out of her underwear beneath him. Legs were shoved out of the way, lifted and moved before her panties were fully off her body. His towel came off much faster. Both ended up in a pile on the floor.

He sat back on his heels and was unwrapping the condom when her legs glided against his, and she was sitting up. "Let me," she said, taking the condom out of his hand.

Watching her clever fingers peel the condom

out of its wrapper and roll it down the length of his dick was one of the most erotic moments he could recall. She seemed to touch all his sensitive skin at once, and with pressure just where he wanted it. He almost came in the condom before it could serve its purpose.

Then, with a look of satisfaction spreading over her face, Mina scooted back down the mattress until she was under him again. She reached out, wrapped her hands around his cock and guided him into her.

Tight, wet perfection surrounded him, and together they fell into a rhythm. Levi's hopes to last longer the first time they had sex burst into a million pieces as his orgasm overcame him in several quick thrusts.

"Oh, man." He didn't have the ability to say anything more coherent. Not "thank you," not "that was worth the wait," not "I could love you." It took all his energy to lift himself off her and stumble to the bathroom, where he could put the condom in the trash and wash his hands.

Those small pieces of business done, Levi crawled back into the bed. He opened his arms, and she tucked herself against him.

Then he waited for the chatter, but all he heard was silence.

"I expected you to be a woman who talks after sex."

Only when he heard the soft puffs of her breath did he realize that Mina was asleep. As he kissed the top of her head, delight filled the empty spaces within him.

CHAPTER FIFTEEN

MINA WAS STILL sleeping when Levi woke up the next morning. She must have been incredibly tired because he'd tried to wake her up a little later in the night to see if she wanted something to eat, and she'd only snorted and rolled over. Even now, all she said when he placed a hand on her shoulder was a mumbled "I'll be up soon," before rooting her head deeper into her pillow.

He shrugged and climbed out of bed. He *had* gotten up to eat something later in the night, so he put on the briefs and shorts that he'd left on the floor and headed down to his kitchen to make coffee. While the coffee brewed, he slipped on the ancient pair of boots he kept by the door and went outside for the paper.

To his surprise, Mina was up and bleary-eyed in the kitchen when he came back in. She had on a pair of wide-legged sweatpants and a T-shirt with the neck cut out, hanging so that it revealed the smattering of dark freckles that dotted her shoulder. No bra, and the points of her nipples against the cotton made him want to turn her back around for another go.

But he'd been raised to offer guests something other than nonstop sex, so all he said after kissing her head was "Coffee's almost ready. Sleep well?"

"I wondered how loquacious you would be in the morning," she said with a smile.

"Yeah? And did I live up to expectations?" He hoped so, though he wasn't sure if that meant he should be talking more or less. It wasn't a measure he'd ever expected anyone to take of him. Especially not using the word *loquacious*.

"Of course you did. And you do."

An odd swell of pleasure rose in his chest, even though he still wasn't certain what he was being complimented on. Or if it was a compliment. "You weren't as much of a post-sex talker as I had expected."

"Disappointed?" Both her eyebrows were raised up to her hair, which was still sexily mussed from sleep.

"By you? Never."

A pleased sound, close to a snort but far more ladylike, came from her nose. "Good. In the future you won't be able to shut me up after sex. But I was really tired last night, for some reason."

"Commentary on how well I did?"

"God, maybe." She looked embarrassed by the thought. "I'll try not to comment on the sex while we're still in bed. All those advice columns say that's a bad idea, but once I get started talking, sometimes I can't stop. But I'll probably just tell you about my day. In more detail than you'd ever hoped to hear."

"Something to look forward to, then," he said, meaning every word.

She yawned and shook her head. "Maybe I'll take a nap today."

The coffeepot beeped. "Stay awake long enough for me to make you breakfast."

"I can do that. So long as you get me that cup of coffee."

"*I* can do that," he echoed, and she giggled.

Mina sat at the kitchen table and flipped idly through the newspaper while he got out the ingredients for a basic bacon and eggs breakfast. "This is the second breakfast that you've made me. I can get used to this."

"I used to make Kimmie breakfast every weekend." Even when she wasn't feeling up to eating.

"Oh? You don't talk much about your wife. Or your marriage. Did you fix her dinner, too? What was she like?"

Usually when people asked that question,

they knew about Kimmie's suicide and wanted to know *how bad was it?* For those people, he only ever said that he didn't like to talk about her, and their eyes would soften, and they would nod and tell him, "Of course," like being married to someone depressed enough to commit suicide had to have been a burden. Those people were voyeurs, and he didn't want their voice anywhere near his memories of Kimmie.

But Mina was different. Coffee had woken up her face, and curiosity brightened her eyes now. Her eyebrows were slightly lifted, as was her chin, and she looked like she genuinely expected to hear positive memories of Kimmie. Levi never wanted to disappoint Mina.

He cracked an egg into the mixing bowl. "Kimmie had the best laugh when she laughed at her own jokes. Stupid puns were the only jokes she ever made, but then she would laugh, and her whole body shook. Everyone always laughed with her, because her joy was contagious."

He paused to crack the rest of the eggs into the bowl and waited for Mina to say something. But when he looked over his shoulder, she was eyeing him, her brows still raised, chin still up, waiting. Waiting for him to talk about himself and his life and his beloved wife.

"She would spend hours thinking of the perfect gift to get a person. When I was mining, she would drag me all over the state, shopping and driving for hours. She'd look in every store and pick up everything that caught her eye." He shook his head as he picked up the whisk and mixed the eggs together. "And if the gifts she got me were anything to go by, she'd spend all that time picking out almost the absolute worst perfect gift. Like all that time she spent in the stores when we thought she was looking for the perfect thing, she was really looking for the perfectly awful thing."

Levi shoved the bowl of beaten eggs aside. Bacon sizzled on the stove. He grabbed an onion to cut. Kimmie had preferred pancakes for breakfast. He hadn't started making scrambled eggs until six months after her death when, one Sunday morning, he'd wanted a leisurely breakfast, and the thought of pancakes had made him want to vomit.

"You really loved her," Mina said from behind him. "Like, a lot."

"I did." He slid the chopped onion to the other side of the cutting board and picked up a pepper. "I do."

"Oh." Her voice was so small and barely audible that he couldn't read anything into her tone.

"Is that a problem?"

"No." Another tiny word said in a tiny voice. "No," she said louder. "No, it's great, really. I mean, I hope that you being able to love someone so much means that you can love someone *else* that much."

With the pepper cut, Levi added butter to the pan and turned the heat on low. He didn't say anything for several seconds while the idea of love sizzled in his head along with the butter in the pan. When the butter had fully melted, he finally said, "I think it does. If I didn't think I could, I wouldn't be here, with you."

"So I'm not only a passing fancy?" she responded.

He was dumping vegetables into the hot pan and had to give them a quick stir, before he could turn around and check if the amusement in her voice was real. Much to his surprise, her eyes were sparkling with humor, and a hidden smile flickered on her lips. "No, not just a passing fancy," he repeated with a smile.

Passing fancy. He turned back to the eggs, half in love with her for the way that she talked.

"I didn't think so. You didn't seem the type."

"What does that type look like?" he asked as he poured the eggs into the pan.

"Well, they don't ask to wait for the perfect moment for sex."

He gave the eggs a stir, still a little embarrassed by his original insistence—made worse by the fact that he still couldn't really explain *why* he had to wait for the perfect moment. It wasn't that he hadn't had sex since Kimmie, but he had known that this would be different. He'd known from the moment he had set eyes on Mina in her short shorts.

"It was a stupid idea," he said.

"You said that last night. I thought it was cute." Which he knew hadn't been exactly true. She'd also been frustrated with him. That much had been clear. But putting a positive spin on the episode was nice.

He concentrated on the way the consistency of the eggs changed as they cooked.

If he couldn't put his finger on why he wanted to wait until some mysterious perfect moment, neither could he put his finger on what about last night had been different than he'd expected. She'd been naked. He'd been naked. That much was par for the course.

But it wasn't just that he wanted to replay the noises Mina had made when she came over and over and over in his head; his feelings for her were intense in a way he didn't understand. Not yet. They hadn't known each other that long. She was funny and light and interesting and had this really cool side job that he didn't think real people actually *did*, so he knew why he dug her.

But he more than dug her. Thinking about her stopped him short, and he had to catch his breath.

The curds in the eggs grew larger and a paler yellow. Done enough for him, but… "How do you like your eggs?"

"A little runny is okay."

"Then breakfast is ready. Can you put some toast in?"

"Sure." She shuffled around him as he plopped eggs on plates and set the bacon aside to drain.

Once everything was finished, he handed her both plates of food, then refilled their coffee cups and sat at the table.

He was being stupid again. If there was one thing he'd learned after ten years of marriage to Kimmie, it was that there was a right time to say things. And usually that right time was now, because you didn't always know when you'd get another chance. Trapped in the mine shaft for forty-eight hours, he'd thought of all the things he had wanted to say to his beautiful wife but had been waiting for the right time. For her to be in the right mood. For him to be in the right mood. He'd made a long list in his head, and as soon as the hospital had declared him fit to be released, he'd bolted to the door, for home and the chance to say those things.

Only his rescue hadn't actually given him the chance he'd thought it had.

Before he picked up his fork, he cleared his throat. Mina looked up. "It was stupid because the moment would have been perfect, no matter what. Because all the moments with you are going to be perfect."

He was about to look back down at his breakfast when her face melted into soft pleasure, and she breathed out a soft "Oh." Then she blinked several times. "You really don't say much, but when you do, you always say the right thing."

"Yeah," he said, knowing he was going to ruin the moment and feeling like he didn't have a choice. "That's not going to be true all the time."

"Hmm. Well, probably like I'll ruin many a perfect moment. But it's a nice thing to say right now."

Had it been last night that they had stopped talking like they were dating, and plans couldn't be assumed, and started talking like there was a long-term future that involved them both? Maybe it had been earlier, and he just hadn't noticed it. Whenever it had happened, it was nice.

He liked the solidness of a relationship much more than the strange fluid rules of *dating*. This, *this* was good. And it was better with Mina.

They spent the rest of their breakfast talking about their plans for the day and what time they would be able to see each other tonight. Some scholar from Russia was visiting the university, and Mina was part of a group having lunch with her. Then she was taking a walk with Echo and that yappy little dog. All of which would give him a chance to draw up some estimates for several clients. Everyone in Missoula seemed to want to redo their bathroom right now.

When they finished eating, Mina helped him clean up the kitchen. Then they shared a brief but intense kiss at the front door, and he watched her walk to her own house, a deep sense of satisfaction swelling in his body because she was in his life.

His profound satisfaction only grew when he got to his bedroom and saw her underwear from last night lying on the floor. Then he hopped in the shower and got ready for a Saturday of work. Only when he was walking out the door did he realize that he'd not looked at his or Kimmie's horoscope today, for the first time in thirteen years.

MINA COULD BARELY keep her eyes open during lunch and Hellie's talk afterward. Unfortunately, it wasn't last night's energetic activities that were wearing her down. Honestly, after Levi had come, she hadn't been able to keep her eyes open, so calling herself "energetic" last night was a bit of a misnomer. This morning, while eating breakfast, she'd fought to be witty and fun. Levi had been telling her important things about their relationship and its future, and she wanted to be present for those.

Worse, her tiredness hadn't been on the bad end of the normal fatigue that came along with her HIV and as a side effect of the meds. This exhaustion was different, sucking energy out of her toes and making her ears feel as droopy as she was certain her eyes looked.

When Hellie finished talking, Mina told her how interesting it was, then slipped out the door at the back of the room and to her car before anyone else could talk to her. She started the engine, rolled her windows down and turned the New Found Glory album she was listening to up as high as it would go. The punk music was barely enough to keep her eyes open and her mind alert until she pulled into her driveway. Once in her house, she stripped down to her panties and climbed into bed. Pulling out a pair of pajamas wasn't worth it.

Her eyes closed, and she was asleep immediately.

CHAPTER SIXTEEN

ECHO WAS WALKING past his house with her irritating little dog tugging on the leash when Levi pulled into his driveway. He didn't think anything of it until his neighbor stopped, and her dog began digging at his grass. When he got out of the car, he slipped under the garage door and went to the road to talk to Echo.

"Hey," he said. That one word was the extent of his interaction with Echo in the three years he'd lived in that house.

"Hey." The dog barked at him with the same enthusiasm with which it had been digging in his yard. "Have you seen Mina?"

"She stayed over last night. Isn't she at some talk this afternoon?"

"She was. We were supposed to take a walk this afternoon. We'd made plans, but she didn't answer her door. I think she's home. I saw her car drive past."

"Oh, right. She mentioned your walk." He looked over at her house, scratching his chin while he thought about what else she had said over breakfast. "You know, she did seem a little out of it this morning. Like talking was a struggle."

"Do you have a key to her house? It's not like Mina to miss one of our walks." The dog barked in agreement.

"I don't. But if you're really worried, I can get into her house without one."

"Could you? I don't know. Maybe I'm worried about nothing, but..." Echo trailed off with a shrug.

"I get it." Levi knew worry like he knew how it felt to hold a hammer while he hit a nail. And how it felt when he missed the nail and hit his thumb. "Let me get some tools."

When he came back out of his house with a lock kit in hand, Echo was shifting her weight back and forth, her little dog momentarily distracted from his attack on Levi's lawn by her movements. She was also chewing on her thumbnail.

"Do you know something I don't?" he asked after she caught up to him on Mina's lawn. Levi was worried, but Echo seemed on the edge of panicked.

"I don't think so." She took her thumb out of her mouth. "I jump to bad conclusions. You know, slipped in the shower, fallen down the stairs, that sort of thing."

His surprise at his chipper neighbor's macabre outlook must have shown on his face, because she shrugged. "I've only been right once. My ex-husband was really leaving me."

"What else have you considered, so we can rule those out?"

"Something involving a fall has been the major one."

They were both standing on Mina's porch, the dog staring at her front door, wagging its tail eagerly.

"Do you have your phone on you?" he asked.

"Yes."

"Call her again. And text her. I don't want to break into her house if she just forgot your plans or something." They were…more than dating…but breaking into a woman's house was a violation, *more* or not.

Echo nodded and started dialing. With the speakerphone on, they could both hear the ring before it went to Mina's voice mail. Echo ended the call and started texting. She looked up after hitting Send.

"We've got to give her some time to answer," he said to Echo's expectant look. Both she and her dog had the same tilt to their heads. Like he was supposed to do something. Or say something. "You're sure you saw her come home?"

"I'm sure." She sighed. "Look, I jump to terrible conclusions, but Mina and I have become pretty good friends. She's not the type to forget a date, even something as simple as a walk. She'd text or call if she was held up."

"You're right." For all of Mina's grandiose hand gestures and her breezy chatter, she was solid and stable. She wouldn't have been able to have gotten her PhD and now to teach, all while writing her comics, if she didn't have dedication and a strong work ethic. All that stubborn desire to succeed underneath the fluff was one of the things he liked about her. He wasn't so mistaken as to think that he saw a side of her no one else did, but their relationship meant he got to see the multiple facets of her personality in a different way.

They waited in silence for what felt like several minutes but was probably only one or two. Echo continued to chew on her thumbnail, and Levi tapped his foot until the dog pounced on his boot.

"Noodle!" Echo yelled, giving the leash a yank. "I'm sorry. I don't know what came over him. He's normally so friendly."

"We're all nervous," Levi said. He looked down. There were countless numbers of reasons for the dog to be shaking; nervous was only one of them. He crouched and stuck his hand out for the dog to sniff. "It's okay, Noodle. Mina will be fine. We'll break into her house, and she'll be mad at us, and this will all be done."

Noodle—a ridiculous name for a dog, but the dog was pretty ridiculous—sniffed his fingers, then stuck out a pink tongue for a tentative lick. He patted the dog on its head, then stood back up to face Echo's open mouth, her surprise giving her thumb and her teeth a break.

"You know, Mina said you were less of a grouch than you appeared to me. Well, to everyone in the neighborhood. Maybe she was right. I was pretty sure you hated my dog."

The dog looked like a kindergartner had cut out pictures from a book on little yappy dogs and glued them to a piece of construction paper. At Levi's stare, it sat. Its body was so long and its legs so short that its sitting didn't look that different from its standing.

"My wife had wanted a dog like that."

"Like Noodle?" The dog's winglike ears perked at Echo calling his name.

"A small dog." She'd brought up the idea before her last depressive episode, and, like a jerk, he'd argued with her. When she'd gotten sick again, he'd offered to go to the shelter and pick out any dog she wanted.

But by then she hadn't been interested in a dog any more than she'd been interested in eating. Every time he'd seen Echo and her dog walk past, he thought about that failure until he couldn't see the dog without being sick to his stomach.

Now it didn't seem to matter. The failure still existed, but in his past where it couldn't hurt him. Mina was in his future, and she liked the dog.

"Any response?" Mina's HIV was not the same as Kimmie's depression had been, but thinking about those last couple of weeks with Kimmie reinvigorated the ache of worry in his joints that he thought he'd worked through since his wife's death.

Echo checked her phone. "Nothing."

He nodded and opened up his lock pick set. It had been a long time since he'd had to pick a lock, and his skills were rusty, but he got the lock undone after several tries.

Mina's purse was sitting in its usual spot on her table, and it looked like she'd kicked off a pair of heels as soon as she'd walked in the door.

She didn't come running at him and Echo, either in greeting or with a pot in her hands for protection.

"Bedroom?" he asked, raising his brow at Echo.

Nothing would be wrong. For sure, nothing

could be wrong. Mina was healthy, with a low virus count and high T-cell count. Plus, HIV wasn't something people dropped dead of. It was a chronic illness she could and did manage.

And God would not be so cruel as to take another woman he loved away from him.

Echo and Noodle, who was insightful enough to figure out that he should be silent, followed him to Mina's bedroom. They all stopped short in the doorway. Mina was in bed, but she didn't look like she had been resting. The overhead light was still on and what covers weren't wrapped around her body and constricting her movements were puddled on the floor on top of her clothes, which she must have taken off right before climbing into bed. She'd left on only a pair of panties. And Echo now knew the color of Mina's nipples and how her ass curved because Mina was twisted in a way that made Levi's back hurt just looking at her. Her skin was an unhealthy pink color and shiny with sweat.

The warmth of Echo's hand seeped through the shirt on his back. "Oh," she said. "I'm so glad we're here."

Levi nodded. He eased himself into the room, Echo and Noodle behind him. When he got to the bed, he scooted Mina's body over enough that he could sit next to her and put a hand on her forehead. "Yep, she's hot. Help me get some clothes on her, and we'll get her to the hospital."

Having a plan of action dampened his worry until he grabbed Mina's hand. She woke up and immediately started coughing so hard that she curled up around his body. He moved his hand to her back, rubbing lightly as she coughed and shuddered.

Echo returned with some clothes. She'd let her dog off the leash, and instead of sniffing around the room, Noodle was seated at the side of the bed watching the activity. Even though he knew it was stupid, the fact that the dog's ears were alert made Levi worry all the more.

Getting clothes on Mina took time and patience. Though she was awake, she sniffed and moaned more than helped as they moved her arms around to get a shirt over her head. She didn't argue with them—or say anything at all—which concerned him more than the fever. Her silence sank in his gut like too much fried food and beer. The pair of pajama bottoms Echo had found went on easier than the shirt.

Once Mina was dressed, Levi dug into his jeans pocket for his keys and gave them to Echo. "I'll get her downstairs. You get my truck out of the garage and bring it round front."

"No. I'll run home, drop off Noodle and get

my car. I can drive us to the hospital, and you can sit in the backseat with her."

"Okay." Her suggestion made sense, especially since the goal was helping Mina. And as much as Levi hated being a passenger, he liked the idea of holding Mina more.

Noodle's light and quick feet hit the floor between Echo's heavier footfalls as they both ran down the stairs and out the front door.

Levi turned his attention back to the sick woman collapsed against him. "Mina, honey. Can you get up?"

She shook her head, then convulsed with coughs. "I can."

"Okay. On the count of three, we're going to stand. One…"

"I don't want to," she said. Her voice was so small, barely audible above his breathing.

He tucked her head against him, running his hand down her damp, sweaty hair. "We've got to get you to the hospital. You're burning up."

"Okay." She said the words, but she didn't make any effort to stand.

"I'll carry you down."

"That's better," she said, her body seeming to lose more muscle control the longer they sat at the side of the bed. As she sank deeper into his arms, Levi wondered if she would eventually melt into a puddle on the floor.

"Do you have a coat downstairs?" She would need more clothes to go outside, and he didn't think he'd be able to get a sweatshirt over her head without Echo's help.

"In the closet."

"Okay. We'll get you to the couch and then get that coat on you. Echo's driving us to the hospital."

"Echo. I was supposed to go walking with Echo. I didn't call her."

"I know. She knows that you're sick. It's okay. She understands."

Mina's head looked heavy as she nodded in understanding. She also looked like her bones were no longer doing their job holding her upright. Before he stood, he nudged her around so that she was leaning against her headboard. Then he gathered another set of clothes and some toiletries he found in the bathroom into the gym bag on the top of her dresser and set it on the bed.

Mina was dead weight when he gathered her into his arms, and he got hot just touching her. Before he bent down for her overnight bag, he dropped a quick kiss on her forehead. He took the stairs one careful step at a time, checking that he'd placed his weight properly before shifting down. The rag doll in his arms was precious and worth all the time he would ever need to take for her.

By the time he got her coat on her and got her back in his arms and out the door, Echo was waiting at the curb, her car running.

Once in the car with the heater on high, Mina showed more life. Besides coughing, she pulled at the neck of her shirt and complained about being hot.

Levi and Echo both let out a sigh of relief when they pulled into the circular drive in front of the hospital, and they snagged Mina a wheelchair. The process of checking in to the ER had only gotten worse since the last time Levi had been in one. He was opening his mouth to decline face masks for both him and Mina when he remembered that HIV was an immune deficiency virus. Then he accepted the two white masks the attendant was handing out.

By the time Echo came in from parking the car, Levi had completed all the paperwork that he could and was concentrating on how much he cared about Mina in an effort to push the sneezing, coughing and moaning happening all around him out of his head.

No one talked much in the ER waiting room. By the time Mina's name was called, they were all stiff from the uncomfortable chairs. Only one of them was allowed back, though, so Echo sank down while Levi pushed his rag doll through the swinging doors.

It took what felt like hours and an amazing journey through hallways, into rooms and back to the waiting room before they were in a small exam room where the physician's assistant came back with a diagnosis of the flu. "Do you know if she's had the vaccine?" the woman asked.

He looked at Mina for her to answer, but she was lying on the bed with her eyes closed. She probably wasn't sleeping—he didn't know if anyone short of death could sleep under all the fluorescent brightness and the buzzing—but she didn't move to answer. "She never mentioned it."

"It doesn't really matter. Only that she should have been one of the first people to get a vaccine. And she should get one every year." The woman shook her head. "It's so important for people like her, and they can be so careless with their health."

"People like her?" Levi asked, raising an eyebrow. "College professors?"

"I'm right here," Mina said weakly, her eyes still not open. "And I got my thirty-percent-effective flu vaccine. I also read the news. There are a couple strains going around that the drugmakers didn't anticipate. Looks like I got one of them."

"Looks like," Levi agreed.

"Well," the PA huffed, her only acknowledgment that she'd judged too harshly. But she did turn her attention to Mina. "The most common flu the vaccine doesn't cover is a particularly bad strain, especially for those already at high risk. But you don't need to stay in the hospital. I've got a prescription for an influenza antiviral for you. Take it for five days. Get lots of bed rest. You're dehydrated, so drink lots of water."

The PA turned back to him. "You're her...?" The question trailed off, so Levi could supply an answer.

"Her boyfriend," he supplied.

If the PA was inclined to make more comments about "people like her," she didn't. The woman kept her face neutral. "Make sure she drinks fluids. One of the side effects of the antivirals is diarrhea, and I don't want to see her back in here for dehydration."

"Oh, good," Mina said from the bed. "More drugs that cause diarrhea."

"Any other instructions?" Levi asked.

"Come back within the next forty-eight hours. Twenty-four, if there's been no improvement."

"We will," Levi assured the woman before slipping the prescription into his back pocket and gathering Mina up for the slow walk back to Echo and the waiting room.

WHEN SHE WOKE up the next morning, Mina had only vague recollections of the night before, but those were enough for her to know that she'd been to the hospital. Every piece of her body ached, like her skin, muscles, bones and joints were all being pulled in different directions. She couldn't gather them together to stay with her in bed, and she certainly couldn't get out of bed to go get them.

The back of her throat started to tickle. Then she started to cough so hard that she wished she could take off to parts unknown with her skin cells. Instead, she was stuck curling into a ball while tears and snot made their escape.

"Here," her favorite voice said as the coughing fit slowed. Levi was holding tissues in one hand and a glass of water in the other. "I want to make sure you get your meds before I leave for work. Then we'll get you downstairs in front of the TV for the day. I bought some cans of chicken noodle soup, so lunch should be easy for you to reheat. And I'll be back after work with real, non-canned food."

"Oh." The melting in her body now wasn't due to her fever, but from Levi's thoughtfulness. Despite still feeling like crap, she ral-

lied herself to sit up on her bed with her back
against the headboard and accepted the tissues
first. Luckily, the movement caused only a little coughing. Once she'd wiped her eyes and
blown her nose, she held out her hand for the
glass of water. Levi gave her a pill from his
hand and then grabbed the container of pills
labeled "morning" from her nightstand.

It took her entire glass of water to get everything down her throat. "Sometimes I think
about the fact that I'm twenty-seven and take
more pills than my dad, and I wonder what
happened."

"I think that I was lucky you were born in a
time when pills exist that will keep you alive,"
he said, with far more cheer than anyone should
be allowed in the morning. In fact, that was
even more cheer than she'd heard out of him
when she'd been lying in his bed in scarlet un-
derpants.

"I must have been really sick."

"You scared us last night. I don't know how
quickly those retroviral pills they gave you are
supposed to work, but you look a million times
better this morning than you did last night."

"But I still look like shit," she finished for him.

"You look like you've been sick and will be
sick for another week at least."

"Do I need to call the university?"

"No, I took care of that."

"You're really good at this 'taking care' thing."

He shrugged, and she could tell she'd embarrassed him. "I did it for years for Kimmie."

With those words, the pleasure she'd taken in his gestures dimmed a little. Suddenly she was just another sick person he took care of. As those thoughts raced through her head, she knew she was being ungrateful and incredibly stupid. The other chronically ill people he'd taken care of in his life were his wife, whom he still clearly loved, and his best friend. The company she kept in his caring circle should humble her, not make her feel like just one of the crowd.

Between wanting to be in a hot tub and an ice bath simultaneously, yearning to cut off her nose in the hopes of being able to breathe and wishing she could pump Icy Hot directly to her joints, those little thoughts were minor. If they were still dancing around in her head in a week, when she no longer felt the need to be separated from her body, then she'd worry about them. Right now, she accepted his help as she stood and held his hand as they walked down the stairs to her living room.

Levi guided her to her couch, set her up with a blanket, pillows, a glass of orange juice, a bottle of water and all the medicine she might ever need or want. Sinking into the cushions, she pulled the blanket up to her neck and pressed the cool bottle of water to her forehead, watching him walk to her kitchen.

When he came back, he kissed the top of her forehead and smoothed her hair. "The soup is in a bowl in the fridge. All you need to do is microwave it. There's tea on the counter, and the electric kettle is full. I'll call you at lunch to check on you."

Then he slipped out the door while she was gathering her breath through her snot to say thank you, leaving her alone with Netflix and her own sickness.

CHAPTER SEVENTEEN

AFTER LUNCH, LEVI sat in the cool afternoon for a few moments. "To collect his thoughts," his sister had always said when he'd walk away from the group to stare at a tree. Or a flower. Or a piece of grass. He hadn't ever really cared, so long as it was a plant.

The worst part of being stuck in the mine for forty-eight hours had been that there was no place to walk away *to*. And the darkness meant there had been no distance to stare into while his mind cleared. And once they had established the basics of their situation, assigned duties and rationed out supplies, there had been nothing to *do*. Tahoma had led the group in sing-alongs— the man must have memorized every stupid camp song ever—and that had been their entertainment until the ground shifted again, and they were either going to be rescued or they were going to die.

Not that he had thoughts of death to collect himself with right now, but at some point this morning taking care of Mina had felt awfully close to taking care of Kimmie. The words he used. The tone of voice. The gentle touch.

There were differences, too, and they were important. The flu was not a depressive episode. HIV was not clinical depression. Mina was not Kimmie, and neither of them were their chronic illnesses.

He was the common point they shared. If he was feeling a sense of living his life over again, then, well, that was his problem to work through. He picked out an aspen in a neighbor's yard and watched the leaves sway in the breeze. It was unsettling to realize that not reading the horoscope one, now two, mornings had not actually been the sign that he was completely over Kimmie's death, which he'd been hoping for.

Even worse, he might never be over Kimmie's death. And wasn't that a horrible thought. Especially since he wanted Mina. No question that he wanted Mina.

His phone buzzing in his pocket was a welcome distraction. "Pardo," he said as he swiped it on.

"Have you had your flu shot?" his sister asked.

"Hello to you, too."

"I heard from a friend that you were in the ER with a woman who has the flu. I assume that woman was Mina," Brook said. "You need to get a flu shot."

He shook his head at the speed with which gossip traveled. "It's the beginning of flu season. Lots of people have the flu."

"That didn't answer my question."

He sighed. "No, I haven't had my flu shot. I'll get it. I promise."

Brook had called to remind him to get his flu shot every year since Dennis's illness. Though usually she waited until the first flu death in Montana was announced. "It might be too late. You've probably already been exposed."

There was too much panic in her voice for this conversation to actually be about the flu. His sister could worry with the best of them, but she was not afraid of germs. "Brook, what's up?"

"Dennis took the job in Bozeman."

Levi blinked in surprise. "That's great news, right?" *Right?* "It's a promotion and a raise. And just a better job."

He and Dennis had been friends for, God, thirty years, since Dennis and his family had moved into the house next door. They'd both decided to follow Levi's father's footsteps and go into the mines together. They'd been trapped during the mine accident together. They'd decided to move away from it all and come to Missoula together.

"I don't know anyone in Bozeman. I don't know the doctors in Bozeman. What if I can't get a job in Bozeman?" The worries poured out of Brook's mouth thick, like escaped mercury and probably as poisonous, if not to Levi, then to Dennis.

"You don't like your job here." His sister loved deeply and thoroughly, but she didn't *like* anything. Her natural inclination to criticize was one of the reasons he hadn't been too worried about her initial reaction to Mina. If Mina had had red hair, then Brook would talk about redheads and their tempers and their tendency to sunburn. Once Brook warmed up to someone, she still complained, but she would also drive cross-country to get them a bowl of chicken soup if they were ill.

Unfortunately, he didn't know how much of Brook's current complaints—about Dennis's new job, about Mina's illness, about anything— would make the switch to complaint plus support.

"That's beside the point," she said, and he could hear the way she waved her hand in the air, dismissing any argument that didn't support her agitation. "Maybe this was your idea. Maybe you put him up to this."

"Really, Brook?" He was ashamed to admit that when Dennis had told him about the job interview, a small part of him—one bigger than he was willing to acknowledge to himself—had hoped Dennis didn't get the job. Not that he didn't want his friend to get a better job, especially a better job that wouldn't have such a detrimental effect on his health. But Dennis's leaving would be a door shut on his past.

A bird taking off on the tree next to him startled him and shook the ridiculous thoughts out of his head. The past being over was in the definition of the past. Ending was what the past did.

He'd just never expected Friday nights at the bar with Dennis to be in the past.

"Yeah," she said, her voice as sharp as it ever had been when they were teenagers. "Get your last connections to Kimmie gone before whatever future you think you might have with Mina."

The uncanny way his sister nailed thoughts he wasn't fully willing to admit to himself made the back of his neck tingle. "That was uncalled for," he said. Even if he had been thinking some variation of it, it wasn't called for. And it wasn't true, not really.

Or he didn't want it to be true. This morning, he'd been taking care of Mina. They hadn't been hanging out, they hadn't been trying to impress each other or be their best selves, and this evening wouldn't be any different.

And still the first thing he wanted to do when he got off work was see *her*, in all her coughing, snotty, feverish mess. Not that he wanted to take care of her, but that he wanted to see her. Seeing her made the world better.

Which made her like Kimmie, yet different. Seeing Kimmie had made the world better, but he'd also gone home wanting to take care of her, rather than just to be with her most nights.

When he'd been young, love had meant caring for someone, like you care for a child or a pet. Setting out Mina's lunch this morning had been taking care of her, but that wasn't what their relationship was based on, or what it would be based on.

At least now he was old enough to recognize that he'd done that to Kimmie; it wasn't something she'd brought on herself.

"It will be weird to sit around the table at Thanksgiving with Mina instead of Kimmie."

"It was weird for us to have a Thanksgiving with no Kimmie. I'm not sure this will be any stranger, and if it is, it will be because you're determined to make it that way."

"Why couldn't Dennis have gotten a job here?"

"Brook? What is wrong?" It was clear in

the way she jumped around in her upsets that something besides moving was at the root of it all.

"His cough is getting worse, Levi," she said, accusatory, like he should know. But then her tone softened. "He's not talked with you about it, either?"

"No." Dennis's coughs at the bar seemed— maybe—to be worse, but Levi had written it off as the end of the long day, the drying effect of the alcohol, etc. And he only really saw his friend once a week. Who was he to notice if it was different during those couple of hours at the bar?

Then the other shoe dropped. "Either?"

"He thinks I don't know." The fear in Brook's voice broke his heart. "But I hear him at night, even when he gets up to sleep on the couch. And I saw the doctor's bill. It wasn't his regular checkup appointment. He *made* an appointment. Dennis *never* makes an appointment to see the doctor."

Did his sister and her husband never talk to each other?

"Maybe he's…" Levi started that sentence but had no idea how to finish it. He hadn't been to the doctor in well over a year, and most of the men he knew didn't go to the doctor until they were at the ER for a heart attack. Knowing better didn't translate into action.

"Have you talked with him about it?" he asked, trying for another tactic. His partner had headed back inside after their short break, and Levi really should follow; but Brook was upset, and another ten minutes on the phone wouldn't kill their timeline.

"I've tried," she said, the words coming out in a long whine. "He says it's a better job, and I should be happy for him."

"Not about the job. About his lungs."

Silence on the other end of the line was all the answer he needed.

"You have to talk to him about that. What are you afraid of?" The wind was picking up, and branches with their dried leaves clacked together. A crow cawed.

"That it's cancer. That we're moving, and it's cancer, and he won't admit it to himself, and he'll be slowly dying, and I won't be near anyone who can help."

Cancer. The word stuck in his throat like a boulder that he couldn't dislodge. Before he suffocated, he thought through what Brook had said. They didn't know if it was cancer. She was worried that it *might be* cancer, and that Dennis wasn't telling her. "Talk to him, Brook."

"He always says not to worry." She sounded

so dejected, and he wanted to strangle both of them. Dennis for not talking to his wife. Brook for being hard to talk to. His brother-in-law hadn't complained about the weight of Brook's worry, but she was Levi's sister. He didn't need Dennis to complain for him to know.

"Then maybe you shouldn't worry," Levi said, stepping into worry and hypocrisy at the same time.

"Can you talk to him?"

The tree blurred as his eyes lost their focus. This conversation was blurring the entire world. "I don't know what you think he'll tell me that he's not telling you."

"Please," she begged.

"All right," he said, knowing already how that night at the bar would end up. "When do you move?"

"His job starts in a month."

"I'll talk to him the next time we're at O'Reilly's." Hopefully Dennis wouldn't get *more* drunk than usual. God, he wasn't looking forward to this.

"You're the best brother ever."

"I'm your only brother."

"Still…" Brook was apparently trying to lighten her voice, to make everything sound better, but all that did was make the attempted compliment sound more fake.

"Maybe you should let go a little. Trust Dennis to take care of himself."

"Yeah," she said, her voice snapping right back into negative territory. "I know you're going to be at Mina's, taking care of her while she has the flu."

"Brook, that's different. You know it."

"Do you trust her to take care of herself?"

"She's an adult. She takes her meds. She got her flu shot. What more do you expect her to do?" The realization that his sister had pulled him back into talking about her fears about Mina punched him in the gut, and he spit the bad taste of it all out of his mouth. "You know what? You're mad at Dennis, not at me and not at Mina. Go talk to your husband. Call me back when you've worked out the moving problem."

"You could be a little nicer."

"It's hard to be nice when you're questioning my girlfriend."

"But…"

"There is nothing more we can say to each other right now. And I've got to get to work. You'll probably figure out when I've talked to Dennis, but I'll text you anyway. Goodbye."

Levi hung up and slammed the phone into his pocket, irritated with Brook and irritated with himself for letting her get on his nerves.

LEVI OPENED MINA'S front door and slipped in quietly, careful not to wake her if she was sleeping on the couch. She was an easy patient. Or maybe, Levi considered, it was that he wanted to be around her, even when she was sneezing, piling snotty tissues on the bedside table and complaining about her aches. While she was sick, he had been spending nights sleeping on her couch, helping her down the stairs in the morning before going to work. In the evening, he came back to her house and fixed her dinner, then went back to sleep on the couch. He took her to her doctor's appointments.

On Wednesday morning, when she felt well enough to shower, she insisted on doing that on her own, despite Levi's request to help. When Levi got home from work on Wednesday evening, Mina was sitting up on the couch, alert and animated through her sniffles. As he went into the kitchen, she shuffled along behind him, a blanket wrapped around her like a giant cocoon that dragged along the floor.

"Can I help?" she asked as he set the groceries on the counter.

"No. Hang tight and I'll get you a chair."

He didn't have to be facing her to hear her slight grunt and know she was dissatisfied. "I've been sitting all day."

"You're sick." He set the dining chair on the

hard kitchen floor with more force than he'd intended. He'd had to break into her house with Echo and then carry her down the stairs. The limp weight of her in his arms wasn't anything he was likely to forget soon. "You shouldn't even be up yet."

She still looked pale, except around her nose and the red of her eyes. A shower this morning had helped remove some of the ashen look of fever sweat on her skin, but she was still in worn pajama pants and a ratty, heather-gray T-shirt with a *Crime and Punishment* book cover on the front. None of the easy, comfortable clothing he'd seen her in before had been so ragged.

The slight wheeze in her voice didn't help. He'd had the flu years ago and hadn't wheezed. Maybe this was related to her virus. Not just that it made her more at risk for illness, but that anything she caught was likely to be worse.

"I'm bored," she whined, eyeing the chair with disgust.

"You're sick," he repeated. "The doctor said rest. So I'll insist on rest."

"Tomorrow I'm helping with dinner." She was still negotiating with him, and she sounded put out, but she was also sitting in the chair he'd gotten her, so she probably felt worse than she was willing to admit.

"We'll see about that tomorrow." The bag crinkled as he pulled out a head of garlic and some carrots.

There was a moment of quiet from Mina, enough that he started to worry until air rasped behind him. "Did you force Kimmie to stay in bed when she was sick?"

Not only was Mina more tired than she let on, but she was more irritated, too.

"If Kimmie was sick, she never had to be reminded to rest." Kimmie had been the type of person who was on or off. She'd not had any middle gears. Part of his joy in Mina was watching her not just exist in different gears of life, but shift between them.

"Why do you think I needed to be reminded to rest?"

"Because you're getting up and moving around," he said, much louder and with more exasperation than he had meant. He turned to face her, carrot in one hand and peeler in the other. "You're weak and you're sick, and who knows what other viruses are in your body, plotting against you."

As she crossed her arms, the blanket lifted up from the chair like great wings she was flapping, and he knew that he'd fallen into the trap she'd laid for him. It wasn't fair, really. She'd had all day to plot through her bored sickness, while he was only learning about this now.

Then she said, "Is all of this extra care and attention because I have HIV?" And he'd been walked right on top of a hole without realizing it.

He turned back to the cutting board. "No."

"Can you look at me when you say that?"

The knife clunked on the counter as he set it down. He held himself stiff as he turned. "No. This extra care is not about your HIV. It's about the flu I had to take you to the emergency room for."

She made another unhappy low grunt at the back of her throat, like she didn't believe him. "Would you give this much care to me if I didn't have HIV?"

His hands came out in front of him, his hands fisted around the knife. It was all he could do not to toss his hands—and the knife—in the air and go home. "I've never taken care of anyone with the flu who didn't have HIV. I have nothing to compare it to."

The truth was that he really didn't know. Removing Mina's illness from who she was wasn't fair, but neither was focusing on it. His conversation with Brook only made matters worse as her words lingered heavily in his mind. He trusted Mina to take care of herself, but the thought of what could happen if she didn't was a weight he couldn't push off his heart.

"Why are we even fighting about this? What are we even fighting about?"

"I don't…" She sighed, her shoulders drooping and looking as weary as he had seen during her illness. "I don't know."

"Can we stop? HIV or no HIV, you're recovering from the flu. And I've been working all day. Can I just make dinner, and we eat dinner and watch a movie or something?"

She closed her eyes. When she opened them, she pasted a smile on her lips. "You're right."

The smile was fake, the admission was half-hearted, but both would do for tonight.

CHAPTER EIGHTEEN

On Thursday, Mina felt well enough not just to take another shower, but also to poke around her kitchen for something other than chicken soup for dinner. She was grateful for the care Levi had shown her over the past week—Lord knew that being sick alone and single was a miserable experience—but she wanted something for dinner that took effort. Not effort from the cook but effort to eat. Something she had to chew.

Unfortunately, she didn't have anything in her kitchen other than bread, carrots, butter and cheese.

Grilled cheese and carrots it would be.

Her front door opened and closed as she was topping each sandwich with its second piece of bread. She reached into the drawer for a spatula and pressed down on the bread.

"Feeling better?" he asked, with a kiss on her cheek.

She coughed into her shoulder before answering. "Well enough to make you dinner.

Thanks for taking care of me." The butter in the bottom of the skillet sizzled when she pressed on the sandwiches again.

"It was my pleasure," he said, rubbing her back. Her muscles and joints were still sore, but at least his touch felt good. When she'd been really sick, she hadn't wanted anything touching her skin, especially his warm hands.

"Anyway, I enjoyed doing it." He gave her bicep a squeeze.

The only way to get a good crust on a grilled cheese sandwich was to use moderate heat and keep pressing the bread into the butter. If she was paying more attention to Levi's touch than to her cooking and pressing down a little harder than necessary, then the crust would only be better. "You enjoyed taking care of me while I was laid up with the flu? That's a little weird, don't you think?"

Especially after last night's conversation and feeling like an invalid in a Victorian novel, she'd had plenty of time to think about his comment about "years caring for Kimmie." The corrosive thought that she was the chronically ill replacement for his beloved wife was probably the fever talking. But, like the soreness in her joints, the thoughts lingered, sinking deeper and deeper into her marrow. And him saying things like "I enjoyed doing it" only gave the thoughts sticking power.

She probably should have let it go, but what if it were true?

He was close enough to her that she could see the confusion on his face from the corner of her eye. "I liked being with you. Even though you were sick, not *because* you were sick."

She flipped the sandwiches. Both had a perfect golden crust, and the cheese inside already looked gooey. A few more minutes and dinner would be ready. She pressed the sandwiches into the pan again. "Can you wash a couple carrots? Dinner is grilled cheese and carrot sticks."

When he stepped away from her to the sink, his brows were still crossed. "That sounds good, but I would have made you dinner."

"I needed something other than soup," she said. Her words were harsh and ungrateful, even to her own ears. Water poured out of the faucet. She closed her eyes. The water turned off. Levi still hadn't said anything.

"I'm sorry," she said, looking over her shoulder at him.

His shrug was loose, uncaring, which immediately made her suspicious. Levi wasn't a loose, uncaring kind of guy. "You were sick of soup. Nothing to be sorry about there."

"I'm not sorry for being sick of soup. You ate

soup every night with me, so you're probably also sick of soup."

His head tilted in what she thought was agreement, but he seemed to be concentrating so much on peeling carrots that she wasn't sure.

"I'm sorry for sounding ungrateful. All you did was take care of me. You didn't have to."

"No," he said, finally putting down the carrots and the peeler and turning around to face her. "I didn't have to. I wanted to. Because I care about you, not because you needed me to. It was a simple thing I could do that would make your life easier. Up until this week, I didn't think that was a bad thing."

"Up until this week?"

"Dennis got the job and is moving to Bozeman. We have lived in the same town since we were kids. We went into the mines together. We were in the mining accident together. And, hell, he married my sister."

Taking the carrots out of the sink and getting them to the cutting board seemed to absorb all of Levi's attention, but she didn't press him. Nor did she remind him that she knew most of this information. This seemed like the kind of story someone would stop and start and finish in their own time.

"Brook called me on Monday and accused me both of being with you because you're sick and

of pushing Dennis to apply for the job in Bozeman because he's sick." The fall of the knife on
the cutting board as carrot tops skittered on the
counter underscored what he thought of both
those ideas.

"And did you?" Mina asked, before pulling
the sandwiches off the heat. She'd gotten lost
in the conversation and had left their dinner
on the pan too long. They weren't burned yet,
thank God.

"Push Dennis to move?" The knife chopped
off the pointed bottoms of the carrots. "No. I
don't want my best friend to move. Or my sister."

She got a paring knife out and cut the sandwiches into triangles, then pushed the two halves
of the sandwiches apart to make room for a
nice pile of carrot sticks. Only when she set the
plates on the counter next to Levi and the cutting board did she realize that they were having
this stressful conversation, and *it was okay.* She
wasn't worried about him walking out of her
house, of saying that she was too stressful or
too much work or talked too much. They would
talk through their problems and eat their dinner
and—if she weren't sick—they might go up to
her bedroom and make love.

Was this love?

As if they had made grilled cheese sandwiches together for years, Levi scooped up the carrot sticks he'd cut and plopped them on the plates. He took a plate in each hand, turning to follow her. When they sat down, he sighed, and she looked up from her plate.

"I did some thinking while you were sick."

Her heart froze, icing around the panic about their relationship that the fever had brought on. Only, maybe it wasn't that he had this strange fetish about caring for sick people. Maybe, like he'd said when they'd first met, he'd been in a relationship with one person who'd had a chronic illness, and he didn't want to do it again.

Her rational mind pointed out that all he'd said was that he did some thinking, but she was too tired and too sore, and her nose was too stuffed up to pay attention to rationality.

"Nothing to be panicked about," he said, and she realized that her knuckles had turned white as she gripped her plate. "I realized spending time with you was nice, and that neither of us had to be perfect for it to be nice. That the time itself mattered."

"Oh." The ice that had formed around her fears cracked and melted away. She'd been an idiot. A sick, frightened idiot. "That was really nice."

He nodded. "You're a good way to end a day of work."

She smiled, sniffed, then smiled again. As they ate their dinner, and in between fits of coughing, Mina talked about the escapades of daytime television.

She was going to assign those courtroom dramas as a drawing exercise at one of her drink and draws. That would be funny.

MINA TOOK THE plate Levi had rinsed and put it in the dishwasher. Then she turned to him and said, "I need food in the house for tomorrow." She felt better, but not well enough to stand and teach a class just yet. She'd return to work next week. "Something that's not soup."

"You also need to get out of the house."

The truth of his words hit immediately. Being sick with the flu hadn't been the only reason she'd latched on to her fears. Being stuck in the house, and her existence shrinking to what Levi was able to give her, had warped her understanding of the world. Shockingly, it had taken only a couple of days.

"Yes." Her body tensed, and if she could have dashed out of the house, she would have.

"Go change. I'll finish cleaning up and take you to the grocery store."

She went upstairs and found a pair of jeans.

But they were not the forgiving pajama pants she'd been wearing all week. Not only did they feel stiff as she put them on, but the rougher fabric tingled her skin. Remains of the fever, probably. Even before her diagnosis, fevers had seemed to linger in her bones. Still, she didn't lose her breath trying to get them on, and her fingers worked well enough to button them, so that was all a plus. She'd make it through a trip to the grocery store, and Levi wouldn't even have to carry her.

"This was a good idea," Mina said for the fifth time on the drive to the store. She would have been bouncing in her seat except that she wanted to save that energy for shopping. Between making dinner and getting pants on, she'd had enough activity for the day to fall asleep as soon as she got home.

She might even fall asleep in the car on the way back. Like a puppy asleep on its ball.

Once in the store, Mina leaned on the grocery cart and started her slow slog through the aisles. She picked up an apple from one of the bins, examined the weight and the skin and felt for chances of mushiness, while examining the variety and comparing prices. She did the same for oranges and pears. The selection of potatoes was disappointing, especially this close to Idaho.

She was shuffling her feet through the bread when she noticed Levi wasn't behind her. She stopped, looked around and smiled at the surprise on his face when he caught up to her. "You're wearing slippers," he said. The scruff on his face couldn't hide the wrinkles in his cheeks as he pulled his lips to one side in disbelief. And those wrinkles were no match for the crinkles of his forehead.

She smiled, sticking one foot out for his inspection. "Sure am. I couldn't face putting on anything where the shoe would be tight along my skin." The jeans were bad enough. Yoga pants would have been a better idea, but she had wanted to prove something to herself. And she had; she'd proved that yoga pants would have been a better idea.

"But they look almost like loafers. Plus, you're the only one who's going to look at my feet long enough to notice."

She was pretty sure the wrinkles and scruff were now hiding a smile.

After putting her regular brand of bread in her cart, she stopped in front of another and pulled a bag off the shelf, then turned it over to look at the back.

"You already have bread in your cart," he said.

"I know. But this is a new brand, so maybe

it's a better one." It wasn't, so she put it back and moved on to the peanut butter.

"What were you looking for?"

He sounded genuinely curious, so she answered. "Fiber content. My meds mess with my digestive system. Eating a proper diet helps."

"And with the peanut butter?" he asked.

She had two jars of peanut butter in her hands and was comparing the ingredients. "Sugar and salt content."

She decided to stick with her regular brand, then picked up a jar of almond butter. "I never buy this because it's too expensive, but I think I deserve it today."

She didn't stop at the luncheon meats—all too salty and guaranteed to upset her stomach—and instead turned her shuffle down the first aisle. "I should have made a list," she said, grabbing a bag of dried apricots even though she wasn't sure if she was out. For good measure she added some dried cranberries and an expensive bag of dried blueberries. Again, the flu provided some justification.

"I never go to the grocery store without a list," he said.

"Do you buy only what's on your list?" she asked. "Never mind. I'll bet you do." Did she have salad dressing? Not this kind of salad dressing, she was sure. "I don't. The list is more of a guiding principle, rather than a rule. Ideas, suggestions and opportunities, but not restrictions. Never restrictions. The grocery store is a place of possibilities. Why would I limit myself?"

Oil was one thing she was certain she didn't need, so she was able to pass by those bottles with only a quick glance before turning down the next aisle. Again, she had the sense Levi wasn't following her. When she traced her steps back to find him, he was shaking his head, and there was a smile on his face that his scruff couldn't hide.

"What?"

"I always thought the grocery store was a chore. It's, uh, great fun to come with you."

"Stick with me, baby. I'll make everything an adventure."

He laughed. "I plan to. Stick with you, I mean."

"Well, hurry up, then. This is the second time I've had to turn around to get you."

He chuckled again, still shaking his head, and followed her down the next aisle.

"I wish Lucky Charms weren't so full of sugar," she said, reaching for Cheerios to add to her yogurt in the mornings. "But I've never understood why anyone would want chocolate cereal. What do you eat for breakfast when you're not making your girlfriend pancakes?"

"Oatmeal."

A pleasure shimmied through the exhaustion lingering in her body. He hadn't corrected her when she'd said "girlfriend."

"Packet or freshly made?" She picked two boxes of granola bars off the shelf and turned them over.

"Packet. I'm a single man. And apple-cinnamon, before you ask."

"You never just go for it and buy a mixed box."

"No," he said, his voice amused.

"Then you haven't lived." She sighed, putting the more exciting box of granola back on the shelf.

"What was the sigh for?"

"I love these granola bars, but they have so much sugar I might as well eat a candy bar. One of these days I'll turn the box over, and that sugar number will be reasonable. Then I'm going to buy every box on the shelf. Maybe drive to every store in Missoula and buy all their boxes. Stock up, just in case they change the formula again."

"You do this every time you come to the store?"

"Every time I come to the store to buy granola bars. Does this mean you'll never come with me to the grocery store again?"

"No. Like everything else we've done together, I'm fascinated by the process."

She beamed at him. "That was sweet." Then she reconsidered what he'd said. "I think."

His left shoulder lifted in an easy shrug. "It was meant to be. I don't think you have the ability to be boring."

"I was probably pretty boring when I was lying on my couch complaining and coughing."

"Eh," he said, waving her concerns away. "You were sick. Everyone gets leeway when they're sick."

"Thanks." She leaned against the rail of the cart and pushed. Talking back and forth with Levi was fun, even if they were only loafing around the grocery store, but it was also wearing her out. She'd overestimated how well she actually was. The soles of her slippers shuffled against the linoleum like she was ninety years old.

"Do you want me to push the cart?"

"No. It's holding me upright," she said, which was only a partial exaggeration.

"Do you need to get more things?"

It was Mina's turn to stop and contemplate. She had fruit, stuff for salads, bread, granola bars and peanut butter. She could survive off what was in her cart for the next week.

But the blanket on her couch was starting to

stink from fever sweat and sick-person coughing, and there were snotty tissues under the bed
and buried in the couch cushion she would have
to retrieve sometime. The whole house had become suffocating. And she'd be stuck in it tomorrow.

"No, but I want to keep going. I'll lie on the
couch," she said, trying not to grimace at the
thought, "while you put everything away. I can
direct."

He didn't say anything, just gave her a sideways look, his eyes full of a faux sense of im-
position.

She stopped in front of the pasta sauces, grabbing only the one she knew she wanted and not
looking at the more interesting vodka variety
that had appeared on the shelves since the last
time she'd bought sauce. "I'd better not push my
luck. There's still half the store left and plenty of
time for you to decide that we're a better couple
when we don't grocery shop together."

"Maybe. But I'm thinking instead that I need
to rearrange my schedule so that I have enough
time to come back with you."

Her heart swelled with so much pleasure that
she coughed and had to clutch the bars of the
shopping cart to keep herself upright.

Confident in herself, in Levi and in their relationship—and amused that he was amused with

her shopping—Mina kept up a running commentary through the rest of their grocery-store adventure. And even though her eyes were closing on their own and her shuffling went from active retiree to a retiree after knee surgery, she explored every aisle.

CHAPTER NINETEEN

MARY O'REILLY SET Levi's beer on the table as he was sliding into the booth across from Dennis. Then she set Dennis's drink in front of him. Dennis was starting with a beer, no added whiskey—that was a good sign. The sour look on his face was not.

"So," Dennis said as he raised his beer to his lips, "what do you have to say that will convince me not to move?"

"I'm supposed to convince you not to move?" Levi asked, keeping his tone light to match his brother-in-law's.

"Brook said you were going to talk to me and set me straight. I figured, since she didn't want to move, that's what this was about."

Dennis's sentence stunned Levi, and he had to set his pint glass back on the table. "Do you two ever talk to each other?"

His best friend shrugged and knocked back half of his drink. The night had started off okay and, as Levi had predicted, was quickly headed downhill. "Sure. I told her I was applying to a job in Bozeman. She said she didn't care. So I took her at her word."

No, you didn't, you idiot. "She doesn't want you to move. But the reason is she saw a hospital bill that you didn't tell her about, and she's afraid you have cancer. You seem to be coughing more."

As if on cue, a coughing fit overtook him. When he finally stopped, he said, "This is why I drink whiskey. Beer doesn't do a damn thing for my cough."

"Do you have cancer?"

"No." They stared at each other in silence, Levi's chest heaving in relief, until Dennis relented. "The test was for cancer. I'm clean. The doc thinks it's too much bad food, too much alcohol and not enough exercise that's making me feel worse. Oh, and I'm old. Apparently age doesn't help coughs."

Levi let the bitterness in Dennis's voice slide. "Have you told Brook?"

"She hasn't asked." His second coughing fit after finishing his beer was gentler but still looked painful. He signaled to Mary, and she nodded, reaching for the whiskey behind the bar.

"Do I need to pass you a note from her?"

"I didn't ask you to get involved in my marriage."

Levi sighed. "No, you didn't. My older sister did. Tell her the truth. She'll lighten up."

Dennis didn't respond until he'd taken a long sip of the drink Mary had brought him. "God, that feels better."

They nursed their drinks in uncomfortable silence. Only when Levi waved off another beer did one of them say anything.

"What do you think about me moving?" Dennis asked.

Levi almost changed his mind and signaled for another beer to ease the second surprise of the night down his throat. "It's your life. Move, if you want to move."

That wasn't at all what he wanted to say. He wanted to say that he would miss Dennis. That he wished he wouldn't go. That he didn't know what he would do with his Friday nights. Those were all things he could think of to say and even tell Mina. He had no effing clue how to say them to the man he'd known most of his life.

"That's it?" Dennis said, looking wounded and pissed at the same time. "I'm moving to a new town, taking your sister and your niece and nephew, and all you can say is 'Have a nice life.'"

Yes. "No." He opened his mouth, but "I'll miss you" still didn't come out. Hell, he wasn't sure it would be true if he said it. Their regular nights at the bar had become...not routine, but tedious. Until Mina had come into Levi's life, and then Dennis had decided to move, they hadn't said anything new to each other in over a year. Regret, anger and sadness were as regular at their table as whiskey and beer.

Instead he said, "Missoula's a good town."

"Missoula was supposed to be a new start for both of us. No more mining. But it was only a new start for you. Here I'm still the sick friend married to your sister. Hell, Brook's more *your sister* than *my wife*. I want a fresh start, and I want one on my own terms."

Levi blinked several times, then signaled to Mary for that other beer. "I didn't realize being my friend was that awful."

Dennis ordered another whiskey, and Levi got some fries to absorb the alcohol so that at the end of the night, he'd be able to drive his friend home.

"It's not awful," Dennis said after their liquid courage had arrived. "But I'm not your friend. I'm your sick friend. I'm the friend who didn't make it through the mine accident untouched. I'm the friend who struggled to find work when we moved. And I'm sick of being that friend. I'm moving on my own terms. I'm taking my wife and kids with me. Anyway, it's a better job. I can make it a better life."

"I didn't come out 'untouched.' Kimmie

thought I was dead, and the jolt jimmied her out of her depression enough to commit suicide."

Dennis sat back in the bench as if he were going to argue, but thought better of it. "You're right. But I'm right, too."

Brian brought out their fries, and as if by mutual agreement they ignored all the uncomfortable things they'd left unsaid to talk about last night's football game and the upcoming game on Sunday until it was time to go.

Levi dropped Dennis off at his house, and they settled on a time to go back for his car. On the rest of his drive home, all Levi could think about was that Dennis was his *sick friend*. Worse, had he thought of Kimmie as his *sick wife*? And was he thinking of Mina as his *sick girlfriend*?

Was he the sick one?

LEVI COULDN'T GET out of bed when his alarm went off on Wednesday morning. A million little nails weighed him down, poking into his skin at the same time.

"I should have gotten a flu shot," he said to the emptiness.

Only his room wasn't empty, because a voice responded back. "You didn't?"

He turned his head to face Mina, too tired to turn the rest of his body toward her. "I meant to." Then the back of his throat tickled, and the mountain of nails couldn't stop his body from curling up as a cough beat its way through him. Mina rubbed his back, maybe making the cough worse, maybe making it better, but he didn't want her to stop.

The fit finally over, his head fell back against his pillow, his body more exhausted than it had been when the alarm went off.

"Let's get you to Urgent Care."

He closed his eyes. When he exhaled, his breath came out like a groan. Uncomfortable plastic chairs. Face masks because it was flu season. Probably a needle. There was always a needle. "I don't need to go to Urgent Care. Give me five minutes, and I'll be out of bed," he said. Maybe the wheeze would hide the lie in his voice.

"Okay." Mina's voice was light, offering him something, and he was immediately suspicious. "Tell you what. I'll reset your alarm for ten minutes. Notice that I'm being generous and giving you extra minutes. I'll go make coffee. If you are in the kitchen, seated, with your hands around a coffee mug in fifteen minutes—I'm setting my alarm, too—then no Urgent Care." She patted him on his back, and he winced. "Do we have a deal?"

Talking felt too much like work, so he nodded and grimaced at the headache that accompanied the movement.

He was never going to make it out of bed.

"Good. I'm setting the alarms now. You've got fifteen minutes."

A cool breeze slipped under the covers as she slipped out, taking both her warmth and the magic she carried with her out of his bed. He didn't open his eyes to watch her put a robe over her sexy body.

I must be sick.

The alarm going off ten minutes later jolted him awake. The jolt kicked off a coughing fit. And even though he managed to get out of bed—under his own power, thank you—get his pajama bottoms on and get down the hall to the kitchen, the time he'd spent coughing and the time he'd spent recovering from coughing meant that he was late to his seat. Two whole minutes late, according to the alarm on Mina's phone, which she didn't turn off until he'd wrapped his hands around the warm mug and shoved his face into the steam.

"So, Urgent Care?" He didn't have to lift his head to know there was an arch to her eyebrow.

"I hate Urgent Cares. And ERs. And doctors' offices." As stupid as it sounded, even in his own mind, he'd rather be sick.

"But you went with me. Echo would have taken me."

That was enough to make him look up. "I'm not a jerk."

"I'm not a jerk, either, which is why I'm going with you."

Something was off in her thinking, but he couldn't concentrate long enough to point it out. Instead, he shoved his nose back in the steam.

"Do you want a bowl of hot water?"

He took as deep a breath as he could. The moist air didn't smell like anything. He took a sip. His coffee didn't taste like anything, either. This sucked. "No."

"Are you a terrible patient?"

The legs of one of his chairs scooted across the linoleum floor. A mug clinked on the table. And then he could feel Mina and her magic next to him, the liveliness she carried around with her like most people carried their phones. "Yes," he admitted.

"I'll let you drink your coffee and put on real pants, if you want them, before we leave. It would have been far worse for both of us to be sick at once. And the antivirals really help."

She was silent long enough that he looked up.

Her face faced him, but her eyes were off in the distance. When she shook her head, her hair bounced about her face, and she blinked a couple of times before focusing her gaze on him again. Then she shrugged, like whatever she wanted to say didn't matter. Like it was easy and casual.

Like he would believe that. Especially after the shrug.

"Of course, I have to believe in antiviral medicine. They're what's keeping me on the poz side of the diagnosis instead of shifting over to AIDS."

For all the pressure on his head, there should be a giant with a giant-sized vise squeezing his temples. Worse, the giant should be squeezing his brains out his nose. He hunched back over his mug, resigned. "You're right."

"Of course I am. Now, finish your coffee, and let's get you to Urgent Care and on your way to recovery."

Levi drank his coffee as quickly as his nose would allow. He couldn't even be mad at her for being relentlessly chipper. She'd just come out of what he was about to get into.

ONCE MINA HAD gotten Levi back to his house and tucked into his bed with his own prescription for antivirals medicine and a thermos of hot tea by his side, she curled up on his couch with her tablet and emailed two students to reschedule the appointments she'd missed today. Then she followed the instructions from the department secretary to reschedule the classes she'd missed when she was sick.

All her immediate work concerns taken care of, she put her tablet aside and stared at her phone sitting on the coffee table and the task she'd been putting off for over a week. Her parents knew she'd had the flu, and they were worried, which was reason enough to avoid calling them. Her mother would continue to insist that Mina look for a job closer to home, like a tenure-track position in Russian literature was easy to find. They'd go back and forth, their argument following its predictable course, and then Mina would tell them that the reason she was home at this time of day to call them was that Levi also had the flu, and she was going to take care of him.

Ignoring her phone, she got up off the couch and went to the kitchen to make herself another pot of coffee. While that was brewing she dug around in Levi's cabinets until she found what she was looking for. When the coffee was ready, she poured herself a ridiculously large mug and carried it and the chocolate chips back to the living room and the phone.

If she was going to have a predictable conversation with her mother, she might as well make a game of it.

"Mina," her mom exclaimed into the phone.

"What a surprise to hear from you. I'm glad we were home."

Her parents each had cell phones, but her mom said those words every time Mina called them, and they were at home. Even though it wasn't technically a score, Mina helped herself to a chocolate chip.

"Are you still home sick?" her mom asked, her worry almost strong enough to melt the chocolate on the table.

"No, Mom. I went back to work on Monday." And, even better, had been back to drawing on Friday. Antivirals really were a magical thing.

"Good." Her mom clucked. "Mina's feeling much better," she hollered back to her husband, not moving the phone away from her face. "No, she says she went back to work on Monday. No, I don't know what she's doing calling us now."

Mina winced. "Mom, if you're going to yell at Dad, could you at least move the phone away from your mouth?"

"Hmm? Oh, of course, honey." There was a slight shuffle of noise and then more hollering. "I don't know. I'll ask her."

Whatever her mom had done to the phone had helped. A little. Though it wouldn't get Mina out of the next question. She helped herself to two chocolate chips as a precaution.

"What are you doing home? Are you home?"

her mom asked as an afterthought. "Honey, maybe she's calling us from work." Again her mom forgot to move the phone away from her mouth.

Mina looked at the bag of chocolate chips and all the promises it offered her. Delicious escape. Delicious calories. Uncomfortable stomach reactions if she ate the whole bag.

She sighed, then popped the two chips in her mouth. "I'm not at work today because Levi woke up with the flu. I took him to Urgent Care, and I've stayed home with him for the day. Like he stayed home with me."

"You could get sick," her mom said.

"I've already had the flu. Levi took care of me. Took me to the ER. Made me dinner every night. Remember? I texted you and told you I was being taken care of."

"You don't know what other diseases you could have caught at the Urgent Care."

"Mom, I work with college students who live in dorms. If I'm going to catch something, it will probably be from them, not from the strangers I didn't interact with at the Urgent Care while wearing a face mask." Mina hated the face mask but recognized the prudence of it. Despite what her mother seemed to think, she wasn't a complete idiot.

"I just think you should move closer to home.

Like your brother." Throwing "like your brother" into the sentence made that one worth five chocolate chips.

"I'm not moving home. I have a good job that I like. I bought a house. I have a boyfriend." She bit her tongue against saying *and I think we're serious,* because the first conversation she had with someone about the seriousness of her relationship with her boyfriend wasn't going to be with her mother.

"You're supposed to be happy for me," she said, unable to control the whine in her voice. Going away to college had been hard, and her mother had struggled to let go of her youngest child. Her mother had given up struggling when Mina had been diagnosed. Since then all their conversations had been a constant refrain of "when are you coming home?" And at every opportunity, Mina had moved farther and farther away. She wanted to tell herself it wasn't acting out, just taking the best opportunity available, but that wasn't the entire truth.

She could have applied to graduate schools close to home, and she hadn't. Though she hadn't told her mother that.

She reached for the bag of chips, anticipating her mother's next response. But it didn't come, and Mina was left leaning forward, her fingers rustling the plastic of the bag when her mom said, "I am happy for you. I'm just scared that something will go wrong, and we won't be there to help you."

"What could go wrong?" Mina asked before she could stop herself. Then she leaned back on the couch, not taking any chips for this one. Even if she would need the chocolate when her mom started in on her list, she didn't deserve any for speaking without thinking.

"You could get sick again."

"Of course. So could anyone. Luckily my virus count is almost undetectable, and so me getting sick isn't that much different than you getting sick. And you'd be insulted if I said I had to live near you because I was worried you'd fall and break your hip. Right?"

"You could lose your job."

"So could Michael. Actually, it seems more likely that Michael would lose his job, given the instability in his industry right now." She had to grit her teeth as she said the words, even though her brother would probably never know that she'd thrown him under the bus.

"And what really do you know about Levi's intentions? All those other boyfriends said they would stick with you, but they couldn't honestly handle the repercussions of your illness. How do you know he's different?"

Mina grabbed the whole bag of chips from

the coffee table and set it on the couch next to her. Screw a later upset stomach. Screw a few extra pounds. Screw having to explain to Levi where all his chocolate chips went. This conversation was only getting more stressful.

She popped a chip in her mouth. "I don't know that he's going to be different any more than you know he's not going to be." And not all of the men she'd been with had broken up with her because of her HIV. A couple of times they broke things off because it just wasn't *right*.

Mina didn't know exactly what *right* was, but she'd known that it hadn't been with those guys. And she also knew it was *right* when she looked at a sick Levi with the same swelling sense of affection and—dare she think it?—love that she felt when looking at well and robust Levi.

Because he was Levi.

"Your father and I are too far away to mend any broken hearts. And you've been dating this boy for a couple months now. Longer than anyone since…"

The bag of chips crinkled when Mina set her hand on it.

Since Enrique. The boyfriend who had nearly literally broken her heart. Enrique had been poz, too, which her mother knew, and seemed unable to understand how that had been part of the problem. Not that Mina had anything against dating someone with HIV—that would be self-hatred, and she wasn't into that—but Enrique had an activist streak she respected but wasn't ready for.

He had wanted her to be out, to be loud and to be proud. And she wanted that, too, eventually.

But first she wanted to be known for herself. She didn't want to be Mina Clements, the chick who drew autobiographical comics about HIV. She wanted to be Professor Mina Clements, who taught, studied and drew Russian literature.

What she'd admired about Enrique was that he'd been open about his HIV status and still managed to define himself, rather than let other people—and his poz status—define him.

Mina didn't know how to do that. She'd wanted to. Hell, she still wanted to. But the *how* of it eluded her.

Their breakup had sent her to her bed and, at her roommate's urging, to a therapist's couch, because she'd been brokenhearted but also because she'd felt like a failure. By the time the relationship ended, she'd felt like her desire to keep her status on a need-to-know basis meant she was a weak-willed, cowardly person, and it had been a relief when Enrique had finally dumped her.

Her therapist had told her that her status was her own business, that Enrique seemed to want a partner in his activism as much as a partner in his life, and that the fact that she'd withstood his pressures to out herself made her the opposite of weak-willed. Mina got to define herself as she chose, the woman had said. And, the woman had said, that definition was allowed to change over time.

Which was good, because often Mina felt "Who am I?" was one of those questions that would elude her until she died.

She gave in to the chocolate, popping a few chips in her mouth. Repeatedly asking herself these questions was probably why she was a professor of Russian language and literature, instead of something practical like…well, almost anything else. If one wanted to contemplate the existential questions of life, there were few better texts than the Russian classics.

As the chocolate slid down her throat, it served its purpose. Her shoulders relaxed. Her jaw relaxed. And she was able to refocus on her conversation with her mother.

"Since Enrique. I know." Mina waited, her hand in the bag of chips, for the wave of self-doubt and indecision that always followed mention of Enrique's name. When it didn't come, she eased her hand out of the bag without a single chip.

She wasn't the same person she had been then. She was a stronger person. A person who didn't need chocolate chips to get through a tough conversation with her mom.

Her hand darted back into the bag for one chip.

She might want the treat, though.

Putting the last chip she would have today in her mouth, she took a deep breath. "Mom, Enrique was over two years ago. Yes, he broke my heart. Yes, part of the reason we broke up was because of my HIV. But I'm a different person now. The job. The house. The boyfriend. I got my life together. And sometimes—" she paused, looking at the bag of chocolate chips but not reaching for any "—sometimes when you worry about me so much, I wonder if the real problem is not my HIV, but that you don't have faith in me."

There was rustling on the other end of the phone, but no words.

Mina could imagine what her mom was doing, though. Her mouth was probably open. Her dad had probably looked up from some Micah Blackwell interview on the National Sports Network, decided that the open mouth was a scary sign and looked quickly back at the television before she could notice and say something he might have to respond to.

"You're just so far away," her mom said with a heavy sigh. "I'd feel better if I could see you once a week."

Mina's head fell back against the couch. Her stomach was already starting to revolt against the number of chips she'd eaten, and the conversation wasn't over. She'd have to hang up on her mom for the run to the bathroom, which would only worry her mother more.

Because everything Mina did worried her parents. And had, starting since she'd been the kid with an interest in Archie comics, rather than her brother. Obsessively reading *Crime and Punishment* while sporting black eyeliner that she'd applied with a trowel had only made her parents worry more.

They had never fully understood their young daughter. HIV had only given them something tangible to worry about.

Of course, knowing this didn't help everything. Her mom's comments still felt more like lack of faith than they did lack of understanding.

"I'm not moving back. You're coming to visit over Thanksgiving. You can meet Levi. You'll feel better. Especially because he's nothing like Enrique." *He's more like you*, she realized. Solid. Hardworking. A doer, not a thinker. Except that he seemed to love that she was a thinker. He at least wanted her to keep talking about her thoughts, ideas. She would have anyway, with anyone she dated, but it was nice to be encouraged.

"Who's Enrique?" said a raspy voice from the hallway.

Mina looked up. Levi was leaning heavily on the doorjamb. The flu didn't seem to have had any effect on his ability to grow stubble. And his hair was a complete mess, each strand attempting to escape his head by a new path through the universe.

He looked adorable.

"I've got to go, Mom," Mina said into the phone. "Tell Dad that I love him."

"Do you really think your father and I don't have faith in you?" her mom asked.

"Let's talk about this over Thanksgiving," she answered. "You're coming, right? Email me your ticket information."

"I don't want you thinking that your dad and I don't have faith in you from now until Thanksgiving."

"Then stop questioning everything I do. Or start saying things like 'that sounds like a good decision' or 'you really put a lot of thought into that and I'm sure you know best.'"

"But…" Her mom paused. Mina waited for her to say she was sorry or that they were proud of her and all she'd accomplished in her life or something.

Instead the "but" danced in Mina's ear. Alone.

Levi made his unsteady way from the doorway to the couch.

"Mom, I really do have to go."

"It's not that your dad and I aren't proud of you. It's that we worry about you."

Levi put a hand on her shoulder. Mina closed her eyes. "I know, Mom. And it would be easier if I were closer." Doing something they understood.

He gave her shoulders a squeeze, his concern adding to a pile of irritation that he hadn't caused and wasn't really a part of. She was just sick to death of people worrying about her.

CHAPTER TWENTY

MINA HUNG UP the phone and tossed it to the coffee table. Then she straightened her shoulders, put on as real a smile as she could manage and looked over at Levi. "How are you feeling?"

He opened his mouth, probably to say something, and coughed in response. She nodded and patted his knee. "I get it. I was there, too. Want some tea?"

He shook his head, still coughing. When he was finally able to wheeze out a couple of breaths, he asked, "Who's Enrique?"

She patted his knee again, distracted.

They hadn't talked much about their past relationships. Mina knew about his wife, and that they had gotten married pretty young, so she might be his only significant past relationship. He'd said that he hadn't dated much since Kimmie's death. But Levi hadn't asked, and Mina hadn't told, about her past boyfriends.

Plural.

Of the men she'd dated in the past, only

Enrique compared for significance, not only length of relationship, but also depth of feeling.

"Enrique was a boyfriend," she said. It wouldn't be enough. Levi wasn't so sick that he wouldn't recognize the dodge.

He gave one brief and almost insignificant nod. "Serious enough for your mom to mention him again."

Her lips twitched. She should be honest. Enrique was in the past, Levi was in her present, and she wanted Levi to be in her future. But... She sighed. *But* didn't matter. If she wasn't up-front, Levi might think there was something she was hiding. She sighed again. "I was in love. And he broke my heart, because I wouldn't announce to the world that I was positive."

She must have startled Levi, because he leaned away from her, though the coughing fit his surprise started was short-lived. "Why?"

"He was positive, too, and active in community activism. He wanted us to be this power couple, doing speaking engagements, writing articles, etc. I didn't want that. I just wanted to be a professor and an artist and live my life."

"Who dumped who?"

"Oh, he dumped me. Called me a coward. Sometimes, I wonder if he was right."

"Because you wouldn't tell the world your own medical business?"

"I guess." When Levi put it that way, her position seemed so reasonable. It *was* her business to tell or not tell, not everyone's business to know. But when Enrique had dumped her, she'd felt just the opposite. And some of those doubts lingered. What if she hadn't made the right decisions? What if she'd been unreasonable?

It hadn't helped that her parents had loved Enrique, especially her mom. Strangely, they'd seemed to find comfort in his positive status, like he could understand her better, or life would be easier if they were both positive.

Meanwhile, she'd just been annoyed that her disease seemed to define their entire relationship. And maybe she'd been unreasonable about that, too.

No, she thought, looking at Levi. Or even if she had been unreasonable about Enrique, she was in a good place now and the past was worth the present.

"Was it easier to date someone who was also positive?"

"What do you mean?"

He shrugged. "They would know how you feel."

She sat back as if slapped. Had he not been

listening? She'd just said how Enrique didn't understand her, and how she didn't understand him. That they'd fought over what he thought a person with HIV should do with their lives versus what she wanted to do.

"By that logic you should date men."

He blinked several times. "That's not," he said slowly, rubbing his eyes with the heel of his hands, "what I meant."

"What did you mean?" she asked, arching her voice.

"I guess..." He rubbed at his face again, then shook his head like he was clearing dust out from between his ears. "I guess I'm not sure."

"We still had to use condoms, if that's what you mean. There are different strains of the virus, you know."

"I know." Levi made strange clicking noises in the back of his throat. "Sometimes, I would look at Kimmie on the days she couldn't get out of bed, and I wondered what it felt like to be her. I would know in my mind that depression was an illness, and she needed treatment, and treatment wasn't an instant fix or even a permanent fix, but I still wondered why she couldn't just put her feet on the ground and walk out the door."

He sniffed. "Those thoughts weren't fair to either of us. I guess I wondered if I would better understand what she was going through if I could go through it, too."

She arched an eyebrow. "That may be one of the most self-centered things I've ever heard. Do you want to get HIV so you can understand me better? That can be arranged," she said, before her sense caught up with her mouth, and she stopped talking.

He blinked several times, then rubbed at his eyes again. "I'm not making myself clear."

"I don't know what you could say that would be any clearer. You wanted to be sick so that you could understand your sick wife. You have the flu. Do you understand what I was going through last week any better?"

He coughed, and Mina's words sank into her head like a thousand pieces of glass, tearing her apart. "I'm sorry." She curled her legs under herself, and the bag of chocolate chips fell to the floor, fortunately not spilling any. "I had the flu last week, and I could barely think through my name. I shouldn't be yelling at you for not being able to enunciate a complicated feeling about you and Kimmie. I should be offering to make you tea."

She put a tentative hand on his shoulder. "Do you want some tea?" she asked, the lack of empathy she'd shown in her anger holding her back from showing more affection. She'd been an ass, and it embarrassed her.

"No. I just came down to see if you were still here."

"I'd planned to stay the night, like you did for me." As she said the words, the reality of what Levi had been trying to say sank in. There was something whack about wanting to share your partner's disease, but that wasn't what Levi had been trying to say. At moments in his marriage where he'd struggled with empathy and compassion for his wife, he'd fantasized about an extreme solution. Just another version of dreaming of winning the lottery or hoping the floor will open up and swallow you when you've made an ass of yourself or wishing the person tailgating you on the highway will be late to work. Not that you want any of those things, really, but the fantasy fills an immediate emotional need.

"Oh. Thank you," he said.

"And I'll make you dinner. 'Cause I appreciate when you did that for me."

"Chicken soup?" he asked, both his eyebrows rising when he coughed.

"I hear that's what's best for a flu patient," she answered with a smile.

"And I'll complain when I'm sick of it."

"Fair." She looked at Levi with his watery, red eyes and sleep-sick messed hair. "And it wasn't easier dating someone who was also positive. Maybe he understood the havoc the meds can wreak on your stomach, but he didn't seem to have any sense that I might have a different relationship with my disease than he did."

She put her hand on his upper thigh, where she'd wanted to put it earlier, when her mouth had gotten ahead of her brain. His thigh was warm, and the muscles under her hand were hard. She'd underestimated him. Or overestimated herself and not stopped to think before talking and acting. The same things that usually got her in trouble.

"Really, you are much better at understanding *me* than Enrique ever was."

He shrugged. "I worry, sometimes."

And that seemed to sum Levi up completely. His stoicism and constant scruff protected a heart that felt so deeply that she was often in awe. That he felt those emotions for her sometimes brought tears to her eyes, even if she was sick of people worrying about her.

"Well, don't worry right now. Right now, let me take care of you."

"I'm not very good at letting people take care of me."

"I know." She stood and held out her hand. His skin was warm—too warm—as he slid his palm into hers. She planted her feet and pulled, helping him off the couch. Levi leaned on her as they walked into the kitchen. He collapsed into a chair and buried his face in his arms while she heated up a can of chicken soup for them both.

CHAPTER TWENTY-ONE

AFTER THEY WERE both recovered from their fights with the flu, the pattern had been set. They weren't living together, but they weren't living apart, either. If Mina was the one who was out late, then as soon as she'd parked her car, she slipped her key into Levi's door, brushed her teeth in his bathroom and slid into his bed. If Levi was the one out late, then he came to her house. When they were both home for dinner, negotiations just seemed to work themselves out.

Tonight, after Mina shook her toothbrush in Levi's sink and crawled into his bed, she would fall asleep immediately. Maybe even as soon as her head hit the pillow. Between work and Levi, she was doing too much, and she didn't want to give any of it up. Which basically meant she felt like she could barely keep her eyes open every night. The plus side was that she slept like a rock, even if she wasn't getting enough of it.

She shed her clothes, then grabbed her pajamas from the floor next to Levi's bed and pulled them on. He shifted a bit when she lifted up the blankets and crawled in, but as soon as she pulled the covers back over herself, his arm came around, and he was pulling her in close to him. She wondered if he sensed how tired she was lately. He gave her sideways glances sometimes when she yawned but hadn't said anything.

Well, he was tired these days, too. Working all day and then going over to Brook's house and either helping her pack or helping Dennis with repairs.

They'd have a free weekend before her parents came for Thanksgiving. A free weekend to hang out, sleep and recover. Then they'd be okay. Trying to hold on to the thought, Mina closed her eyes. Sleep came immediately.

MINA HELD LEVI'S hand tightly as they stood in the baggage-claim area of the airport waiting for her parents. People exiting the terminals in a steady stream were all variously dressed for the weather, and she almost overlooked her parents. Her mom was dressed for an arctic expedition, her thick coat complete with a fur-lined hood. Clearly her mother hadn't been kidding when she'd said that she wanted to visit at Thanksgiving instead of Christmas because she was nervous about the weather. Her dad was dressed more reasonably in the same winter coat he wore in Virginia in February.

"Hi, Mom," Mina said, the fur of her mom's coat brushing against her cheek as she leaned in for a hug and kiss. "I'm so happy you could come."

Tension flowed out of her in a rush as soon as she said the words and felt her mother's arms wrap around her. The anxiety she'd felt in anticipation of this meeting disappeared completely when she embraced her dad, and he gave her his usual hesitant pat on the back. While she knew that her mother's gushing worries came from a place of love, they often felt like a tsunami that knocked Mina off her feet and didn't let her get back on her feet long enough to recover her balance.

As a kid, her dad's more hands-off approach to parenting and praise had left her wondering if he even noticed his children. Now she was old enough to understand that his hesitancy was directly related to her mother's overbearing nature. The more her mother overflowed with worry, love and affection, the more her dad pulled back, as if he knew he couldn't compete, so why even try.

But the cool, dry skin of her dad's cheek felt as good against the top of her hair as a cool pillowcase on a warm summer's night. And Mina felt his love for her in the way his fingertips lingered on her arms as they pulled away. All her anxiety dropped to the floor the instant her dad's fingers lost contact with her.

"Mom, Dad. This is Levi." She looked back and forth between the people she loved most in this world, her face beaming with so much pleasure that she was afraid her cheeks would crack. "You'll be seeing a lot of him this weekend."

"Nice to meet you," Levi said, shaking hands heartily with her father and more delicately with her mother.

"Come on," she said, the fabric of Levi's coat crinkling as she slipped her arm through his. "Let's get your bags and head home. I've got the slow cooker going, so dinner is waiting."

The cold night air felt good after the heat and milling bodies of the airport. As they walked to the car, her mom talked about their flight, the people they'd met and what they were doing in Missoula. There were college students home for the holiday, some parents visiting their children, also for the holiday, and a couple of "crazy"—her mom's word—people for whom spending a cold weekend camping in the wilds of Montana was their dream vacation.

"Why's Levi driving your car?" her mom asked as she climbed into the passenger seat beside Levi. "Not that I mind you driving," she said, leaning over and patting his leg, as if to reassure them both, "but Mina has always been very independent."

"I'm still independent, Mom. But I've been tired, recently." She put all the excitement she'd felt at seeing them in the airport into that sentence, and still it came out halfhearted to her ears. When she smiled—to cover up the frailness in her voice—that came out weak, too. "Dinner is split-pea soup with smoked turkey, and that will make everyone feel better."

And it did. Mostly. Though Mina went to bed almost immediately after dinner, leaving Levi to entertain her parents with information about Montana and Missoula.

"SHE SEEMS MORE tired than normal," Peg Clements said to Levi as Mina dragged herself up her stairs to her bedroom.

"She's been working a lot," he responded, brushing off Peg's concerns as easily as Mina had brushed his off over the past month. *Because* Mina had brushed off his concerns. She'd bristled every time he'd mentioned how tired she seemed and how busy she was. Mina didn't want him to worry; and, every time she spoke on the phone with her mother, she complained that her parents worried too much, so he'd tried not to add to it.

Even if the light in her eyes was dimmer tonight than he'd ever seen it.

He didn't stay much later at Mina's house, and, despite how much he wanted to crawl into bed next to her and wrap his arms around her, he walked across the lawn to his own house after saying goodbye to her parents.

Though he did stop in his driveway to look back at her dark bedroom and hope she was okay.

OVER THE NEXT two days, Mina pretended to have energy. She expressed an opinion when her mom asked what size turkey they would get. She said she wanted pumpkin pie over pecan, even though the thought of eating either sounded exhausting. But she didn't even have enough energy to smile when Levi said he didn't know stuffing and dressing were different, and her mom sucked in her breath.

As three of them walked and one of them shuffled down the aisles of the grocery store, her mom double- and triple-checking her lists every five minutes, it took all her energy to wave to a French professor they passed near the apples. She just dragged behind them, with barely a comment on what the best cheeses were to get for a vegetable tray.

Though he'd been up with her parents through

the produce, now Levi was hanging back. When her parents turned the corner, he finally said something. "Are you okay?"

She'd been waiting for and hoping to avoid that question all week. "I'm tired," she said, her fingers trailing over the price tags as she made her way down the aisle.

"I know." He stopped. She made it almost five feet before she noticed he wasn't following and stopped, too. He didn't speak until she turned around to look at him. "You've been tired for over a week. Almost flu-tired. Is something wrong?"

Mina looked up at the row of canned soups, something she hoped to never eat again after living off them during both her bout with the flu and Levi's. She touched the can of split pea and ham. Maybe that would be okay...

"Mina," Levi said, his irritation clear in his voice, as was his attempt to hide it.

She didn't want to talk about it. Not here, in the *grocery store* with her parents in the next aisle and some unknown student hovering behind her. Not ever, because she was twenty-seven and should know better and should be able to talk about such things with her boyfriend with a sangfroid that every French woman could be proud of.

But instead she wrinkled her nose until he

marched up to her. His body trembled with the effort he was making to hold in his emotions. Those emotions she loved to watch spill over and out when he thought no one was looking. The overflow of love he felt for the people closest to him that he could only keep contained when he thought people were looking, but which came out like a river when he didn't think anyone was paying attention.

Only now, those emotions weren't positive. Frustration was what he wound so tightly around himself that a small touch would set him off. "Mina, whatever is going on, we have to talk about it."

She lifted her head, so that she could look him directly in the eyes. He was right. Of course he was right. Only...

"There you are," her mother exclaimed from behind them. "We were wondering where you had gotten off to. I was thinking of trying something new. What do you think about wild-rice stuffing?"

She didn't think much. But arguing with her mother sounded too much like work, and she needed to save her energy for arguing with Levi. "Sounds good, Mom."

STILL ON EASTERN Time and seemingly determined to stay that way, her parents went to bed early, leaving Mina alone with Levi. Since they hadn't spent any time alone together since her parents had arrived—the couple of minutes in the grocery-store aisle didn't count—she should be thrilled. Instead, she kept thinking about her bed and her down comforter and her soft pillow.

And she couldn't ignore the fact that her reluctance to talk with Levi wasn't simply emotional cowardice. He was right; her tiredness was unusual and a sign that something was wrong.

As soon as her parents shut her guest bedroom door, Levi turned to her with a brow raised.

"Can we at least sit down for this?" she asked.

Normally the fact that he wasn't saying anything wouldn't seem like a big deal, but his gesture at her couch felt like they were back at the beginning of their relationship. With her about to babble on and on, standing on his stairs while he stood there, silent and with his brow raised in an expression she couldn't pinpoint.

And which only made her talk more.

Which didn't set this conversation up for success.

But she followed his outstretched hand to her couch and sat. Communication was key to relationships. She'd read enough women's magazines to know the truth of that statement, even if she'd never made it fully work in relationships past.

"What's up?" he asked, sitting next to her. He was close enough for her to reach out and touch, his jeans covering thigh muscles that she knew would feel magnificent under her hand. With her parents here and her tiredness, feeling the way his thigh muscles clenched when her hand touched them might be all the action she got for a while.

"I've been tired recently." She waited for him to agree or nod, but he sat there, his face impassive and not even a lift of his brow to ease her nerves. She sighed. "It's not the HIV. I mean, it's related because the meds and the virus don't help, but I think I'm anemic."

"Anemic?"

"A shortage of iron in the blood."

"I know what it is," he said, his voice teetering on the edge of insulted.

"Oh." The floor above them squeaked, and she looked at her stairs to see if her parents were coming down. She wasn't quite so lucky.

They sat in silence for several minutes. The trouble was that she knew she was being ridiculous but couldn't seem to stop herself. Between this and the flu, she didn't want to be Levi's sick girlfriend, and that was how she felt. Especially with him looking at her like he did, with patience making his face placid when she wished he would get frustrated with her.

"Are you going to tell me why?" At the cutting edge to his voice, her shoulders relaxed. Maybe it seemed silly, but so long as he could get mad at her, she wasn't the sick girl to be treated with extreme gentleness and caution. People could get mad at those they loved, but they didn't get mad at those they pitied.

More than the disdain and the judgment, she feared the pity if her health condition were ever revealed. The "Oh, I'm so sorry" people who took an unconscious step back in case what she had was catching.

Of course, what she had *was* catching, but that wasn't the reason they stepped back. They'd step back for Echo and her breast cancer, too. The people who stepped back from her didn't want to face the possibility of illness and death in their own life. She'd dated a guy like that once. And even when she'd broken up with him, he'd been sympathetic and understanding to the point of pitying. Because if he pitied her, then he wouldn't have to think about the possibility he would be chronically sick sometime in his life, too.

"Anemia isn't new for me." She shrugged. "When I was a teenager, I got these awful periods, and my doctor put me on iron pills." Which had helped, but the side effects had been uncomfortable. "Now I get anemic when I'm stressed, and my period hits. I probably would have grown out of it, if it weren't for the HIV, but who knows? Maybe it's related. Maybe it's not."

"Your period started on Monday." He stated the words as a fact, not as a question he was asking. The man was quiet, but she should never forget that he noticed the world as it went around him in intricate detail. He'd probably had her cycle pegged within two months of their dating, which was when he started showing up with particularly well-timed bags full of ice cream. "What is stressful?"

God, what wasn't? "Grading has gotten out of control, which is my fault because I keep assigning all this work, and the kids are doing a great job, and I want to give them lots of feedback. I have a deadline coming the first of this month for that book of poetry, which is turning out to be harder to craft and draw than I'd anticipated. It had seemed like such a great idea, and now I don't think it was. Russian poetry in comic-book form. God, nobody reads poetry anymore. Why do I think that my sketches will change it?"

She took a deep breath, both to slow herself down and to ensure that she had air to keep talking. Because she wasn't done.

"That would be enough, but I'm also behind because I had the flu. And because you had the flu, and I was taking care of you and taking care of me when I should have been working."

"Why haven't you said anything?"

There had been so many moments when she should have said something. As the pile of papers to grade and the number of panels she needed to draw had gotten bigger and bigger, and yet she'd still gone over to his house to watch football. "Because I want to spend time with you. And I know the right decision for us is to take a break, so that I can get caught up."

A small wrinkle appeared between his eyebrows as he considered what she'd said. "Did you think I'd be upset?"

She shook her head. "No." She worried that he'd be exactly the opposite. That he'd be understanding and sympathetic. That the time they spent apart would be easy, so easy that he would notice how much better it was.

The very worst of it was thinking these things and *knowing* how ridiculous they were, but acting on them anyway. Because what if she made the wrong decision? What if she kept going on her current path without stopping to think about it? She'd done that before, many times, and had messed everything up.

"Yes," she said, because that was closer to

the truth. "Not that I thought you'd be angry, but that I thought you'd feel pity for me and try to take care of me."

"Is that so wrong?" The wrinkle in his forehead got in line behind a million other things she didn't understand. Was he upset? Confused?

"I don't want to be the sick girl you're dating." She tossed her hands up in her own mix of upset confusion. "I want to be the woman you're dating."

"What makes you think I see you as a 'sick girl'?" Obvious confusion dragged out the sentence, which was understandable, because she'd confused herself.

"I just…" She didn't know how to finish that sentence. "I didn't want to disappoint you."

His eyes closed for the briefest second. The side of his jaw twitched.

"I've disappointed you," she said.

If she hadn't studied him so closely for the past several months, she might have missed his barely-perceptible nod. "I think you disappointed yourself," he said.

She sucked in her breath. "That was patronizing." She was a grown woman, and despite their ten-year age difference, she didn't need to be told when she'd disappointed herself.

Her indignation escaped from her lungs in

a loud, long puff of air. The truth was she *was* disappointed in herself. She'd gotten caught up in her fears and what she thought was important for someone else, forgetting what was important for her and for her own body.

"How angry are you?"

He sighed and it was worse than a yell. "I'm not angry. I'm..."

Great—she'd caught Levi at a loss for words. She was used to him not talking, but usually that was because she was the one talking, or because he didn't have anything to say, not because he didn't know *what* to say.

"I've had three people who I care about in my life have health problems. I'm sure I'll have health problems in the future, and someone, hopefully you, will be a part of my life and help me figure out what I need to do to take care of myself. And I hope I will trust you more than you trust me."

His accusation stung hard enough that she had to lean away. "What do you mean trust you? How does me not sharing this information mean I didn't trust you? Maybe it just means that I wanted to keep my own health information private. Because it's *my* health information."

From his slight flinch, it was her turn to have insulted him. "I thought we were at a place in our relationship where we shared important things with one another."

She sighed. "We are. I have no good excuse for not telling you why I was feeling so tired. Worse, I have no excuse for not facing up to the information myself. Anemia is easy for me to fix. I can eat a steak and some spinach and take iron pills. It's not even anything I need to go to the doctor for. It's happened enough to me that I can treat myself, and if it doesn't go away, then I can go to the doctor."

Knowing that she'd been stupid, and that she'd hurt someone she cared about and potentially jeopardized a relationship, didn't make facing this any easier.

She knew better.

She closed her eyes for a moment, to give her brain time to catch up to her idiocy. "Everything in my life was feeling so perfect. I guess I didn't want to admit that something could go wrong."

"You being sick isn't something going wrong. It's life. Your life. My life. The vows say 'in sickness and in health,' and I wouldn't be in this if I didn't see marriage in the future. I'm not dating you casually."

She snorted. "I know. And I agree with you."

His eyebrows were lifted. She'd tried to explain too much away.

"This too shall pass," she said.

One brow came down. "I used to say that to my wife. She never thought it was all that helpful. Having it said to me, I can see why."

She gave him a rueful smile. "People only say it during bad times, but that's not what Rumi meant when he said it. He meant bad things will pass and change, but he also meant good things will, too. The good times will change into bad as surely as the bad times will change into good."

"That's depressing as hell."

"I used to think it was reassuring, but then I had something really good, and I was so afraid to mess it up that I think I messed it up." She bit her lip. "How badly did I mess it up?"

"Honestly, I don't know. I didn't react well to your HIV in the beginning. I know that. And the thing I was more afraid of than anything was watching helplessly as you got sicker and sicker, and I was on the sidelines, unable to do anything and, worse, unable to get you to do anything." He had a small dimple in his cheek that just appeared when he was concentrating, only she didn't like what he was concentrating on, because he was concentrating on how she'd messed up.

"But I realized that was selling you short. You're not Kimmie. HIV isn't depression. And it was patronizing of me to conflate both of those things. I needed to treat you as you, and HIV as HIV."

Understanding rang in her head like someone was pulling ropes on church bells. "And I went and didn't take care of myself. I made your worst fears come true."

He inclined his head. "Not the worst. As you said, anemia is easily fixed. I'll make you a steak every night for the rest of your life if that's what it takes. But if you don't trust in me and in us, how can I?"

"I don't know." She tucked her legs under her, but curling up into a smaller ball didn't make her feel any better. Now she was physically smaller, along with feeling small. In an effort to keep everything in her life together and exactly where she wanted it, she might have ruined the best thing she'd ever found.

The deep breath she took traveled through the crevices of her body, searching for the distrust he'd accused her of. When she exhaled, she came up blank. "I do trust you. I couldn't be here if I didn't. I don't take sex and relationships and this," she said, waving her hand at the space between them, "lightly."

"I don't, either." He rubbed at the back of his neck. "Do you trust us?"

She opened her mouth to answer, "Of course," but it didn't come.

"Is your silence a no?"

"No." It wasn't. She felt that deep in her soul, down to the tips of her big toes and full out where her arms extended. "I've just never asked myself that question."

He raised an eyebrow. "You've asked yourself if you trust me?"

"Of course. Haven't you asked yourself if *you* trust *me*?"

She understood his short snort to be a yes.

"I've dated men before and had serious boyfriends, but I've never had an *us* to trust before. At least, I don't think I have. It's different." Scarier, but also wonderful. "Did you trust in the *us* of your marriage?"

"Yes." His lack of hesitation was heartening. The depth of his love always comforted her. It had been possible in the past. It would be possible in the future, for them.

What a strange concept. *Them.*

"Again, what now?"

He shrugged. "We have Thanksgiving plans here tomorrow, and Dennis and Brook are coming over, too. We'll keep doing that. No reason not to."

"We're not broken up, are we?" It wasn't until

she'd said the words that she realized how much it revealed the little trust she had in *them. Us.*

She turned her head to look at him while he answered and was surprised to see a look in his eyes that she could only describe as pure fear. He might be trying to hide it, but he held himself so stiffly that she thought he'd shatter if she tapped his shoulder.

But he held himself together, taking a deep breath. "Honestly, I don't know where we stand."

Horror made her suck in her breath so quickly that she coughed. "What does that mean?"

"When you told me about your illness, I thought the worst thing in the world would be caring about someone as they suffered through something I couldn't fix. Worry combined with caring and fear and... Just because I wouldn't go back and change any of my life with Kimmie doesn't mean I want to go through that again."

His hand gripped the edge of the couch, tightening around the cushion so that his knuckles turned white. "But we might not even make it there because you can't decide if you trust me enough to talk about feeling tired. I could learn not to pile all my worry on top of you, but not if I never know if you're hiding something from me."

Mina wrapped her hands around her torso, this time trying to keep herself from splintering. "That wasn't what I meant by this at all. I just didn't want you to worry."

Worry smothered, and she needed to breathe. "I know. But you've got to give me a chance. You've got to give this whole thing a chance."

"So what does 'I don't know' mean?" she asked again. "Do I get a second chance?"

She needed all the help she could get figuring out solid relationships. God, she was twenty-seven years old. She should know more about what it meant to be in love and to be settled with someone than she did.

She'd dated. She'd even been in love, but she'd always been too busy thinking about what would happen to her relationship when she graduated and went on the academic job market, she probably hadn't put much effort into any of those relationships. Maybe she'd let them fizzle out before their time. Inertia, or lack of it.

Or the fates were giving her a chance to grow and meet Levi. Now she needed them to give her the opportunity to make this right.

"I need to think about how long I can stay with someone who has to think about how much faith they have in a relationship with me," he said bluntly. "I'm honestly not sure what the answer is."

"Are we broken up?" she asked again.

"No. But I'm thinking. And you should think, too. After we get through Thanksgiving, maybe we should spend that time thinking in our own houses and our own beds."

She blinked away the tears that came into her eyes at the thought of this relationship ending, while she repeated *We're not over* again and again in her head, as if that phrase were a lifeline she could cling to.

"I don't need to be apart from you to think," she said, her voice cracking over the words.

"I need to be apart from you." With that blunt pronouncement, he stood and looked ready to walk out on her. Then he seemed to think better of it, stopping to put his hand on her head. She fell against him, wrapping her arms around him, pressing her lips into his torso and trying to store as much of his scent into her memory as possible.

With a quick kiss to the top of her head, he was off. The door shutting quietly behind him snapped her composure completely. She made it to her bedroom before she burst into tears. He said they weren't over, but that wasn't even what she was crying about. This was hard, harder than she'd thought love would be. She'd messed up, and that was hard, too.

But she wanted him to come back so that they could keep working on *us*. Just because it was hard didn't mean that she wanted to quit.

CHAPTER TWENTY-TWO

LEVI'S FOOTSTEPS ACROSS their two lawns felt as heavy as his heart did. He loved Mina. He didn't doubt that. And he was a relationship kind of guy, which meant that love came with a desire to settle down. Marry. Have kids, if that was what they both wanted.

Frozen leaves crunched under the soles of his boots, sounding like a death knell, even though they were only the sounds of fall. He'd been reading too many of Mina's overly dramatic Russian stories. Though his thoughts leaned toward the death of their relationship, because if she didn't trust in *them*, how did *they* survive?

At least now he had more sympathy for Brook and her worries about Dennis.

His front door squeaked when he opened it, like it did every November. At least he could fix this. He went for his WD-40 rather than going directly to bed.

MINA WAS NAPPING when he arrived at her house the next day at the appointed time, which probably meant her anemia was still affecting her; but she had texted him in the morning to say that she'd gone out for iron pills and was grateful to the poor drugstore staff who were working on a holiday for people like her. It was a step.

Peg accepted the basket of rolls, with a smile, saying, "These smell delicious."

"Pillsbury hasn't failed me yet," he said.

"Well, they smell homemade," she responded. "And it's nice of you to take over the responsibility of them." Peg Clements had welcomed Levi wearing a nice sweater, skirt and heels, quite a contrast from his jeans and T-shirt. After their trip to the store yesterday, she'd spent the afternoon going through her "plan of attack" for the holiday, cooking and preparing dinner according to a schedule she'd drawn up before leaving Virginia.

But, for all that, he doubted she cooked Pillsbury crescent rolls for herself—based solely on watching her prepare for Thanksgiving. The fact that she didn't turn up her nose made Peg Clements good with him.

"How long has Mina been asleep?"

"A half an hour." Peg shook her head. "She's seemed so tired this entire trip. Her father and I worry about her."

Levi glanced over to Mina's living room,

where the top of Jimmy's head was barely visible. If he heard them, he didn't show it. Though, with the football commentary coming out of the television, he probably hadn't heard them.

"She's been working a lot," he acknowledged. Mina hadn't wanted to share her anemia with him, and it was a fair bet that she didn't want him to share the information with her parents. Peg Clements was a nice woman, but she was also a champion worrier. Brook could learn to worry from Peg.

Mina's mother pulled a kitchen towel out from one of the drawers and placed it over the rolls. "She was never good at taking care of herself, even as a little girl. Never stopping when she needed to stop. She was on the track team in high school, and she would run until she barfed, and then she would run again. Even though she didn't have a chance of winning. She just wouldn't quit."

He leaned against the counter and watched Peg move about the kitchen, blissfully unaware of what she'd just implied. "You wish she would quit at more things?"

"What?" To her credit, Peg pulled her head out of the fridge and looked at him, her eyes big with horror. "No. No. My baby's no quitter."

"But you just said..."

She closed the fridge with a sigh. "I wish she

didn't push herself so hard. I wish she took better care of herself. That's all."

"Does she not regularly take care of herself?" he asked. He'd assumed that Mina ignoring her anemia was an aberration, not a pattern.

"She must not be." Peg shook her head as she stuck it back in the fridge and rummaged around, her voice muffled. "She's so far from home, and she's working too much, and she's trying to fix up this house, and it all must be wearing her down. If she lived closer to home, Jimmy could help her with the house. And she could come over for dinner on nights when she was too tired to cook."

No wonder Mina had wanted to move farther away from home. And if this was what she expected every time she showed any physical vulnerability, then no wonder she hadn't wanted to tell him about her anemia.

Having all this worry directed at you all the time would be as bad as... Well, he knew what it would be as bad as because Brook was doing it to Dennis.

He pulled back from his own worries, both about Mina's health and about their relationship. "She seems to be doing okay to me. I've never seen her miss taking her pills, and I'd be tired, too, if I were under her deadlines."

Peg set out stuff for mashed potatoes, and

then she looked straight at him. "That's because you don't know her like I do. If you knew what she looked like when she was really feeling good, then you wouldn't think that."

He was glad she turned her back to him to cut up potatoes, because he didn't think she would appreciate the mystification on his face. "When was she 'feeling really good'?" he asked, knowing he wouldn't like her answer.

"Back before she got sick, nothing stopped her. Nothing."

Did she realize that just five minutes ago she had been complaining about Mina not knowing when to quit? "Did getting sick change her that much?" *Or did it change how you thought of her?*

"She'll always be my little girl," Peg said, as the knife sliced through potatoes on the cutting board.

But now she is your sick little girl.

Levi couldn't wait too long for Mina to decide if she had faith in them and their relationship, but this conversation with Peg Clements meant he would wait a little longer.

"You're right. I didn't know her before her illness, but I know her now. And now she seems pretty great. I can't imagine her being better."

Peg stopped cutting potatoes and looked over

her shoulder, a smile on her face. He glimpsed Mina in that smile.

There were some quiet footsteps and a little shuffling behind him. Mina had woken up from her nap and stood, her head cocked and a thoughtful look on her face, in the doorway. When he caught her gaze, she smiled and mouthed, "Thank you."

He smiled back.

THANKSGIVING DINNER HAD been a heavily negotiated affair. Mina had done most of the negotiating, though Levi had needed to step in when Brook had announced that she didn't want to intrude, and they would just have a family dinner in Bozeman.

As Dennis seated their son at the table and Brook seated their daughter—managing the entire negotiation without saying a word to one another—Levi wondered if letting his sister and Dennis stay in Bozeman would have been a better idea. The legs of Levi's chair bounced against the floor as he scooted toward his dinner, which was more noise than had passed between his brother-in-law and his sister since they'd walked through Mina's front door.

They hadn't said so much as one word to each other, from what Levi could tell.

"Would someone like to say grace?" Peg Clements asked.

"I will," Brook offered.

Everyone around the table bowed their heads. "Our Heavenly Father. We thank You for the food we are about to eat and for the blessings of family. We are grateful for the bounty of Your love and pray that You continue to bless us with good health and keep us safe from harm."

Levi's head snapped up. Across the table, he caught Dennis's eye. Brook had volunteered to give the Thanksgiving blessing every year of her life since she was eight years old, and she'd been giving the same one since she was twenty-one.

The reference to health was new.

He shook off the strange thoughts bouncing around his head. Dennis's health was still probably on Brook's mind. The reference was nothing more or less than that. Plus, even a person who hated change as much as Brook did was allowed a shift or two in her life.

"Thank you," Peg said. "What a wonderful blessing. Before dinner, we always go around the table and say what we're grateful for. If you don't mind…" Her voice was gentle but still firm enough that everyone around the table knew they were expected not to mind. "Mina, why don't you start?"

"I'm grateful for my move to Missoula." Her hand landed on his knee, and she squeezed. "The move has been everything I'd hoped it would be and more than I could have imagined."

"How nice." Peg beamed as she looked between Levi and Mina.

"I'm grateful for the chance to have gotten to know Mina," he said. Her grip on his knee loosened, and her fingers slid off as the mediocre words came out of his mouth. There was more he meant to say, more he could say, but he hadn't had enough time to think.

Peg didn't seem to notice the hollowness of his words. She continued to beam as she moved on to Solstice, and Levi felt a little sick. Last night, when he'd been talking with Mina about going through with their Thanksgiving dinner, he hadn't thought about what it would feel like to sit here, next to her. To have talked about how wonderful she was with her mother and then not be able to say something similar, in public, in front of his sister.

How fake everything felt. Because if she wasn't sure their love was real and worthy of her trust, how could he be sure about anything?

Gratitude went around the table in a wave, with mostly predictable answers. The kids had trouble saying more than that they were happy to be back in Missoula to see their friends. They were obviously struggling with the mid-school-year move.

Brook was last. "I think most of what I'm grateful for this year I said in the blessing. Health is probably the biggest thing. I hadn't realized how important it was until this year. And like the kids, I'm glad to be back in Missoula, among people I love."

Levi still wasn't sure if the references to health were pointed at Dennis or Mina, but he could see the wound the remark about being among friends left on Dennis's neck.

Thanksgiving was going to be a long dinner. It would be easier if Mina's hand were still on his knee.

"Did you just move?" Peg asked, all innocence. All she'd been told was that his sister was coming in from Bozeman for dinner. No one had purposefully thrown her to the wolves.

"Oh, not even a month ago. Dennis got a new job." Brook was smiling, and her voice was light as she said the words, spooning green-bean casserole onto her plate. But the corner of her mouth was stretched just a bit too wide and her lips a bit too thin.

Levi knew his sister. And none of that was a good sign. He'd had a dog who made the same face thirty seconds before barfing up his dinner.

"How nice for you," Peg said, looking between Brook and Dennis and their kids. "A promotion, I assume?"

"Yes…"

Dennis coughed, and Brook didn't let him recover long enough to finish. "It'd better be a promotion for how much extra he's working."

Given Peg's startled blinks, she had just realized the minefield that she'd stepped into. "Oh, yes," she said, her voice trying to smooth over the bumps that had appeared in dinner. "New jobs do that to you, right, Mina?"

"Oh!" Mina followed her mom's bright tone, even as she looked back and forth between Dennis and Brook, her gaze stopping on their kids and the dedicated way they ate their food without looking up. "Moving is hard, and it takes a long time to build a group of friends. But it's good. Especially today with email and Facebook and texting. You get to keep your old friends, too."

Solstice, Levi's niece, looked up at that remark, and he wondered if all Brook's negative energy had made her forget that she needed to help her kids learn to be happy in their new hometown. "If you kids want to visit friends, you can always stay with me. Or I could meet your mom halfway and drive you," he offered.

"You managed to make friends fast," Brook

said, turning to Mina. "Got any secrets you want to share?"

Mina raised her eyebrow as she took a bite of turkey. Like everything else Brook had said over dinner, the words themselves weren't bad, but the tone and implication were caustic enough to strip paint off a rusted metal chair. "I decided I was going to have high expectations of Missoula and that it would live up to them."

Then she glanced over at Levi, and the tension in her jaw softened. He could see that she had faith in them and their relationship. Why couldn't she see it and just say it? Saying "Missoula and the people in it have exceeded my expectations. I can't imagine wanting to be anywhere else" wasn't the same.

"You have someone to call if you get sick." Brook's voice bordered on the wistful, and, for once tonight, Levi almost felt sorry for her. Almost, because she was coming awfully close to talking about Mina's HIV, and she wasn't able to do that without being horrible. Tonight didn't seem like the night she would change her ways.

"Yes, being able to call someone when you're sick is important. I heard Dennis cough, but I thought that was just a little cold," Peg said, still wading her way through the nasty family business being slopped onto the table. "Or do you have a health problem I don't know about?"

"Dennis…" his sister started to say.

Dennis interrupted her. "Levi and I were in the same mine accident together. I have lung damage from it. It's not cancer. Despite what some people believe."

"Oh. I'm sorry," Peg said. "But it's good that it's not cancer."

"That doesn't mean…" Brook said.

This time Solstice interrupted her. "Mom, can we talk about football? Or something else?"

Every face around the table, even Jimmy's, who hadn't said a word the entire meal, looked immediately guilty before turning their attention to their plates and eating in silence.

It took several uncomfortable seconds of chewing before someone spoke. "Let's hope the game tonight is a good one. The one on Thanksgiving, like the Super Bowl, always seems to be one of the least interesting games of the season."

All the guilty faces turned immediately to Jimmy with relief in their eyes. "I think the Christmas game is the worst, because the Lions are never good," Dennis said.

And the debate was on. Nothing serious was said for the rest of the night. As predicted, the football game was boring.

THE FRONT DOOR had shut behind Dennis and Brook hours before, but Peg and Jimmy had stayed up late to watch television and help clean up. Levi was almost ready to go to his house and fall into his own bed when they finally said good-night and headed to the guest room.

After the tension of dinner, Levi opened his arms to Mina before he remembered that he was supposed to go home and think, without her to distract him. But she accepted the invitation, and he missed the feel of her, so he gave in to the chance to envelop her. As they hugged, all the stress of the night melted away. He didn't forget Brook and her pain and the damage she and Dennis were doing to themselves and their kids, but with Mina in his arms, neither it nor his need to take time apart seemed to matter so much.

"Your sister is in a lot of pain," Mina said, as she pulled away from him.

"They both are." His sister and his best friend seemed to be bent on killing each other, and Levi didn't know why. Or how long it had been going on. He'd been too intent on staying hidden up in his house to notice. "I don't know what to do for them."

That was the worst. He couldn't fix them. He'd tried serving as the go-between, but that seemed only to make Brook suspect him as much as she suspected Dennis. Like Dennis was having an affair instead of applying for jobs and going to the doctor. Maybe his brother-in-law should have talked to Brook sooner, but her insistence that she should continue to punish him wouldn't help anyone.

Mina patted him on the shoulder. "I don't think there's anything you can do."

"I know. And that's horrible, too."

She laid her head back against his chest. "It's hard to watch someone you love struggle and know the only thing you can do for them is care."

"You're being awfully nice, especially given how terrible Brook has been to you."

"She means something to you, so I can be patient for a little while."

"I hope a little while is all it takes."

It was late. He was tired. But when Mina suggested that he stay over at her house instead of walking the short distance home, he shook his head.

Her face fell. "Still thinking?"

"I'm not the only one who had thinking to do," he said, his fingers trailing down the soft skin of her cheeks as he pulled away. "We don't want to end up where Brook and Dennis are, and both of us have to make that commitment."

"You have to be able to say it. No question

and no hesitation." A part of his heart snapped when he lost the last bit of contact with her. But he walked toward the door, because he had to trust that she would find her faith.

CHAPTER TWENTY-THREE

A WEEK LATER, Levi slid into his bench at O'Reilly's bar, facing Dennis and missing Mina, who seemed to be thinking just fine without his presence in her life, because she hadn't yet come over to talk with him about their relationship.

He'd been assuming she would realize that she could trust their relationship. Realize that she did.

Maybe he'd been assuming wrong.

There wasn't enough alcohol in the world to make him feel better if that were the case.

Mary brought Levi a beer, and he must have been looking particularly thoughtful because she said, "Moose Drool Brown Ale," as she set the glass in front of him. And she said the words with a smile. And a pat on the back.

His head jerked up to look at her.

"Ya' look more relaxed," Mary said. "Love will do that to you."

And he had just been about to comment that

it felt good to have Dennis back for the weekend. That it felt like old times.

"What the hell was that about?" he asked, turning his attention away from Mary to his friend.

Dennis pressed his lips together, and suddenly this Friday night at the bar felt more like old times than was comfortable. "We sold our house," his friend said, the fake chipper tone to his voice ringing uncomfortably in Levi's ears.

"Brook told me," Levi said. Then he waited, letting the silence fill the space between them. Silence was a neat thing. It started small, invisible. If fed, it expanded like a balloon, engulfing everyone and everything in its path.

With the right person and in the right mood, the silence was reassuring. It was soft and warm.

Dennis was not in the right mood. As the silence started to touch against his skin, it must have grown spikes, because his friend started to shift in his seat, like a thorn was poking him in the back.

"Brook told the real-estate agent about Mina's HIV," Dennis said, finally.

The pop of the balloon rang in Levi's ears. "What? Why would she do that?"

"That's not the only person she told." Dennis shifted uncomfortably in his seat. The silence had apparently left the thorn in his back, and it was growing bigger. "From what I can tell, anytime someone asked about the move, she launched into a story about giving you space to deal with your girlfriend's illness and not have to worry about me, too." The last sentence sliced through the air in the bar, leaving a sour smell in the air.

"What the hell is wrong with her?" Brook was his sister, and he loved her, but he couldn't think of a justification for spreading Mina's health information all over town. Or making her husband feel like a burden, particularly considering the move put them in a better financial position.

"Never mind," he said as Dennis started to open his mouth to answer. Levi sympathized with how nervous she was about moving and about being in a new place without a support system. They'd always been there for each other.

Brook was killing that support in a way distance never could.

"The more important question is, who all knows?" Even as the words left his mouth, he wondered if that mattered. What was he going to do? Go to each and every person and make sure they understood…that they understood what? Understood that they shouldn't say anything to anyone else? Understood that Mina was an amazing person, and that they shouldn't let whatever misconceptions they had about HIV cloud their impression of her? Threaten them with physical violence if they said something unkind to her or about her?

If he did those things, he wouldn't be supporting his girlfriend; he'd be trying to protect his *sick* girlfriend, and their relationship would turn into everything she was afraid of.

He couldn't do anything except be there for her. Which didn't feel like it would be enough, but he didn't know what else to do.

He pushed his beer away. "I've got to go."

"Brook's not at the house. She's out with a friend."

Levi slid out of the booth and looked at his friend with disbelief as he rose to his feet. "Brook? I don't give a shit about Brook."

He must have looked angry, because his friend jumped back like he'd been struck. Levi didn't care. "I'm going to Mina's house. You and Brook need to work out whatever problems you've got. It was bad enough when her fears and your silence were affecting me, and she was being a bitch privately, but this isn't acceptable. Not if you want to be my friend and she wants to be my sister."

"I had nothing to do with Brook's big mouth."

"You don't have anything to do with the fact that my sister is scared and feels like she's not getting information and support from her husband? You're totally innocent in that?" His words dripped with sarcasm, burning the inside of his mouth before sizzling on the floor as they fell. "I'm leaving before I say something I regret. But you and Brook need to deal with each other before she kills every relationship she has and you drink until your liver is in worse shape than your lungs."

On his way out the door, Levi stopped by the bar and handed Brian cash for his drink.

"Hey, man, I've never met your girlfriend…"

"You, too?" Levi swore under his breath. "What did Brook do? Drop flyers from a plane?"

Brian raised an eyebrow. "I was going to say that you should bring her in. She sounds like an interesting lady."

Levi's shoulders relaxed, and he took a deep breath. Brian didn't deserve his anger. "She is an interesting woman. I've never met anyone like her."

Brian cocked his head. "I heard the rumor, too. Brook was in here with a friend yesterday. She told Mary. It's not that big of a deal. People who matter won't care."

Levi shook his head. "That's not the issue.

Brook shouldn't have said anything, whether it's an issue or not. And—" he steadied himself before saying the next part "—I told Brook when I shouldn't have. It wasn't my business to share with her, and if I hadn't told her, she couldn't be spreading the news around right now. Ultimately, I'm responsible for this. And I'm sorry to have trusted someone when I shouldn't have. And I'm sorry someone trusted me when they shouldn't have."

"Sorry, man." Brian put Levi's change on the bar.

"Keep it. Put it toward Dennis's cab fare if he needs it. I'm not coming back for him."

LEVI STOOD ON Mina's front porch for several seconds, knocked hard a couple of times, then put his hand on the knob and went in. When she'd first moved here from Chicago, and they'd begun dating, her front door had been locked all the time. A big-city understanding of the world and its dangers. How much of that would change when he told her what Dennis had said, and Missoula stopped being the welcoming, friendly town Mina believed it to be?

Maybe he was selling his hometown short.

Or maybe he knew that he couldn't protect her from this. This was something Mina would have to face mostly on her own. What was it

she had said? He could care for her, but he had
to let her take care of herself?

He sighed, rubbing at the whiskers on his
face as he walked through her house. He still
didn't fully understand what she had meant by
that, but he was determined to give her what
she needed. That was what love was, as far as
he had always understood it.

In her kitchen, Mina was singing to Taylor
Swift, her hips swaying as she chopped carrots.
It was that catchy song about never speaking to
an ex again, and Mina crooned it like it was an
ardent love song, rather than a breakup song,
which didn't seem to bode well.

Or maybe he was letting years of astrology
reading trick him into believing that mundane,
everyday things like singing along to a pop
song were signs of a fated future. He didn't actually believe anything like that, but old hab-
its die hard.

"Hey," he said as soon as the song ended,
pitching his voice to be heard over the next
song on the album.

"Oh!" She flipped around, one hand holding
the knife up, the other clutching her chest in
surprise. "I didn't hear you come in."

"No, not over Taylor."

"I didn't expect to see you tonight." She rubbed
her teeth across her bottom lip. "I miss you."

"Then why haven't you come over? Or called? Or texted?" Being apart from her was physically painful, a heavy weight that sank him.

She blinked; the pleasure of singing slipped off her face. "You said you needed to think. And you needed to think apart from me. I was trying to give you that time."

She was battling something internally, because she blinked again, and a small smile crossed her face. "Especially since Dennis is in town, I didn't expect to see you tonight."

The pleasure wasn't just from singing, he realized stupidly. She was happy to see him unexpectedly, when she hadn't thought she would. If he hadn't already felt like a dick, he did now. Especially because he could see the moment where something *he'd done* built up to the pain he was about to cause the woman he loved.

All his fault. And nothing he could fix.

"I came home to tell you something."

His face must have been reflecting the disaster he felt because her smile fell, and she set her knife on the counter, turning fully to look at him. "What's wrong? This is more than 'thinking.'"

"I didn't think Brook would say something. But…"

Mina leaned against the counter, her face blank. "But she has."

"She has," he replied, bracing for her justifiable anger.

"How many people has she told?" The words left Mina's mouth with a slow crackling burn that scorched the hair off the back of his neck.

"I don't know. The worst of it is that they've told people."

"And they've told people," Mina said flatly. "So I don't know how many people are out there who know I'm HIV positive and who they're all telling. And what they know about me. Levi's girlfriend? College professor? Author and artist?" Her voice rose with her list. "Even if none of the people currently spreading my health information around know who I am, they might tell someone who not only knows but cares. Who thinks their kid shouldn't be in my class or who believes they are compassionate, but that they can be more compassionate if we're not touching the same utensils at the coffee shop."

Levi wanted to be able to argue with her, to tell her that the AIDS panic of the nineties was over, but Brook was a prime example that he would be lying. It was true that people weren't as panicked as they used to be when AIDS first spread, but the people who accepted it as a disease, understood the risks of exposure and treated those with the virus like people were offset by those who let fear crowd their reasoning.

Like his sister. Even though Brook said that she understood how the virus was caught, she was still cold and unwelcoming to Mina. It had taken Levi a while to realize that Brook wasn't so much reacting against the virus, but that she was reacting against her idea that Mina somehow *deserved* the disease.

He couldn't imagine what it would be like to stand up in front of a classroom with even one student looking at you and thinking similar thoughts to his sister. But Mina would do it. She was the bravest person he knew.

"I'm sorry. I set this off, and I'm sorry—"

"You did set this off." Mina's once welcoming face was tight with anger. Her entire body seemed to have folded around her anger. The open, bubbly person he'd fallen for months ago when she'd been standing on his front steps rambling was gone.

"How long has everyone known? How long have I been walking around in ignorance of all this?"

"I don't know. Dennis didn't say. And I haven't called Brook to ask her who all she told and when."

"And why?" Confusion bolstered the anger in Mina's voice.

"And why," he echoed. He knew why, though there was no making sense of it. And *why* wouldn't make Mina feel any better.

She put her hands up to her face, cupping her palms over her mouth. "What am I supposed to do?" she asked through her fingers.

"I don't know. I left the bar early so that I could tell you, and maybe we could figure it out together."

At that moment, he realized that he didn't need her to *say* she had faith in their relationship, but he did need her to have faith. To let him be here for her.

"What are you going to do to help?"

Levi tried not to be hurt at the mocking tone in her voice. She had every right to be angry and scared. Being defensive about his role in this mess wasn't going to help her.

"Stand by you, no matter what."

"What if I don't want you by me?" She spit out the question. "What if I think you and your sister should go leap off a bridge?"

"If there's a way to stand by you while standing on that bridge looking down, I'll figure out how to do it."

Slowly, and with near audible sizzles, his words doused her anger. First, her shoulders fell away from her ears. Then her jaw loosened, and her lips parted a bare millimeter. Finally, the corners of her eyes softened, though that last may have been the tears as much as the dying anger.

"I'm scared, Levi."

"I know." He didn't say "I am, too," because he was scared *for* her, not scared for himself. Those were two different things.

"I can't control this," she said. "It's out, and I can't get it back, and I don't know who knows and who will know and who will judge me and who will be afraid of me and who will still be my friend." Tears dripped down her face, lining her cheeks with all the doors she imagined being shut on her.

"I know," he said again. He couldn't take away her fears, but he could acknowledge their importance.

"I wish you hadn't said anything to Brook."

"I wish I hadn't, either. It's the only thing about our relationship that I wish I could go back and change. The other—" he paused, uncertain of the word to use "—things we've run into can eventually make us stronger. This is a crack in the foundation."

"Is it fixable?"

"That's up to you."

Tears caught the one corner of her half smile. "You're the handyman."

"But you're the foundation."

Her full smile sealed the crack for him, but he needed to get it sealed for *her*. *She* needed to get it sealed for her.

Then her smile faded. "What am I going to do?"

He opened his arms, and she stepped into them, resting her head against his shoulder. He hugged her tightly, the movement of stroking her hair as comforting to him as he hoped it was to her. "You don't have to decide what you're going to do, not right now. Right now, you can have dinner. Maybe watch a little TV. Take a break from it. The problem will still be there for you in the morning."

"It might be worse by morning," she said, her voice muffled by his shirt.

"Hey." He put his hand under her chin and nudged her face up. "It might be worse tomorrow. But it's not likely to be. And you won't be able to solve anything while you're this upset. I'll finish cooking you dinner. You can have some wine. The problem won't look better in the morning, but maybe sleep will bring new ideas."

Mina's face was blotchy, and her eyes were still red, but she looked beautiful. "Let's have sex."

He blinked. "Now?" Sex was the last thing

he had expected, especially since anger and being kicked out of her house took up most of the spots on the "expected" list. He wasn't sure he could count high enough to find a place for sex on that list.

"Yes—now."

He hesitated, and fear dulled the brown in her eyes. "Unless you don't want to," she said.

Then he understood. Mina didn't want sex because she desired him, because she was horny or because he was completely forgiven. She wanted sex because she needed to feel desired. She needed to feel loved. He could do that for her. He *wanted* to do that for her. He felt privileged to do that for her.

He smoothed his palms down her arms until he reached her hands. Once her hands were in his, he stepped back, away from her and toward the bedroom. "I want to," he said, pulling her along behind him. "I'm the luckiest man on earth to be here with you."

The words he'd meant to be sweet and reassuring stopped her in her tracks. "What if you're not?" she said. He had to hold her hands tight to keep her fingers from slipping away. "What if Brook is right, and all this relationship will ever be is one struggle after another? What if this is just the beginning?"

If I drop her hands, she and Brook will both be right. "Faith, Mina. I need you to have faith. You need you to have faith."

"Faith in what?" she asked, looking so broken that he worried neither of them would be able to collect all the pieces and put her back together again. "In one wrong decision after another? Why I want you to have sex with me? Why you are going to?"

"Was introducing yourself to me a wrong decision?"

"No." There was no hesitation in her voice.

"Was our first date a wrong decision?"

She shook her head, quick and immediate.

He squeezed her hands so tightly that she winced. He loosened his grip but didn't let go. "I need you to have faith in us if this relationship is going to go anywhere, but right now, let me be here for you. Because I want to and because you need someone."

"Because you're worried about me," she said, flatly.

He sighed. "Because I'm worried about you. Because I care about you. Because we both know you're strong enough to face whatever life has to throw at you, but because it's easier with someone by your side. Even if it's just for tonight, let me be that person."

He leaned in, and he could feel her tense. "I want to worship you."

Every part of her body seemed to relax at once.

He pressed his advantage. "I don't want to hold you back. I want to help you soar."

CHAPTER TWENTY-FOUR

MINA LOOKED AT the beautiful man beside her. The beautiful sleeping man beside her. Well, he deserved his rest. He'd taken her mind off the unknown number of people who knew her secret, and he'd helped her feel wanted. Back when she'd been diagnosed and there had been a flurry of telling people she thought needed to know—family members, roommates, friends and officials at school, plus that awful call to her patient zero—there had also been a flurry of rejections. Some, like her cousin, were mild. A few had made Brook look compassionate. Most had been tinged with the sense that she'd gotten what she deserved by being stupid enough to have unprotected sex.

As if diseases or cancers had innocent victims and deserving victims, and it was up to the general public to decide who was who and save their sympathy for the former.

Since then she'd been able to pick and choose whom she told, and mostly the tells had gone better. Rejections and judgments were still intermingled among the hugs, but the volume was lower and so easier to ignore. She could concentrate on the acceptance.

Now the bombardment of judgment would begin again. It had been hard the first time. It would be harder the second.

This time, she had someone standing beside her.

Levi snored quietly in his sleep. If she looked closely, Mina wondered if she could see his stubble growing. All the hard edges of his face softened in his sleep, and he looked so peaceful that she wanted to stay next to him, under the covers forever.

His open desire had been a gift, and she intended to use it. As he'd worshipped her body, he'd given her more than orgasms; he'd given her confidence. No matter what, he said he'd stick by her. From that bridge she had wanted to shove him off, even.

That had been what he meant by faith.

She pushed the sheets off her body and swung around to get her feet onto the floor, her toes nestling into the carpet. Levi had meant what he'd said; she believed that, though she also wondered if he'd be able to stick to his big words once he saw the actual fallout of what she intended to do. Standing by someone during a possible shunning was easier said than done.

As she took a deep breath, filling her lungs with cool air, she looked back over at him. The great gift of his confidence was that she wanted him to stick by her side, but she knew she'd be okay if he didn't. Even if Levi couldn't stick by her, that didn't mean the end of, well, the end of anything but her relationship with Levi.

And that would make her sad, but it wouldn't devastate her. She'd move on, find another lover, and it would be okay. That man wouldn't be Levi, but the HIV wouldn't kill her and neither would people knowing about her HIV.

The chill air raised goose bumps on her bare shoulders. That realization scared her, but it also made it easier to have faith in Levi. In *us*, as he had asked her to. She could believe.

And if she believed in *us*, then she could believe in a future.

She could take control over who knew. She could make sure *everybody* knew.

Mina slipped out of bed, careful not to wake the gorgeous man sleeping beside her. Then she wrapped a robe around her and padded down the hall to her office. At her desk, she got out her sketchbook and laid out her pencils and erasers. And pens, in case she hit perfection on the first try.

For a scary ten seconds, she stared at the blank paper. Her hand gripped the pencil like a claw, frozen and impractical for her purpose. But then she took a deep breath and drew the first curve in a body. She drew the second curve, then the third, then the fourth. When she had a full outline of a person, the sandbags in her mind burst and the rest of the panel came easily. The twin beds in the dorm room. The piles of clothes on the floor and the Einstein poster on the cinderblock walls. A small fridge under the window, filled with beer and cheese and nothing else.

In the drawing, Mina stood in her collegeself's idea of sexy clothing. So, basically, she wasn't wearing anything but strips of cloth. She hadn't seen Chase since college, when she'd occasionally pass him on campus, and he remained impossibly young in her mind. Everything about him was easy to draw. All the lines of his body were permanently etched in her memory, like her mind had taken a photo that would never fade. She'd sat in the Planned Parenthood room when the doctor had come in and told her that her HIV test had come back positive and—snap—she'd never be able to forget anything about that night, down to the green, red and yellow plaid of the flannel shirt she'd felt so privileged to remove.

That panel drawn, she flipped the page and started on the next. Chase's smile and the way she'd felt sexy and grown-up, silly to think about now while trying to arrange the speech bubbles in the dorm room in between the posters and clothing on the floor. How to draw his confidence as he said he'd pull out and not to worry. How to draw the wanting. The wanting of sex. The wanting to trust. The wanting to believe.

So different from now, when there was no wanting; there was only believing.

In her drawing, she leaned forward.

Poor naive Mina on the page. She'd wanted to have sex with him because he was Chase, and she'd had a crush on him since their first semester together in calculus. She drew it all, not skimping on the awkward uncomfortable sex that had been college and twin beds.

Mina flipped the page and started another. Another dorm room, almost exactly the same, except piles of clothes on the floor were on only one side of the room, and there was more food in the fridge by the window. Different posters on the walls.

She jumped and gave her roommate a third arm when Levi kissed the top of her head. "You look busy. Shall I finish dinner?"

"Yes," she said, not looking up and scrubbing out Kaitlyn's extra arm.

"What were you making?"

"Carrots." Different clothes on this very different Mina. Nothing sexy. Pajama pants—they had been pink, with daisies—and an old T-shirt of her brother's.

"Anything else?"

"Carrots." Kaitlyn had been wearing pajama pants, too, and a tank top. Blue pants and a light blue tank top. They had both been color-coordinated, so careful in their choice of clothing, even when casually lying in bed, telling each other their dreams. Even if they pretended not to be, Mina with her art and Kaitlyn with her physics, they had both been so concerned with the outside. Even though *in this moment* the virus was already replicating and spreading on the inside.

What was inside was what mattered, and Mina had HIV inside her. She didn't have to let the virus define her, but she needed to start letting people see what was inside. The good, the bad and the buggy.

She leaned back in her chair, bumping her head against Levi, who said, "I'll go make carrots, then," with amusement in his voice. She nodded, only barely aware of the press of another kiss on her head.

The panel had two girls, both sitting on their dorm beds. Kaitlyn, leaning against the wall, legs hanging over the edge of her bed. Mina, hugging her knees, her head resting on her knees. She remembered that moment. She had been curled up against all the bad consequences of unprotected sex. Naïveté meant they'd been worried about only one of the consequences.

"Are you on the pill?" Mina drew in a speech bubble above Kaitlyn's head.

"No." Another speech bubble, lower, with Mina's answer. And then, though it wasn't usually her style, Mina drew in little viruses dancing around her head. Round, space-alien half creatures with suckers sticking out all around. The microscopic portents of death that she hadn't even considered. Because why would she have? She was at an elite private college, and she'd had heterosexual sex. Pregnancy was the worst thing either of them could imagine, and Kaitlyn had convinced her to go to Planned Parenthood and get on the pill, even though Chase wasn't returning her calls.

She flipped to the next page. All the waiting at Planned Parenthood in one panel, tightly divided into three separate spaces. That was how it had felt. Everything, all crammed in. A vise of worry.

A busy, if kind, front desk worker. Mismatched and worn seats in the waiting area. The exam room, cold and hard and sterile, with posters on the wall reminding her about condoms. As if she didn't know. As if she would forget again.

Levi set a plate next to her. Carrots. And rice,

with what looked like one of the stir-fry sauces from her fridge. For a brief moment she wondered where he'd gotten the chicken.

Then she flipped the page. Sitting on the exam room bed, with a white sheet covering her lower body and her feet dangling over, not able to touch the small step at the end of the bed. The door was closed. The curtain was closed. And the doctor was sitting in a chair, her hand on Mina's knee.

"You tested positive for HIV," Mina wrote in the doctor's speech bubble.

"Okay." It had been such a stupid thing to say, but Mina hadn't expected that news. Hadn't known what else to say. The support groups she eventually went to had included people who hadn't been surprised by the news. Hemophiliacs who had been getting blood transfusions during the height of the infection. Gay men who'd had risky sex. Intravenous drug users. All the stereotypes of someone with HIV, and at the back of their brains had been the thought that it could happen to them.

And then there had been people like Mina, who didn't fit the media's portrayal. But the disease didn't care who the media said was at risk for HIV, and it didn't care who the public thought "deserved" it. They had all sat stunned in an exam room, probably saying something as inane as "Okay."

"Is there someone here with you?" the doctor had asked. She'd been kind. They'd all been kind at the Planned Parenthood. Busy, occasionally brusque, but kind.

"No." Kaitlyn had offered to come, but Mina had turned her down. Going alone had been part of Mina feeling grown-up, taking the bus by herself to get her pelvic exam and prescription for the pill. She was learning the hard way that feeling grown-up didn't mean facing things alone, so much as it meant being alone.

At some point when she was editing the panels, Levi came back in, picked up her full plate, kissed the top of her head and said, "I'm going to bed. It's late, and I'm tired, so after I clean up, I'm going to sleep here, okay?"

"Yeah, yeah, yeah."

She erased Kaitlyn's arm and redrew it. Sharper elbows. Kaitlyn had been sympathetic but pointed. Mina redrew her roommate's mouth. Once that was done, she spread the panels out on her desk and leaned back in her chair.

As she spotted minor problems, she pulled a panel toward her, fixed what she saw and put the page back in place. All little fixes. The curve of the doctor's eyes. The sweep of the hair of Chase's Einstein poster on the wall, looking amused at the earnestness of the condom negotiation happening below.

How many times had Chase made the same "I'll pull out" argument, but with a different girl?

Mina hadn't ever considered that she wasn't the first, though she had hoped she was the last. When she'd called Chase to tell him her test results, he hadn't sounded surprised. And she'd never figured out how to tell women he was dating that he was bad news without sounding like a jealous ex-girlfriend. Eventually she'd stopped. Cowardly, maybe, but she'd stopped.

When all the drawings were to her satisfaction, she got out her pens and inked in her story. HIV became as permanent on paper as it was in her life.

She laid the panel out on the table again and stood on the seat of her chair, gaining as much of a bird's-eye view as possible. Something was missing.

The chair rolled back a little on its wheels as she leaned forward, trying to get even more over her desk and her panels. The seat rocked when she moved a little to the left and the right. If she wasn't careful, she would fall on her ass and wake up Levi.

She wasn't quite ready for his soulful brown eyes to see this part of her life in living color.

Color! She grabbed at her face when she realized that was what the drawings needed.

Then she almost hopped off her chair to climb into bed with Levi and be done with the whole thing. Wait till morning, like he'd suggested. Or just hope and pray that people didn't find some Russian literature professor having HIV to be all that interesting, and they started talking about something else.

She crossed her arms, staring at the panels on her desk. She'd decided to take control of the story, and she didn't want to back down now.

Mina drew in black and white. She was known for black and white. All her reviews included something like, "Mina Clements's stark black-and-white drawings capture the soul of the Russian people."

Whether or not that was true was up for debate. However, it was a fact that she wasn't a colorist. Not for public consumption, at least.

Times changed. Her life had never been for public consumption, either. So, instead of hiding from the challenge, she climbed down from her chair and got out her colored pencils. Coloring everything in meant she'd be up until dawn. And if she wrecked one of the panels, she risked ruining the immediacy the frenzy of drawing had brought on.

But her life needed color.

Before she could talk herself out of it, Mina slid a pencil out of her case and added color.

She started with the easy decisions. The blues and pinks of the pajamas. The light greens of the Planned Parenthood. Then she moved on to harder things, like the stripes in Chase's shirt. She didn't color in everything. Her life was in color, but she was still a black-and-white artist. She had to be true to both selves.

Once everything was colored as well as she thought she could do it—not to her satisfaction, but close enough—she put her supplies away. Then she went to the kitchen to hunt down food.

And smiled when she saw the Post-it on the fridge saying, "Leftovers here."

Levi. What would such a public statement do to Levi?

She shook that thought out of her head as she stuck the plate of leftovers into the microwave. Right now she was thinking about herself. Tomorrow she'd think of Levi.

CHAPTER TWENTY-FIVE

THE FIRST THING Levi did after he opened his eyes to see Mina's round face and bloodshot eyes hovering over his head, the light streaming in from the hall giving her an otherworldly look, was glance at the clock.

"Is something wrong?" he asked. He'd slept in, but had she slept at all?

"I need to talk to you," she said, her face so scrunched in worry that he sat up immediately.

"Let me get some pants on." He swung his legs over the side of the bed, feeling for his jeans with his toes. Whatever it was she had to say looked serious enough that he didn't want to be in only his briefs.

"You don't need pants. I just want to show you something." She was shifting her weight from left to right with her thumb between her teeth, an intoxicating combination of innocent and nervous. Much like she'd been when she'd stood on his porch months ago and charmed the hell out of him.

"I want pants." Unpredictable and unexpected didn't go well with underwear.

She didn't wait for him. He was buttoning his fly as he followed her into her office. She didn't bring him to her huge drawing desk to see whatever she'd been working on earlier but instead to the chair at her computer. At the top of the monitor was the banner for her website.

He noticed the color as soon as he sat. Then he realized the beds meant it was a dorm room and the man sitting on the comforter was a boy. The boy who'd given Mina HIV.

Give, like it had been a gift.

Though, he considered, as that thought came angrily to mind, it hadn't been a curse. It just was. Like Kimmie's depression, yet so very different from it.

"Is this what I think it is?" His eyes rolled from the panel with Mina—she'd captured her young self just like he'd imagined her to be—in yellow party clothes looking like she wasn't sure being in this dorm room was a good idea, to the panel with *the guy* trying to convince her to trust him—and basically explaining in a textbook way why Mina shouldn't have.

"It's not live," she said, defensively. "Not yet," she amended.

"That's good." He scanned the next panel, the roommate standing in for every disappointed and judgmental reader of this strip. Only Mina had drawn love in Kaitlyn's face, along with the disapproval.

"You think this is a bad idea?"

He could practically hear the nervous way she was biting her lip behind him. Mina and her open-book face.

"Give me a chance to finish. Then we can talk about whether or not it's a good idea."

He read on. He felt Mina's claustrophobia and fear in the tight panels of the waiting room in the Planned Parenthood and the shock of sitting in the exam room as the doctor told her she was HIV positive. But what really broke his heart was the look of fear on her face as she stared out the window during the bus ride home.

He spun the chair away from the computer. She was biting her lip. Worse, she was hugging her arms like she needed protection. From him. From the world. He wasn't sure, and she probably didn't know, either.

He put a hand on her shoulder. "I know you don't want me to take care of you, but you don't have to be alone anymore. I want to be with you. I want to be there for you."

"I know. I was never really alone, either, even though I had felt so alone at the time. My parents, my brother, Kaitlyn... They all stood by me and made sure the diagnosis didn't get me off the track of my life."

He grunted, like his dad always had when being told something that he didn't want to hear. When she put her hand on top of his, a few of his feelings of being unwanted and unnecessary dissolved.

Her face softened. The muscles under his palm relaxed. She turned her head and kissed where their skin touched. "I woke you up so you could read this, but also because we're partners in this. And you get a say in whether or not I hit Publish. I can take care of myself, but I'm not alone, and so I don't have to."

He squeezed her shoulder, all the fears and doubts and questions melting as sure as the warm sun would melt the frost on the windows. "Is this going to be the end of the story?"

"No. I'm going to do more." She seemed nervous again, and so he nodded, hoping that he looked encouraging. "I hope to tell a complete story, one that includes us." She squeezed their hands together and kissed his again before looking back at him. "If you don't mind, I'm going to write about that in the introduction."

"Mind? Why would I mind?"

"You don't know what it will be like when this gets out, especially like this. For all the people who tell me I'm brave, there will be those who troll me on Twitter. And people will find you, too. And Brook."

"Brook made her bed."

"But did she know what the bed would look like?"

"I appreciate you giving my sister the benefit of the doubt, but she is living and speaking the fears you are worried about. I'd be more worried about her feelings being reinforced than her feeling attacked."

Her hand tensed.

"I'll deal with Brook," he said, though it probably didn't reassure either of them. He hadn't dealt with her well so far. And what his sister needed wasn't anything he could give her.

"I'm not too worried about her. She's already done the damage she can do. And I'm doing this so I control when people learn my secret. I control whether it's a secret or not."

Levi lifted his hand off her shoulder and put his hands on her waist. "You're really not mad at me about Brook spreading your medical information?"

"I decided to forgive and forget back when you told me that you'd shared the information with your sister. It seems unfair of me to be re-mad now that I know the consequences. Like I lied when I said I was okay before."

Her stomach was soft and warm when he

pressed his cheek against her. "I love you. I'm not sure what I did to deserve you, but whatever it is, I'd do it again in a heartbeat."

"You built me a raised garden bed."

He pulled away from her, so that he could smile up at her. "Is that all?"

"So, should I post it?" The light from her computer monitor gave her face an alien glow, and she looked as tired as he imagined she had to be. She'd been up all night, drawing. He'd watched her draw for a couple of minutes before setting her dinner next to her. Mina wasn't a sedate artist. She drew like she did everything else in her life, with her entire body.

He loved watching her.

"I appreciate you asking me, but it's really your decision. I'll stand by you, no matter what."

"Thank you." Her face was soft and her eyes warm as she looked down at him.

"You should warn your dean."

She shrugged. "He knows about my HIV."

"But your students don't and their parents don't. And he won't want to be blindsided about this. Give him time to craft a statement of support for you."

"That's good advice."

"But before you do that, let's go to bed. You need some sleep. In a few hours, you can call

your department chair and write your introduction."

"And you'll still be there for me after." She
said the words with a smile, but he could hear
the uncertainty in her voice.

"Yes. Though I think both of us will need a
nap. Come on," he said, with a gentle push at her
waist so that she stepped back. "When I climb
back into your bed, I want you to be in there
with me."

WHEN MINA WOKE up a couple of hours later, it
was light out, and Levi was still sleeping next
to her. A storm was blowing in from outside,
and she wanted to sink back into a deep sleep
with him warm and comfortable next to her.

She felt safe with him, she realized. Not that
she'd felt unsafe before, but this was a safe that
came from knowing someone deep in his core,
rather than hoping for the best and taking a
leap of faith. A safe that was part of the air she
breathed.

This will all be okay.

She rolled over in bed, and Levi popped awake
immediately. "Good morning," he said with a
lazy, indulgent smile, his arms reaching over
his head in a catlike stretch. "Is it time to call
Thomas?"

The clock on the nightstand said eleven thirty.

It was a Saturday. This needed to be over. "He's got kids. I'm sure he's awake."

"Good." The peck he dropped on her cheek was quick, like this was any other Saturday morning. "I'll go make us some breakfast."

Another bit of worry flaked off. She kept thinking she was done with doubts, and then Levi would do something, and more of the worry would disappear. It was like shedding a skin she hadn't known she had grown out of.

Mina went into her office to call her department chair. His wife said he was leaving for a round of tennis, but she ran out to the garage to catch him when Mina said it was important. She summarized the situation for him, including that the news was spreading anyway, and she didn't know how quickly it would make it back to campus. Or if it was already there.

"Damage control?" he asked. Dean Thomas had been a professor and administrator for a long time, through many different academic crises. As a black man who taught Japanese, he'd been on the receiving end of incredulity, which made him compassionate to others who seemed like they were about to hit a personal wall.

"Control," she said, slowly. "I prefer not to think of it as damage."

"Give me until two this afternoon to make sure everyone who should know knows. Then post away. The department will be behind you, and the university will be behind us. Lord knows we need some good publicity around here."

"You see this as good publicity?" She hadn't expected the university's reaction to be bad, but she definitely hadn't expected anyone to see this as an opportunity. She didn't know whether to be relieved or grossed out.

"I see this as the university standing on the side of education against ignorance. Which is, after all, what we're supposed to be about."

"It sounds like you already have your pitch to the naysayers ready."

Thomas chuckled. "I wrote that down as I said it. It's pretty good, don't you think?"

She didn't realize how nervous she'd been about this conversation until now, when her entire body seemed to release its tension all at once, and she nearly fell over. "Thank you. So much."

"I have a brother who's HIV positive. Everyone knows someone with the virus. They just might not know that they do. And it's just a virus. As a society, we moralize because of how it's transmitted, but a bug is a bug is a bug."

"Sometimes I forget that." Sometimes she also fell into the trap of believing that there were innocent victims, and there were those who deserved the virus, and she belonged in the latter group. But HIV was a virus, not a punishment handed down from on high. God wasn't capricious.

"You've never said how you got infected."

"Nope." Feeling confident, she continued, "And you'll have to wait until two to find out like everyone else."

"That's the thanks I get?" he asked, but she could tell he was secretly pleased. Paula, one of the women who ran the department's office, had told Mina there were worries about her age. Mina had raced through graduate school as quickly as it was possible to do, meaning she wasn't all that much older than her students, and she looked younger than some of them. Thomas always seemed pleased when she asserted herself.

They said their goodbyes, and Mina hung up the phone. Then she sat at her computer, wrote a brief introduction—including her relationship with Levi—and scheduled the post. *The Adventures of Mina* +. She also scheduled Twitter, Facebook, Instagram and Tumblr. Her social media covered, she powered her computer all the way off, so she wouldn't be tempted to look at the post, and went to the kitchen to find Levi.

At the sound of her footsteps, he turned away from the bacon he was cooking on the stove. "How'd it go?" he asked.

"Good. He asked me to give him until two so

he could make the necessary calls. Everything's written and scheduled. Now I just have to wait."

"Waiting sucks. After we finish breakfast, we'll go on a hike."

"But it's cold outside."

"Brisk. You lived in Chicago, so you know this isn't cold. Yet."

She harrumphed.

"If you're cold, you can think of what a bad boyfriend I am for taking you out in the miserable weather." He said the words, then gestured with his head to the window, where the sky was a clear blue, and the sun had a brightness to it that you only got at high altitudes.

"I'll expect hot chocolate when I get back."

"Always negotiating." He tsked. "I'll do you one better. I'll make you hot chocolate, then sit on the couch with you in my arms and a blanket wrapped around both of us while you drink it."

"That will be nice."

He folded his arms across his chest. "On the condition that you're not looking at your phone while I do it."

"Pfft," she said, smiling. "Thank you."

"No thanks needed. I expect to get my own back." His wink looked completely unnatural on his hard-angled face. And she loved him for it. She loved him for everything.

CHAPTER TWENTY-SIX

MINA WAS ESPECIALLY grateful for Levi's imposed internet ban as Saturday evening went on. She wanted to check the comments on her post and her Facebook page and see the Twitter response and do an internet search of her name to see where else people might be talking about her. But anytime she reached for her phone, Levi cleared his throat and raised his eyebrow, and she leaned back. Back against his solid chest as he searched Netflix for another movie. Back into Levi, whose presence reminded her that she would be okay. Tomorrow, she would wake up, and she would still be the same person she had been a week ago, just smarter and more in control of her own message.

She didn't sign in to her computer until Levi left Sunday afternoon to do his laundry and take care of other chores. When he'd asked if it was okay for him to leave, she'd practically pushed him out the door. Wanting him by her side was one thing; having him stand over her shoulder as she read the horrible things people had to say about her was another.

There were ten emails from her family, mostly from her mother, asking what she had done and why. Mina reached for her phone and looked at her texts. Again, most of them were from her mother.

I'm fine. I'll call you later tonight to explain. Sorry for not warning you.

Then she settled back into her chair and read through the rest of her messages. Most of the emails were supportive, which she'd expected out of the people who knew her well enough to send her an email. Other comics artists and graphic novelists, some Russian scholars, librarians and a bookseller or two. Fans. Facebook was much the same. Her fan page was fairly well curated, and it wasn't like Facebook shared posts with everyone who liked her page. She was pleased to see that the university had shared her post, though calling her "inspiring" seemed a bit much.

She responded to the Facebook comments as well as she could, typing "thank you" so often that she finally copied the words so that she could paste them in various replies. She would save the email responses for later. Then she took a deep breath and signed in to Twitter.

Those comments were…less positive. People who were supportive, many of the same people who'd commented on her Facebook post and some of her friends who'd sent her emails, usually offered one Tweet of support. But the people who thought she was a slut justly punished by God posted over and over and over again, arguing with Mina's silence. They flooded her mentions with their hate and lack of compassion.

Before she dealt with them, she sent Levi a quick text, thanking him again for last night. It would be a while before her online life calmed down enough to have another night of peace, and those moments would give her something to hold on to until people forgot and moved on to their next cause.

Back at the blue screen of her Twitter mentions, Mina waded in. She blocked some obviously hateful profiles, reporting the eggs that offered death or rape threats first. She found a few that perhaps leaned more to the "ignorant" than hate-filled, and she responded to those. After sending out a generic Tweet thanking everyone for their support, she ignored the rest of them.

Her work email was also flooded with responses, most of which she would deal with later. The interesting ones were two from the student health center and the Open Aid Alliance, asking her if she would consider speaking to groups on HIV and her experience. The two were similar enough that she wondered if the same person had crafted both messages. Both mentioned that HIV infection rates in Montana were generally low, but that there had been recent outbreaks. Both mentioned that there was a sense among many in Montana that HIV happened to groups of people—gay men, black women, intravenous drug users—and that she was a good example that people got HIV because of risky behavior, not because of membership in a demographic group.

Mina's mouth twitched at the thought of being a good example of anything, and she flagged those emails for a response on Monday and shut her computer down.

Then she called her mom.

Her mother didn't even answer the phone with "Hello," but instead launched in with "How could you post something like that and not tell us? I found out because Michael saw the Facebook post. At least he had the decency to *call* us."

"I'm sorry, Mom. I didn't think."

"You didn't think? You didn't think! You're

in this mess because you don't think about consequences. You didn't think about what would happen if you told some cowboy stranger about your HIV, and you didn't think what would happen if you had sex without a condom with some random boy in college."

Initially, Mina was too stunned by her mom's use of the words *sex* and *condom* to be insulted. Then she heard her father in the background saying, "Hush, Peg," and the full weight of what her mom was saying smacked her upside the head.

"So, you think this was my fault. It's my fault I have HIV?" She said the words slowly and very carefully so that her mother wouldn't miss the implications.

Her mom sucked in a breath. "No, honey. I'm sorry. I didn't mean that. I absolutely didn't mean that."

"What did you mean, Mom?"

"You're my baby, and I've always worried about you. You never ran heedless into the streets, but sometimes you strolled, and you weren't interested in looking both ways. I can't protect you anymore, especially with you so far away. Chicago was at least an easy plane flight."

Their argument never changed. "You haven't been able to protect me for years, and I've gotten by just fine."

"But I wish you were closer."

Mina didn't, though she was smart enough not to say so. "Maybe I didn't look both ways before crossing the street and maybe I got banged up along the way, but I've made it, Mom—about as well as anyone. I've got a good job, one that I enjoy and with a university that has been very supportive. And, you know, professorships in the humanities are hard to come by. Plus, someone pays me to draw pictures. They don't pay me a lot, but they pay me, and most artists can't say that, either. And I have Levi. He loves me, and he's supporting me in this." She took a deep breath. "I just wish you could do the same."

"You think we don't support you?"

"Peg, she thinks *you* don't support her," her father said in the background. "And right now I'm not sure she's wrong."

"Jimmy," her mother breathed out, insulted. Mina's father's shrug was nearly audible through the cell phone.

"What if people say mean things?" her mother asked, her attention and her face turned back to the phone.

Her mom had probably seen only the blog post, where no comments were allowed.

"They've already said mean things. And they said mean things before the whole world knew. But they say nice things, too. I've been invited to be a guest speaker. I might take a break from the Russian stories and finish drawing *The Adventures of Mina* +. Maybe I'll sell that and have a new book out. One with more universal appeal than the stories I draw of Russian literature. This doesn't limit my life, Mom. Maybe to you it looks like I'm trying to cross a superhighway blindfolded, but I found a bridge. Trust me enough to walk across that bridge."

Peace filled her as she said the words. She had drawn the comic in a fit of artistic push and made a quick decision to publish it, but it wasn't a rash decision. Not all quick decisions were rash, and, really, not all rash decisions were bad. She wouldn't go so far as to say that she wouldn't go back to that moment with Chase in his dorm room and walk out when he said he didn't have a condom, but she was pretty satisfied with her life, and she had been for a long time. If she went back in time and changed that one decision, who knows what ripple effects it would have? Not being here, in Montana, with a job that let her be both a professor and a comic artist, without Levi, without everything, didn't seem worth the risk of taking back one poorly-thought-out decision.

"I just worry about you," her mom repeated. "You can still worry about me, now that my secret's out in the open. But I'm hoping you'll worry less."

Her mom grunted. Actually grunted. "I probably won't worry less. But I'll watch my tongue when I'm talking to you. And I won't let my worry worry you."

"I'll hold her to it," yelled her dad, probably from his recliner in front of the TV.

Unable to help herself, she laughed. For a man who hated talking on the phone, he seemed to find nothing wrong with hollering into someone else's conversation.

"Are we okay, Mom?"

"I should be the one asking that. I'm sorry for what I said. Worry is no excuse, and I wouldn't have let it be an excuse for you. You're a good daughter, and I'm proud of you."

The "I just wish you'd be a little more careful" hung on the tail end of her mom's words, but she didn't voice them, and so all Mina said in response was "Thank you."

"Just warn us next time."

"I will. And I'm sorry I didn't this time. I'll do better."

"Me, too. I love you."

"I love you, too. Tell Dad I love him," she added, after hearing her dad call out "Love you" with the television on in the background.

After hanging up, Mina took a deep breath.

This part of her day was over. She might have more comments and emails to reply to, but they could wait. She was going next door to crawl into Levi's arms.

CHAPTER TWENTY-SEVEN

ONLY AFTER MINA opened Levi's front door and heard another voice did she look behind her and notice that there was a car parked on the street. Brook's voice, so probably Brook's car. She glanced around his living room as she tried to decide if she wanted to leave. To leave or to eavesdrop, that was the question. Perhaps a stronger person would walk into the kitchen and announce her presence, but she'd been brave enough today without facing Brook.

Some trolls were easier to face online.

"I can't believe you're defending that post. Telling everyone that she has AIDS. It came across my Facebook feed, and we're not even friends. Some guy from Boise shared it." Despite the hallway muffling Brook's voice, Mina heard every word. And any chance of her slipping out the front door ended.

She sat on the edge of the couch.

"You started telling everyone she has HIV first. You're angry because she has a bigger reach and so told more people. She took *how* they learned the news out of your hands." Levi's voice was strong and clear. "And if you're going to keep yelling about it, it's HIV. She has HIV, the virus that causes AIDS."

"Technicality."

"Not a technicality. I've asked you to learn something about the virus, and you haven't. Instead, you've told everyone you know about a secret that's not yours. Did you do the same with Kimmie's depression?"

"Everyone knew how sick Kimmie was. She couldn't hide it."

"No." Levi's voice sounded so sad that Mina's heart broke for him. "Especially at the end, she couldn't hide it. Everything she did gave her away."

"I saw how hard it was for you to take care of Kimmie."

Mina put her elbows on her knee and leaned forward, into the conversation.

"And I don't want you to have to go through that again. Her death wrecked you." Brook sounded sincere, at least. She did care about her brother, and his wife's death had been hard on all of them.

"At least I know where I get my over-caring from." Brook's sincerity sounded lost on Levi, whose voice was nothing but stabbing sarcasm.

"Mom. You get it from Mom. I get it from Mom." Brook spit out the words, so much like a bossy older sister that Mina almost gave herself away by laughing, despite the seriousness of the conversation. "Don't you remember her last words? 'It's too hard to care for you'?"

"I remember," Levi said. "But worrying until it crushes everyone around you isn't the only alternative."

"I've seen *Philadelphia*. I know what AIDS will look like. And, honestly, *you* looked close to Tom Hanks at the end."

"Brook," he said, back to sounding tired and sad. "I came out from a mining accident to find that my wife had committed suicide. Of course I looked skeletal."

"You looked skeletal before the accident." *Back up, Brook*, Mina thought. *You're hurting him*. "Sometimes I wondered if you were depressed yourself."

"I wasn't depressed. I was sad, and that's different. Caring for Kimmie was hard, but you know what I've learned from dating Mina?"

Mina scooted forward a little on her seat, not wanting to miss what came next.

"No." His voice waved Brook off. "Don't answer that question. I don't want to know."

Mina sighed and sat back on the couch.

"Kimmie's illness was not my responsibility. She was my wife, and I loved her, but she was her own person, and she was responsible for her own actions. I can love someone and care for them and even take care of them without taking responsibility for them. I took too much responsibility for Kimmie."

Mina smiled as Levi repeated almost the exact same thing she'd told him. Maybe he wasn't fully able to act on those words, but lecturing his sister was a close first step. She would have faith in him.

She would have faith in them.

"And you know what?" Apparently Levi wasn't done. "You need to do the same with Dennis. God, we're arguing about me and Mina, when the real problem is that you're afraid something's going to happen to Dennis. Rather than face your own troubles, you're stirring up problems for someone else."

"What's going on between me and Dennis is none of your business."

"You made it my business when you asked me to talk to him."

"Watch *Philadelphia*, and tell me that future doesn't scare you." The abrupt change in topic made Mina's head spin. And made her think Levi was spot-on. Brook was probably afraid and ignorant about HIV, but the meanness was coming from something deeper, uglier, and that had nothing to do with Mina or her illness.

"There are other AIDS movies, you know."

"Like what?" Brook challenged.

"I don't know. There have to be some."

"Are there any with happy endings?"

Mina pushed off the couch cushions. She'd been hiding long enough. Besides, she had come over here wanting to see Levi. And since Levi could spend hours sanding a wall before painting it, and Brook didn't seem like a person who gave up, either, the two of them could be here for a while.

Mina stopped in the doorway, her arms crossed in front of her, getting her first look at the fighting siblings. Levi's arms were crossed, too, his face tight and dark with anger. Even the stubble on his cheek seemed rougher.

Brook's hands were by her sides, like she was relaxed, but her shoulders were lifted up to her ears, and her chin was tucked into her chest as if she were folding into herself. No matter what Brook thought she was doing, her posture gave away that she wasn't listening at all.

"There are other movies," Mina said. "Besides *Dallas Buyers Club*, too. It's not exactly a happy movie, but in *Precious*, the main character is going to change the dire circumstances of her family, and HIV won't stop her. You could watch a romantic comedy like *Jeffrey* or a feel-good friendship movie like *Boys on the Side*.

The story doesn't have to be about death. The story can be about life."

"How long have you been there?" Levi asked.

"Long enough to know you're going to let me be responsible for myself," she said with a slight smile.

"I agreed with you about that before now." Levi's arms had fallen down by his sides, but his brows stayed crossed, this time not from anger at his sister. He actually seemed confused.

"Yes, but you were agreeing with me when I was irritated with you." She shrugged. "I didn't really know if you were agreeing with me to calm me down, or because you actually believed it."

"You didn't think I was being honest?"

"No. Maybe. You care so much, and I wasn't sure how much you could allow me to have my independence and trust me to manage myself." She shrugged. "My mom doesn't trust me to manage myself, but I want my boyfriend to."

"Oh." He looked stricken. "I've always believed in you. I couldn't even take my eyes off you that day you moved in. God—" his laugh had a self-deprecating hollowness to it "—I thought I must be the biggest creep in the world, because I stood at my kitchen window and stared. At least since then I've learned that it wasn't your appearance that fascinated me, though I won't ever get sick of looking at you. You're this amazing, creative and interesting person, and sometimes I look at what you draw and what you do, and I think how I could easily fall into you and never come out. But you would get us out, because you move forward. No matter what, you move forward."

Levi's entire body softened. "And I don't think I've ever met anyone who's impressed me more."

"Oh." Mina's heart was swelling at Levi's words, but the sound came from Brook. "You really love her, don't you?"

"Yes," Levi said, and that simple confirmation was worth as much as the long speech he'd just given.

"It's just…" Brook looked back and forth between the two of them, honest confusion on her face.

"You don't get it," he said. "You still think I love Mina despite her illness. And you probably thought I loved Kimmie despite hers. But it's not about despite or because of. I love Mina. And I loved Kimmie. And their illnesses were as much a part of them as their hair color or their laugh, but never a reason to love or not love them. Their illnesses just *were*."

"But aren't you scared?" Brook asked, fear pulling at the edges of her mouth.

"Of course I'm scared," he said. "I'm terrified. Mina could be hit by a truck. I could slice off my arm. She could meet someone who never worried about whether or not she was taking her pills and realize how relaxing and much better that guy was. But if Mina has taught me not to take responsibility for other people's actions, Kimmie taught me that the fight was worth everything. So long as you were fighting to keep going, then you were winning. I'm not sure I would have been strong enough to love Mina, if I hadn't loved Kimmie first."

Brook's hand shook in front of her, not in anger, but like she was trying to get Levi's words closer to her face, where she could see them and maybe where she could comprehend them. "I don't understand how you can say that. Kimmie committed suicide. She gave up the fight."

"Never say that about her." The fury in Levi's tone sent shivers down Mina's spine. "She didn't give up anything. She won the battle her own way, and I will never judge her for that."

Brook turned to look at Mina. "What do you think about this?"

"I think it's pretty wonderful to love a man who loved his wife so much. I'm humbled that a man capable of so much love has chosen me to receive it next. I'm sorry I ever doubted him *and* us." She made sure she was looking at Levi and that he knew she was directing her words to him. "I'll probably slip, and do it again, but I'll forgive you for future worries if you forgive me for future doubts. And we can work on doing better, together."

Brook threw up her hands. "I just…"

"You're just scared, sis, and it's easier to be angry." There Levi was again, offering a life raft. Quietly searching for solutions and ways to fix the world, ways to make everyone better. He didn't put himself out there for everyone, but when he did, he didn't pull back.

As frustrated as she was with Brook, she admired Levi for sticking with the conversation. A guy with that much stick-to-it-ness was worth the world.

Mina turned her attention to Brook. "I'm not going to die, just because Kimmie died. Levi and I can have children, and I will live long enough to see them have children. Being poz is not a death sentence. And so, you don't have to worry that your brother will have to go through that pain again. He might, but it probably won't be because of the virus."

"I still don't…" Brook stuttered as she shifted to face her brother. "I love you. I can't think about the rest right now, but I know that. And

I'm going home. To Dennis." Levi's sister turned away and nearly ran out the door.

Mina practically ran the other way, throwing herself into Levi's open arms and sinking into his warm hug. His hand was heavy on her hair as he caressed her head.

"I'm sorry," he said, her hair muffling his words.

She had to tilt her head, so that she wasn't speaking into his sweater. "What are you sorry for?"

"For Brook, who can't seem to stop long enough to look at her own problems, but is insisting on creating ones for other people."

Her shrug was lost in their embrace. "She lives in Bozeman, so she won't be close enough for anything she says to hurt me. And I don't care if she tells people anymore."

"I know but…" His weight shifted, and she pulled away, too, so that she could meet his eye. "I'm not going to give up on her. Maybe I should, but I won't."

Mina buried her head back against his chest. "I won't ask you to. But we don't have to talk about that now. All we need right now is each other and to know that we're okay."

"And we're okay?" he asked, sounding ner-

vous, even though she was clutching him like
a life raft keeping her afloat in the deepest sea.

"We're perfect," she said.

* * * * *

LARGER-PRINT BOOKS!
GET 2 FREE LARGER-PRINT NOVELS PLUS
2 FREE GIFTS!

❦ HARLEQUIN®

Romance

From the Heart, For the Heart

YES! Please send me 2 FREE LARGER-PRINT Harlequin® Romance novels and my 2 FREE gifts (gifts are worth about $10). After receiving them, if I don't wish to receive any more books, I can return the shipping statement marked "cancel." If I don't cancel, I will receive 4 brand-new novels every month and be billed just $5.09 per book in the U.S. or $5.49 per book in Canada. That's a savings of at least 15% off the cover price! It's quite a bargain! Shipping and handling is just 50¢ per book in the U.S. and 75¢ per book in Canada.* I understand that accepting the 2 free books and gifts places me under no obligation to buy anything. I can always return a shipment and cancel at any time. Even if I never buy another book, the two free books and gifts are mine to keep forever.

119/319 HDN GHWC

Name _____ (PLEASE PRINT)

Address _____ Apt. #

City _____ State/Prov. _____ Zip/Postal Code

Signature (if under 18, a parent or guardian must sign)

Mail to the Reader Service:
IN U.S.A.: P.O. Box 1867, Buffalo, NY 14240-1867
IN CANADA: P.O. Box 609, Fort Erie, Ontario L2A 5X3
Want to try two free books from another line?
Call 1-800-873-8635 or visit www.ReaderService.com.

* Terms and prices subject to change without notice. Prices do not include applicable taxes. Sales tax applicable in N.Y. Canadian residents will be charged applicable taxes. Offer not valid in Quebec. This offer is limited to one order per household. Not valid for current subscribers to Harlequin Romance Larger-Print books. All orders subject to credit approval. Credit or debit balances in a customer's account(s) may be offset by any other outstanding balance owed by or to the customer. Please allow 4 to 6 weeks for delivery. Offer available while quantities last.

Your Privacy—The Reader Service is committed to protecting your privacy. Our Privacy Policy is available online at www.ReaderService.com or upon request from the Reader Service.

We make a portion of our mailing list available to reputable third parties that offer products we believe may interest you. If you prefer that we not exchange your name with third parties, or if you wish to clarify or modify your communication preferences, please visit us at www.ReaderService.com/consumerschoice or write to us at Reader Service Preference Service, P.O. Box 9062, Buffalo, NY 14240-9062. Include your complete name and address.

HRLP15

LARGER-PRINT
BOOKS!

⊕ HARLEQUIN
Presents®

**GET 2 FREE LARGER-PRINT
NOVELS PLUS 2 FREE GIFTS!**

PASSION
GUARANTEED
SEDUCTION

YES! Please send me 2 FREE LARGER-PRINT Harlequin Presents® novels and my 2 FREE gifts (gifts are worth about $10). After receiving them, if I don't wish to receive any more books, I can return the shipping statement marked "cancel." If I don't cancel, I will receive 6 brand-new novels every month and be billed just $5.30 per book in the U.S. or $5.74 per book in Canada. That's a saving of at least 12% off the cover price! It's quite a bargain! Shipping and handling is just 50¢ per book in the U.S. and 75¢ per book in Canada.* I understand that accepting the 2 free books and gifts places me under no obligation to buy anything. I can always return a shipment and cancel at any time. Even if I never buy another book, the two free books and gifts are mine to keep forever.

176/376 HDN GHVY

Name	(PLEASE PRINT)
Address	Apt. #
City	State/Prov.	Zip/Postal Code

Signature (if under 18, a parent or guardian must sign)

Mail to the **Reader Service**:
IN U.S.A.: P.O. Box 1867, Buffalo, NY 14240-1867
IN CANADA: P.O. Box 609, Fort Erie, Ontario L2A 5X3

**Are you a subscriber to Harlequin Presents® books
and want to receive the larger-print edition?
Call 1-800-873-8635 today or visit us at www.ReaderService.com.**

* Terms and prices subject to change without notice. Prices do not include applicable taxes. Sales tax applicable in N.Y. Canadian residents will be charged applicable taxes. Offer not valid in Quebec. This offer is limited to one order per household. Not valid for current subscribers to Harlequin Presents Larger-Print books. All orders subject to credit approval. Credit or debit balances in a customer's account(s) may be offset by any other outstanding balance owed by or to the customer. Please allow 4 to 6 weeks for delivery. Offer available while quantities last.

Your Privacy—The Reader Service is committed to protecting your privacy. Our Privacy Policy is available online at www.ReaderService.com or upon request from the Reader Service.

We make a portion of our mailing list available to reputable third parties that offer products we believe may interest you. If you prefer that we not exchange your name with third parties, or if you wish to clarify or modify your communication preferences, please visit us at www.ReaderService.com/consumerchoice or write to us at Reader Service Preference Service, P.O. Box 9062, Buffalo, NY 14240-9062. Include your complete name and address.